Looking at her huddled in the chair, Hunter wanted nothing more than to cross the room and pull her into his arms. He couldn't. He wouldn't let her go until he had made her his and once he did that, he wasn't sure if he could ever let her go.

But neither could he let her go through this alone.

Throwing back the cover, he stood. Erin kept her gaze averted. She wasn't going to look. He scooped her up into his arms.

Wide, weary eyes stared at him, caught halfway between surprise and need. The need drew him as nothing else could. "I'll keep you safe."

She relaxed against him, her head pressed against his chest. "I know. At first I didn't want to depend on you, but somehow I didn't seem to be able to help myself." She angled her head up to look at him. "I feel safe with you. But if it bothers you, maybe one of the other men could be with me during the day."

"I get night duty."

"Would that be so bad?" she asked, the desire plain in her eyes.

"Erin, don't. My control isn't very good at the moment."

"Good. I'd hate to be the only one feeling this way." Her lips touched his and Hunter's resistance melted.

INCOGNITO

Francis Ray

Pinnacle Books
Kensington Publishing Corp.
http://www.pinnaclebooks.com

PINNACLE BOOKS are published by

Kensington Publishing Corp.
850 Third Avenue
New York, NY 10022

First Printing: February, 1997
10 9 8 7 6 5 4 3 2 1

Printed in the United States of America

DEDICATION

Carolyn Michelle Ray, my daughter and in-house marketing major, whose insight and ideas were invaluable.

SPECIAL THANKS

Delva J. King—co-owner of The King Group, Inc., a marketing/advertising firm in Dallas, Texas—who took precious time from her hectic schedule to talk with me.

Tina Allen and Jeannye Polk, avid readers who showed me Austin, and by the end of the day had become special friends.

Patsy Day, founder of Victims Outreach in Dallas, Texas, whose courage and faith touched my heart.

Sergeant Roger Martin of the Dallas Police Department's Homicide Division, whose patience and knowledge helped theory become fact.

Bless you and thank you all from the bottom of my heart.

Prologue

June, 1996

She was the most breathtakingly beautiful woman Jake Hunter had ever seen. And in thirty-five years of living, he had seen plenty. None came close to rivaling this woman, whose skin was the color of warm, dark honey, whose svelte body moved with honey's supple, almost hypnotic grace.

If the furtive—and downright frank—male stares were any indication, most of the men in the crowded ballroom agreed with him. More than a few had tried to pick her up. So far she remained elusive.

She wouldn't for long.

With all the instincts of a predator waiting for the opportunity to cut his prey from the protection of the pack, Jake leaned against the wall. His gaze never left the woman in the black-and-white gown as she moved around the lavish room.

So far, he hadn't seen any opportunity to get her alone. But he was a patient man. He knew how to wait.

For once he was glad he'd come to one of Paul's parties. The society scene bored Hunter; the pretense annoyed him. He often wondered if some of the chattering, fashionable people in the glittering room were ever satisfied. The more some of them achieved, the more they wanted. They were always reaching. No matter how much they had, it wasn't enough. Success still left them wannabees.

"Are you enjoying yourself, Hunter?"

"Yes, thank you, Mr. Morris." Paul Morris, rich, influential, and on several civic boards in Chicago, was an exception to the wannabees. He was a man content with himself and who he was, a rarity in Hunter's line of business.

"I'm glad. You work too hard." Smiling, Paul took a sip of amber-colored liquid from his crystal tumbler. "I thought you were going to call me by my first name, since we're partners now."

"Habit," Hunter said. Out of the corner of his eye, he saw the woman move into the arms of a tuxedoed man on the dance floor. Hunter's eyes narrowed as the man's hand moved down from the graceful curve of her back to the swell of her hips.

Her slender fingers moved the man's hand up. Seconds later, it descended again. Hunter straightened.

"I've seen that look before," Paul chuckled. "Whose head are you about to take off?"

Hunter started. Usually, his thoughts were unreadable. In his previous line of work, they had had to be. "One of your guests is having trouble remembering where to keep his hand."

Paul's questioning gaze followed the direction of Hunter's. "Erin can take care of herself."

Almost before the words were out of Paul's mouth, the man on the dance floor yelled, grabbed his foot, and began hopping around. Even from fifteen feet away, Hunter could hear Erin's sultry voice proclaiming that she was a poor dancer and that she was sorry. The sharp glitter in her eyes said otherwise.

"Another one bit the dust," Paul said with a shake of his graying head.

Hunter was about to ask what he meant when Paul's wife came up and hooked her slender arm through her husband's.

"Mind if I borrow Paul for a minute? Some friends of ours just arrived."

"No, of course not, Mrs. Morris," Hunter said, his own plans forming in his mind. Erin had just stepped out on the balcony.

"Come along, Paul," Grace said, her three-carat diamond sparkling on her hand as she increased the pressure on her husband's arm.

Paul paused a second longer, his speculative gaze going from his new partner to the balcony. "Hunter, I'm—"

"Excuse me; I think I'll get a bit of fresh air." Hunter heard the worry in Paul's voice, but chose to ignore it. Paul might as well learn that, although he had a say-so in their business relations, Hunter's personal life was his own.

With practiced ease Hunter moved through the throng of laughing partygoers until he was outside. If her sleeveless evening gown hadn't had a draped white satin collar, he might have missed seeing her. She stood at the farthest end of the stone balcony, gazing out at the lighted tennis courts.

"Hello, Erin," he greeted her, purposely keeping his voice low so he wouldn't startle her.

The dark eyes that slowly turned and studied him showed no fear, only wariness. He wasn't surprised. At six-feet-three and tipping the scales at two-ten, he tended to intimidate more than reassure. It didn't help that he was brawnier and taller than the man on the dance floor had been.

"You're safe with me, Erin."

She continued to regard him speculatively, as if he were some wild animal that had unexpectedly strolled across her path and she couldn't decide whether she wanted to pet him or run. "How do you know my name?" Her sultry voice was even more captivating at close range.

"Paul."

Her chin lifted. "I don't like men asking questions about me."

Spunk. He had always admired that in a woman. "I didn't

ask. Paul volunteered when we saw what was going on on the dance floor with the octopus."

"You've been watching me all evening. Why?"

"I couldn't help myself." He barely kept the frown from his face as he heard his words aloud. They hadn't been what he had planned to say, but they were the truth, nonetheless. She possessed an effortless sensuality that beckoned and called to him as no woman ever had.

Something flashed in her eyes. Instinctively he knew she had made up her mind about him. "If you'll excuse me, I think I'll go back inside."

"Don't." His hand tentatively touched her bare arm; he felt her tremble, felt his own body leap in response. Her skin had the smoothness of porcelain, the softness of a rose petal. He had never felt anything like it before. He wanted to feel it again.

She looked up at him with wide, uncertain eyes.

It was suddenly very important that she stay and that she trust him. "You're safe. Don't go. Please, dance with me." Slowly, gently, he pulled her into his arms.

After a moment's hesitation, her stiff body relaxed. With each note of the slow love song drifting through the open balcony door, her body seemed to shift and mold itself against his, fitting softness to hardness effortlessly.

She was heaven on earth, and her flowery scent was as alluring as she was. "The . . . the music stopped," she whispered.

He glanced down. He watched while she swallowed nervously, watched her tongue trace her lush lower lip. Raw desire struck him low and fast. He was powerless to keep from lowering his head and repeating the motion with his tongue.

She shivered like a leaf caught in the wind; her eyes drifted shut. She tasted sweet, hot. He wanted more. Hunter had learned to take what he wanted.

With firm pressure, his mouth settled over hers; his tongue slipped inside. The tentative touch of her tongue meeting his sent a shaft of need surging through him. The kiss deepened, each taking, each giving, until kissing was no longer enough.

Forcing his mouth away, he grabbed her hand and started for the door. "Come on."

Her heels clicked on the stone pavement. "Where?"

"My place or yours. Just so long as there's a bed."

"What?" Shock and anger were evident in that one sharp word.

Hunter let out an exasperated breath. He stopped and turned to face her. Her withering stare wasn't reassuring. "We're both adults."

"But I'm not a slut." She jerked her hand free.

"If I thought that you were, I wouldn't be here," he told her. Nothing about Erin said she was easy, but the chemistry between them was impossible to ignore. He had never come on to a woman so strongly in his life.

Her eyes widened at his statement, but the anger remained. He tried again. "Look, we both want to make love to each other. Why are we standing here arguing?"

Her anger turned to fury. "I don't even know your name. You barely know mine."

"It's enough to know that we set each other's bodies on fire."

"Not for me."

Hunter's frustration hit the boiling point. He had never wanted anyone like this before. Yet he kept his voice modulated: "Your body wasn't complaining."

She flinched, then looked at him with pure disdain. "A correctable mistake."

Head held high, she walked back inside, leaving him hard and frustrated. He started after her, then stopped. What was the use? She wanted something he couldn't give any woman. Commitment and his line of work didn't mix.

Hunter wanted to howl at the quarter moon; instead, he jammed his hands in his pockets. With brisk movements, he went down the steps and took the long way around to the front to get his car.

He was in time to see an attendant assisting Erin into the passenger seat of a Rolls-Royce. The car pulled off, and in the light Hunter could easily see that the driver was a man.

Hunter cursed softly under his breath. Questions about the man's identity swirled around in his head. Paul would know. But Hunter wasn't going to ask.

He'd have to remember Erin as the one who got away. He knew his body would.

Chapter One

Seven months later
Austin, Texas

Something was wrong.

Erin Cortland knew it the moment she entered her father's study and saw two men she'd never thought to see again rise hastily from their seats. The last time she had seen them they had both been smiling. Tonight their smiles were noticeably absent.

"Come on in, Erin," Marcus Cortland said as he came from behind his massive, hand-carved desk. "You know Police Chief Tolliver and Detective Grimes."

Erin barely nodded at the policemen. Her entire attention was centered on the unusually grim face of her father. Deep lines furrowed his dark brown brow. "Dad, what's the matter?"

Instead of answering, he drew her into his arms. The scent of his spicy cologne and the raspy tweed of his favorite jacket against her cheek were achingly familiar. His refusal to meet any problem head-on was not.

He hadn't built Cortland Innovations, one of the largest

African-American advertising firms in the country, by refusing to face problems. And while hugs were common in her family, more so since the death of her mother a year ago, this one seemed almost desperate.

Her unease quickly escalated to fear. Since she had matched her father's height by the time she reached the sixth grade then had grown another two inches before her body decided five-feet-nine was enough, she easily glanced over his tense shoulder to seek an answer from the silent policemen.

Their gazes refused to meet hers. A knot of terror began to coil and tighten in her stomach. With trembling hands, she eased away. "Dad, please tell me what's bothering you."

Troubled brown eyes lifted and studied hers. Marcus Cortland inhaled slowly, as if his breath and his strength were somehow connected and he was having difficulty maintaining both. "Erin, I'd give anything for this not to have happened."

"What? What happened?" As his silence continued, her gaze returned to the policemen. "Won't somebody please tell me what's going on?"

"Scanlon escaped," her father finally said.

Erin couldn't tell if she or her father flinched; she only knew terror whipped through her. She had thought it was all over, thought she had awakened for the last time with a scream locked in her throat. "When? How?"

Police Chief Tolliver and Detective Grimes rushed forward. The senior officer spoke first.

"A little over three hours ago at the Diagnostic Evaluation Unit in Huntsville. At countdown, a guard counted an ink-colored pillowcase for Scanlon's head. No one caught the mistake until Scanlon was seen going over the fence ten minutes later." Chief Tolliver rushed on to explain. "Writing materials are issued to all inmates upon entering the unit. It wasn't foreseen that Scanlon would somehow get his hands on enough ink pens to pull this off."

"Wasn't foreseen," Erin repeated softly in disbelief. She swallowed and fought the panic. She knew she had to control it, or it would control her.

Detective Grimes said, "Ms. Cortland, I want you to know everything is being done to put Scanlon back behind bars."

"Then you expect to pick him up shortly?" Erin asked, hating the almost pleading note in her voice.

"Yes, Ms. Cortland, we do," the younger policeman assured her. "Scanlon will be back in jail by morning. We'll pick him up as quickly as we did last time."

Erin shivered. A vivid picture of the reason for Scanlon's arrest came to her. After five months, nightmares of the time she'd stopped at the convenience store to use the ATM machine continued to haunt her.

Just as she'd pulled up, a bleary-eyed man had run out the door and had been caught in the beams of her headlights. In one hand he clutched a bloody paper sack. In the other, a gun. For a long moment both of them had been unable to move. The robber recovered first. He ran to the passenger's side of the car and got in.

"Drive or I'll kill you."

She had backed out of the parking lot just as she heard the wail of the police siren. She was shaking so badly she missed the next turn and smashed the driver's side of her car into a light pole.

Her head bumped against the steering wheel. Dazed, she heard the man next to her yelling and cursing. She instinctively turned toward the sound. As her vision cleared, she fought back a scream.

The deadly black hole of the gun was inches from her face. "Stupid bitch," he yelled, and pulled the trigger.

The click of the empty chamber elicited another string of foul oaths. His angular, unshaven face contorted in fury. He raised the gun. The increasingly loud wail of a police siren sent him running down the street, instead.

It hadn't taken the police long to catch him. A previous police record for multiple auto theft, two assault charges, and one count of manslaughter as a juvenile made the trial blissfully short.

Now, instead of being in a maximum security prison for

killing the two store clerks in the robbery, Scanlon was free. As he was forcibly taken from the courtroom, he had shouted death threats to the only witness against him, Erin, and to the judge who had sentenced him.

"What about Judge Hughes?" Erin asked.

"Judge Hughes has been notified, but he has confidence in the police," Tolliver said.

"You'll forgive me if I don't share his opinion," Marcus said. "I believe my daughter's life is in danger."

"The patrol car in her area has already been alerted," the police chief said. "I wish we could offer around-the-clock protection, but we're short-handed."

Marcus's sharp eyes narrowed. "I was told that with every hour Scanlon is free his chances of staying that way become better than yours are of capturing him. Is that true?"

For a long moment Tolliver looked uneasy. "Who told you that?"

"I have my sources," Marcus said, his voice curt. "Is it true or not?"

Tolliver's pursed lips relaxed a fraction. "Ordinarily, yes, but in this case we have something else in our favor. The weather."

"What has that to do with anything?" Erin asked.

"To lessen the chance of detection, Scanlon left his clothes behind. The white coveralls the prisoners wear would have reflected light and made him easier to spot," Chief Tolliver explained. "That ruse may have gotten him over the fence, but it's now in our favor. The temperature will be in the low thirties tonight in Huntsville. He'll have to surface to seek shelter. When he does, we'll get him."

"If he's still in the area," Marcus pointed out.

"He is," Detective Grimes said with confidence. "We found the truck he stole from the visitors' parking lot a couple of miles from the prison."

"Could you tell the direction he was heading?" Marcus inquired.

Sadly, the young policeman shook his head. "Escapees usually try to lose themselves in a big city. Houston is the closest one to Huntsville."

"Then you don't think he's coming here?" Erin asked, glad her voice had lost some of its panic.

"No, ma'am, I don't. Scanlon's been on the streets since he was fourteen, and the foster homes couldn't control him. He was a two-bit hood always looking for the easy big score. He has no friends here," Detective Grimes explained.

"No one will help him if he returns here," said Chief Tolliver. "Scanlon's known to be cruel and vicious, especially to women. His name has been linked to several drive-by shootings that left the victims dead. He pulled the convenience-store robbery as a gang initiation. The tragic thing is that our sources indicate it was some sort of sick joke. The Desperadoes considered Scanlon a loser."

Erin shivered again, her free hand sweeping up and down her jacketed arm. "They're as guilty as he is."

"I agree, but proving it in court is another matter. He was trying to make a name for himself, and he didn't care who got hurt," Detective Grimes told her. "We'll get him."

"You haven't so far," Marcus said. The words hung in the room.

The junior policeman's lips pursed. He faced a silent Erin. "If you're concerned, Mr. Cortland, perhaps your daughter might consider spending a day or two with friends out of town."

Her hands clenched. "I thought you said he'll be picked up soon."

"It's just a precaution," Chief Tolliver soothed.

"Perhaps you could change a business trip to an earlier date."

"No. I'm not going anywhere." Scanlon had taken enough from her. "I'm staying."

"Erin, you could go to our home in Aspen or move back in with me," Marcus suggested.

Erin shook her dark head. The night of the robbery, her father had picked her up from the hospital and insisted she spend the weekend with him. A month later she was still there. She hadn't felt safe unless she was with other people.

Returning to her empty house had taken all of her strength, and several sessions with the Victim Recovery group. She wasn't giving up the independence she had fought so hard to regain.

"I'm not going anyplace but home, then to work in the morning," Erin told her father. "Daddy, you know Hodges retired the end of the year and until I can name a replacement for his vice-president's position, my work load has almost doubled. It's going to get worse in February with Black History Month here."

"Baby—"

"I'm sorry, Daddy. You put me in charge of Cortland Innovations, and I'm not running away from my responsibilities," Erin insisted.

Marcus turned to the police chief. "Can you guarantee my daughter will be safe?"

"We'll do all we can."

"That's not what I asked."

"No."

Marcus nodded. "Gentlemen, will you please excuse us while we have a little talk?" Taking Erin's hand, Marcus moved to the chairs facing the fireplace. Flames leaped on the hearth. Neither noticed.

"Sit down, Erin," Marcus said, indicating one of the Chippendale accent chairs.

"Dad—"

"Sit down," he repeated. The uncharacteristic hesitancy she had sensed in his demeanor earlier was gone. The fear was not.

Erin sat in the brocade-covered chair, sure she wasn't going to like what her father would say.

"I had hoped this wouldn't be necessary, but it appears I don't have a choice." Hands behind his back, he paced in front of her. "I hired you a bodyguard."

Erin sprang to her feet. "I don't need a bodyguard. You heard the police."

''Yes, I heard them. They ''hope.'' They ''think.'' Obviously you weren't listening to them. It's their fault Scanlon is free in the first place,'' Marcus accused tightly. ''Starting this moment, wherever you go, your bodyguard goes.''

Hearing the determined tone in her father's voice, Erin realized that this was one time when she wasn't going to be able to talk him into letting her have her way. Concern for his daughter ruled him now.

Her shaky fingers closed into fists. She couldn't let this happen. She had to think of some plausible reason for not wanting a bodyguard.

If her father had any idea how frightened she'd been, how she'd fought nightmares until a couple of months ago, no power on earth would keep him from bringing her back home and using any means possible to keep her safe. He might be able to keep her body safe, but not her mind.

She had to do that herself, and the only way was to face her fears and not act like a victim. She couldn't depend on anyone. She had to do it alone. ''But, Dad—''

''No buts. I don't want you out of his sight until this killer is back in jail, and that's final,'' Marcus told her with unbending finality.

''How do you suggest I run Cortland Innovations with someone trailing behind me, let alone explain why he's doing it, without causing a disruption?'' she questioned hotly. ''His presence is bound to affect business.''

''You're not the president of the company for nothing. Once you get it into your head this is the way it's going to be, you'll think of something.'' He stopped and pinned her with a look. ''Besides, I don't care if every client walks. You're what's important.''

''I care,'' she flared. ''When you turned the company over to me last year, it was at the top, and it's going to remain that way.''

''I thought you'd be stubborn about this. You're too much like me.'' He looked into the leaping flames in the fireplace.

Erin's body relaxed. He was going to listen.

He lifted his head, and Erin knew she had celebrated too soon. She braced herself without realizing it.

"Either you accept the bodyguard or I'll use my power as CEO to remove you as president and transfer you to our Chicago office."

Stunned. There was no other word for it. "You . . . you can't."

"I can and I will. I love you too much to have you hurt in any way," Marcus said, his voice gruff. "You may hate me, but you'll still be alive."

"You're bluffing," she said, but her voice lacked conviction.

Marcus shook his balding gray head once. "This is the way it's going to be, Erin. I care too much about you to take a chance on any harm coming to you."

Anger and fear shimmered in his brown eyes. "You heard the police. They can't offer around-the-clock protection and after their bungle with Scanlon, that's fine with me. This man is supposed to be the best. And, believe me, Erin, against a man like Scanlon, you're going to need the best."

"Daddy, please don't do this," she pleaded. "Scanlon isn't going to risk coming back to Austin. He's too well known."

"What if he does? I don't want anything to happen to you. Losing your mother was hard enough. Sweetheart, I . . . I couldn't stand to lose you, too."

All the fight went out of Erin. Warmth flowed through her. Her father hadn't called her sweetheart since she'd asked him not to on her twelfth birthday. A rush of childhood memories washed over her.

She and her parents had always been close. The wrenching pain of losing Charlotte Cortland after she had had an aneurysm, had taken its toll on both of them.

Erin went into her father's arms. He held her as tightly as she held him. Her father had been through enough. Somehow she'd manage.

She lifted her head. "I'll do as you ask, Daddy."

"For as long as it takes?"

"For as long as it takes."

"You'll follow his orders regarding your safety?"

Erin gritted her teeth. Her father was really pushing it. "As long as his *requests* are reasonable and he realizes I have a business to run, yes."

Marcus's robust body relaxed. A soft sigh slipped past his lips. "Thank you." His arm curved around her shoulder as he walked back to his desk. "I'll feel better knowing he's with you."

"I'm glad someone will," she muttered under her breath.

Marcus seated Erin in the chair behind his desk facing the policemen, then stood by her side. "After consulting with someone who knows about this sort of thing, I've decided," he paused and glanced at Erin, "with my daughter's permission, to hire a bodyguard."

It didn't make Erin feel better to see the look of relief cross the chief's face, nor the look of irritation twist the young detective's.

Marcus continued speaking in the others' ensuing silence. "He's waiting outside. If you don't mind, I'd like for you to fill him in on Scanlon."

"That's confidential," Grimes quickly said.

Erin didn't have to see her father's face to know that he wasn't pleased with the detective's answer, or to know that he wouldn't be dissuaded easily from what he wanted.

"Is that your answer, also, Chief Tolliver?" Marcus asked, the softness in his voice a gentle warning. "Or should I make a couple of phone calls?"

"No, that won't be necessary," the police chief quickly said, then glared at the younger officer. "You have the Austin Police Department's full cooperation."

"Glad to hear it," Marcus told them. "Because if anything happened to my daughter because of someone else's mistake, well . . ." He let his voice trail off, the implication clear.

Both men sat straighter in their seats. Erin almost felt sorry for them. Marcus Cortland hadn't worked his way from a two-room shanty in a bayou of Louisiana to a twenty-room mansion by rolling over. He might look soft and cuddly as a teddy bear, but he could unsheathe claws when he needed them.

''You have our full cooperation,'' Chief Tolliver repeated.

Marcus's smile was a tiny flash of teeth. ''Thank you.'' Crossing the room, he opened the door. ''Come in, please.''

''Thank you.''

Erin leaned forward as she heard the deep male voice. Something about it . . . Her thoughts stumbled to a halt as the man stepped inside the room and her father closed the door behind him.

She came to her feet without realizing it. *It couldn't be.* Then he looked straight at her. Breath stalled in her lungs. It was the man from the party in Chicago. The man who'd turned her body into a throbbing mass of need, then insulted her.

She had never wanted to see him again.

Hell! What had she committed herself to? And how was she going to get out of it?

Chapter Two

Hunter couldn't believe his eyes. After she had haunted his dreams for seven months, he was finally seeing her again. She was as beautiful as ever, and just as angry. When she looked at him there was no indecisiveness this time as to what she wanted to do.

She'd string him up by his thumbs or another part of his anatomy if she could. Hunter barely repressed a shiver. It was an unsettling thought. Especially when he knew he deserved her condemnation.

He had acted totally out of character and out of bounds. Since he didn't believe in excuses from other people, he made none for himself. He only knew that for the first time in his life or in his career he had let impulse rule him.

His parents hadn't been around to teach him much, but they had taught him that a man who couldn't control his body or his tongue put himself on the same level with an animal. That night on the balcony in Chicago with Erin, he had forgotten that lesson, and sunk to that level.

Pure animal instincts to possess, to mate, had guided him. Nothing else seemed to matter. He had wanted Erin with a growing urgency that had overshadowed every other consideration. A fire had burned in his blood, a fire that could only be quenched in one way, with one woman.

In his thirty-five years, he had never wanted or needed anything like that before. Or since. He didn't like to remember his lack of control, or to know that the woman across the room still got to him.

"Come on in, Hunter; I want to introduce you to everyone." Marcus quickly made the introductions. If the elderly man noticed that no one gave more than a brief nod, he didn't comment.

"You indicated you needed the firm's help," Hunter said, wishing he had had a chance to speak with Paul before he took this job.

"That's right, and Paul said you were the perfect man."

Hunter nodded, still trying to figure out what was going on. He had been checking out of his hotel room in Dallas when he'd received Paul's message. All it said was: *Urgent. Go to Austin immediately. Contact Marcus Cortland. Newest client. Most valuable asset.*

So Hunter had contacted Marcus Cortland before leaving Dallas. Their conversation had been about police procedure and Hunter's background. He hadn't thought anything about it, since people often wanted to know about the person they were hiring. Promising to give him all the details when he arrived, Cortland had asked him to get to Austin as quickly as possible.

Instead of driving back to Chicago with the vintage Mustang he had just purchased, he had driven to Austin. At the time, he had been thankful for the reprieve. Snow and ice had been forcast for the Great Lakes.

He hadn't been looking forward to driving in that kind of weather with his newest acquisition. But if the job had anything to do with the beautiful woman shooting daggers at him, he'd gladly take his chances with the treacherous roads.

"The police will fill you in on the details, but I need you to be Erin's bodyguard," Marcus told him.

"I beg your pardon," Hunter said, unable to keep his gaze from straying back to a stiff-backed Erin.

"If you'll take a seat, we'll answer your questions."

"I'll stand."

"Very well," Marcus said. "Detective Grimes."

Detective Grimes repeated everything. He finished by restating his confidence that there would be a quick arrest.

Hunter wasn't taking this case. No way. Too many conflicting emotions were churning through him. None of them objective and impersonal.

He wanted to take that look of vulnerability from Erin's eyes by hunting down the creep who had terrified her, then have the satisfaction of pounding his fist into him. Hunter wanted to hold her in his arms.

He could do none of those things. Neither could he be her bodyguard. The case was too similar to the last time he had tried to protect a woman and failed.

"I know of another agency. They can probably have one of their best men here by morning," Hunter said tightly.

Marcus rounded the desk. "According to Paul, you're the best man."

"I'm a security expert. I don't take these kinds of cases. We specialize in guarding valuables."

"I can't think of anything more valuable than my daughter."

Hunter had to agree, but he still wasn't taking the case. He would need a clear head to protect Erin and that's exactly what he didn't have, around her. "Mr. Cortland, you have—"

"Let him go, Daddy. I don't want him."

Hunter's head came up like an animal scenting fresh prey. Erin stared back at him, defiant and regal. For a second he thought of staying and helping her, then he pushed the idea away.

He couldn't go through losing again. He turned to Marcus. "I'll call the other agency."

Marcus crossed his arms. "Call who you want, but you're still the one I hired to guard my daughter. The retainer is in your bank. The signed contract has been faxed. The deal is made."

Hunter's eyes narrowed. He'd been duped. Apparently with Paul's full knowledge. Paul knew Hunter wanted nothing more to do with that kind of work. Too many variables could leave the innocent dead and the guilty free.

A fierce pounding started in his temple. "What's Paul to you?"

"A close friend and Erin's godfather."

The trap closed tighter around Hunter. Paul Morris, first as a client and later as a business partner, had helped Hunter as no one else had. Paul's patronage had been one of the key factors in the success of Hunter Security. The company had been Hunter's salvation at a time he wasn't sure he was worth saving or sure he wanted to be saved.

Hunter owed the older man and he always payed his debts. But not at the price of his soul. Then Hunter looked at Erin, scared spitless and doing her best to hide it from everyone.

He might have found a way around the contract, gotten over Paul's disappointment, but not the growing need to see the lines of strain and fear gone from Erin's beautiful face.

Erin needed protection and, once, he had been the best. "I'll take the case."

"Thank you," Marcus said, and extended his hand again.

Hunter clasped it without hesitation. Now there was no going back. This time when he'd accepted the job of bodyguard he'd known full well what he was getting into.

Marcus turned to the policemen, shook their hands, then showed them to the door. As soon as it closed, Erin hurried around the desk. "The deal's off, Daddy. I don't want your hired gun anywhere near me."

"You gave me your word, Erin," Marcus reminded her. "Or did you want to see Chicago?"

Erin whirled toward Hunter. He was leaning negligently against the back of a chair, his eyelids at half mast as if the entire proceedings were boring him. She knew his pose was a facade.

Her godfather wouldn't send an incompetent to guard her. More important, she remembered too well the intensity and intelligence of those eyes, the quickness of his movements. His name suited him. He was one of the most compelling men she had ever met.

And he scared the hell out of her.

His dark brown face wasn't attractive in the conventional sort of way. His nose was too broad, his jaw too square. But once you saw him, you'd never forget him. The irresistible lure in his coal-black eyes wouldn't let you.

They invited, beckoned, promised. Countless women probably had been caught in the magnetic snare, just as she had. He could make a woman burn with an unquenchable desire, then just as quickly humiliate her beyond belief.

Erin didn't plan on giving him the opportunity to do either to her again.

"Don't you have anything to say?" she questioned hotly. "You've made it clear you don't want this assignment any more than I want you to have it."

His hooded lids lifted. Once again she was snared by his piercing ebony eyes. "Hired guns do as they're told."

Erin started as he tossed her unfair words back at her, but she didn't back down. It would be amazingly stupid to spend any time with a man who disturbed her as much as Hunter did. She had learned that undeniable truth the moment he spoke her name seven months ago. Time had only increased the unshakeable knowledge.

"You only do as you're told if it suits you." Her father had taught her always to finish what she started.

"Have it your way," Hunter said with irritating nonchalance.

"I won't forget this," Marcus said, his relief obvious.

"I have a feeling none of us will." Hunter straightened. "If you're ready, Ms. Cortland, I'll see you home."

She had to try one last time. "Daddy, can't you find someone else? It's obvious Hunter and I are not going to get along."

"That makes him ideal. Until this mess is over you and he are going to be living out of each other's back pocket's. You're a beautiful woman. At least I won't have to worry about him walking in his sleep,'' Marcus finished bluntly.

Hunter snorted.

It was too much of a reminder to her of his wanting her only for a one-night stand, and her uncharacteristic behavior to give him that impression. She shouldn't have kissed a complete stranger. No matter how compelling he was. But she had been so unexpectedly drawn to him that she had let her emotions rule instead of her head. Big mistake.

That night on the balcony, *before* his callous assumption that they would be bedmates, he had completely mesmerized her. Now he acted as if he barely remembered her. His control and her lack of it annoyed her to no end.

Draping her wool cape around her shoulders, she yanked up her briefcase. ''I'm calling your bluff, Daddy. I'm going home. *Alone.* Good night.''

''Erin, please wait,'' her father pleaded, his worried gaze flickering from Hunter to his daughter.

''I love you, Daddy.'' Brushing her lips against her father's cheek, she turned to leave.

Out of the corner of her eye, she saw her father glance toward Hunter again. Her pace increased. A few feet from the door, Hunter's voice pulled her up short.

''My orders are to protect you. That includes from yourself, if necessary. So think long and hard about going any farther without my permission.''

Erin spun in three-inch-heeled boots. Her cape swirled furiously around her. ''Your permission? Who do you think you are?''

''Erin, please—''

''Walk out that door and find out.'' Hunter's voice cut through Marcus's placating tone.

Her damp fingers tightened around the handle of her case. She knew that, beneath the brown suede bomber jacket and indecently tight-fitting blue jeans, his muscles were poised and waiting for her next move. It didn't take much to remember their strength or her urgent need to feel his heated flesh beneath her searching fingertips.

"Unless you want to be charged with assault, *you're* the one who should think long and hard before you try to stop me." Her chin lifted. She started for the door.

Her father reached her first. Hunter was a step away, his stance rigid.

It registered in her mind that he had covered twice the distance she had, in half the time. Seeing the blazing intensity of his black eyes, something else registered. She had finally elicited a reaction from him. Only now she didn't know how to handle him. She almost felt as if she had teased a wild animal in a cage, then found out that the cage door was open.

Marcus's placating voice cut through the tension-filled room. "If the police are right, you'll only have to have Hunter around for a day or two."

"I'm not sure I could stand him that long." She tried but failed to block out Hunter's hovering presence less than a foot away.

"My daughter could do anything she set her mind to." The pride and love in his voice were unmistakable.

Love and warmth swept through her. Dropping her case, she went into his arms. Her own tightened when she felt her father tremble.

Over his shoulder, she gazed into Hunter's enigmatic eyes. Her stomach muscles clenched. His gaze narrowed, then he walked over to the French doors and stood looking out over the estate. She was unable to keep her eyes from following.

She didn't know what to think of a man who seemed to be so self-contained, so emotionless one moment, yet so dangerous and compelling the next.

She was aware of him even when she didn't want to be. Every time she'd turned to him tonight, he had been looking at her without a trace of emotion, yet she sensed he could close his eyes and describe her in the most minute detail. She knew she could describe him.

She mentally shook herself. Hadn't she promised herself not to run away from anything else in her life that frightened her?

And that included Hunter. Her insecurities were no reason to make her father suffer. He had been worried enough.

Straightening, she tried unsuccessfully to bring a smile to her face as she picked up her case. "You can still negotiate with the best of them."

He smiled. "And don't you forget it. Now remember your promise to follow Hunter's orders regarding your safety?"

"No" sprang into her mind, then died on her lips. This was Hunter's field of expertise. She grudgingly admitted that if she had to go into a dark alley, Hunter would be the one she would choose to go in with her.

"Don't worry, Daddy. I'm sure we'll manage." She glanced toward Hunter, unsurprised that he was watching them again. His instinct for timing was uncanny.

Without a word, she walked slowly from the room, knowing he was close behind. Outside, she hunched her shoulders against the biting January wind and quickened her steps to her car. She reached for the handle of her Mercedes parked in the circular driveway.

"We're taking my car." The voice came from directly behind her.

Erin glanced at the dark blue prehistoric Mustang. Too small. Too intimate. Too slow. "I prefer driving mine."

The door she opened banged shut under the force of Hunter's hand. "Look, Ms. Cortland. Huntsville is only 150 miles from Austin. In the four hours Scanlon has been free, he's had more than enough time to get here and find you. He'd have no more compunction about killing you than he did the couple in the convenience store."

A chill ran down her spine. Her voice wobbled. "So nice of you to remind me."

The lines around his mouth deepened. "I'll do whatever it takes to help you remember that that creep is playing for keeps."

"Maybe the police are right about . . . everything," Erin said, needing reassurance. She didn't get it.

"And maybe that's what he wanted the police and everyone else to think." Hands on hips, Hunter stared down into her uncertain face.

"Since he only made a verbal threat in the courtroom, the police fulfilled their obligation by notifying you of his escape. If you weren't Marcus Cortland's daughter, you probably would have been lucky to receive a phone call. But because some guard was rushing to get back to a card game and screwed up, the police are trying to cover his sorry behind and theirs. Scanlon is out there. Forget it for an instant and he wins."

Erin shivered. "If he wins . . . I lose."

"He won't." Hunter spoke without hesitation. "We'll pick up your car tomorrow. In the meantime, do you need a garage or gate opener to get into your place?"

"I live in a house. The garage remote is in my purse."

He glanced around the estate. "What about getting back in here?"

"The gates are manned twenty-four hours a day by security guards. They know me."

A dark eyebrow arched. "Staying here would be a lot safer for you."

"It's not my home. No criminal is going to make me feel powerless again." She hadn't meant to reveal so much. Her lips clamped together.

"Where do you live?"

She gave him the address. "It's a twenty-minute drive from here."

"I know."

Surprise narrowed her eyes. "You've been to Austin before?"

"Once," came the terse reply. It didn't invite questions. Erin took the hint.

He opened the door to her car, pressed the lock, then slammed it shut again. Taking her arm, he led her to his car, parked in front of hers. "Get in. I know what it can do, and Scanlon won't recognize it."

She resisted when he attempted to put her in the car. Instead, she studied his harsh face illuminated by the lights shining from the multi-paned windows of her father's two-story Georgian mansion. "Why are you telling me *now* why you wanted to take your car?"

"Because from now on there's no turning back for either of us. Your life may depend on your following my orders the first time. There may come a time when I don't have time to tell you twice or to explain. Now you'll understand and remember everything I tell you has a reason." Applying just enough pressure, he urged Erin inside the car. Clearly, he considered their conversation to be over.

Seated, Hunter shoved the key into the ignition, then flicked his wrist. The engine roared to life, then took off like the proverbial bat out of hell.

The corners of Erin's mouth lifted wryly. So much for judging on appearance. She should have know a man like Hunter wouldn't have anything, machine or woman, that didn't respond to him immediately and completely. That left her out.

Her nails bit into the soft leather of her purse as she looked out the window at the passing Austin traffic. Todd Randolph, her ex-husband, had called them incompatible. He had been too much of a gentleman to call her cold. She had found out too late that she had confused fondness for love.

Todd had been patient with her, but after a year he had cut his losses. Ever the gentleman, he took full responsibility for the failure of their marriage. They had parted friends and still kept in touch both professionally and socially.

She had never responded to him as she had to Hunter. She hadn't known she could. She had been filled with part hope, part fear, that she had found a man who could finally set her body free. Hunter had only wanted her body. Not the woman.

Forcing her mind away from the night they met, Erin watched

the light in the dome of the state capitol as the Mustang roared through the night. It didn't surprise her that he cut the driving time to her house by six minutes. Apparently he didn't want to be in a small space with her any more than she did with him.

For the first time since the robbery, Erin was actually glad to see her house. Apparently, Hunter was not.

"You live in a forest."

Erin almost smiled. Something besides her had irritated Hunter. The single-level dwelling sat a hundred and fifty feet back from the meandering street. In the immense front yard were twelve mature oak trees, some with two or more trunks, towering over bare seasonal flower beds. Ornamental shrubbery ringed the house. All the homes in the exclusive subdivision were on one-acre lots.

"Blame my parents. Coming from Louisiana, they were both used to a lot of trees and water."

Hunter stopped in front of the attached garage. "I don't see any water."

"In the back there's a cascading pool leading to the swimming pool, a Japanese fish pond, and a creek." Erin pushed the control to open the garage door, but not before she saw Hunter's grimace. "You don't like water."

"There are too many places for a man to hide." He pulled the car inside the garage.

Erin's smile died. For a split second she had forgotten.

"Where does that go?"

She glanced at the door to her right. "To a walkway leading to the back yard. Mother had it built so she wouldn't have to open the garage door to get her gardening tools."

"Is it kept locked?"

"Always." Opening the car door, she started to get out. Hunter's hand on hers stopped her. Puzzled eyes lifted to his.

"Let the garage door down first."

Erin hit the control. The double door came down as smoothly as it had gone up.

As soon as the garage door shut, Hunter opened his door and got out. "I noticed the alarm sign. Did you arm it before you went over to your father's?"

"Yes." Erin got out and was about to open the back door when Hunter stopped her once again. Erin waited for the next question or command.

"Do all the windows have sensors?"

"I believe so. The system was already installed when I moved in three years ago after my parents found a house Mother fell in love with," Erin told him. "They didn't want to sell this house or rent it so I moved in."

"You live here by yourself?"

"Yes."

"Give me the code."

"Why do—" Her words abruptly stopped when he pulled a gun. Big and black, it was too closely connected to her nightmares. She couldn't seem to take her eyes away from it.

"Ms. Cortland? Erin? Look at me." The unexpected softness of his voice reached through her fears. She lifted her gaze. "If you don't have sensors on every window, someone could break in and the alarm wouldn't sound."

She moistened her lips. "Wouldn't the motion detectors have set off the alarm?"

"Motion detectors are usually in the hallway or the main room, because a thief doesn't stay in one room," Hunter told her.

"Unless he wanted something in that room or was waiting for someone," she quickly reasoned. Scanlon wouldn't want to rob her, he'd want to kill her. A chill swept through her.

"Give me the general layout of the house and the code."

She bit her lip. "Isn't there another way?"

He looked as if he wasn't going to answer, then he responded, "If it were daylight or you had less of a swamp outside, I'd check the windows from the outside."

"I did have some of the shrubbery trimmed back." She hadn't the heart to cut down the trees. Her mother and father had planted every one. According to them, four-year-old Erin had helped.

"The code and layout."

Determined. Impatient. Two more terms to add to the growing list that described the hard man watching her without a trace of emotion on his face. She quickly gave him what he wanted.

"Stay here." Taking the key from her hand, he opened the back door and snapped on the light. He waited for the sharp shrill of the alarm to sound before he punched in the code.

Blood pounding in her ears, she watched him move through the kitchen, gun raised, then disappear into the den.

After what seemed an eternity, Hunter returned, his gun nowhere in sight. "All clear," he reported, and held the door open.

"What if it hadn't been?" she asked as she slowly entered and walked through the kitchen to the living room. Everything was as she had left it that afternoon to visit her father. The drooping fern still needed watering. The pile of magazines she never got around to reading still cluttered the cherry-and-glass cocktail table.

Hunter didn't answer until he faced her again. "Then I would have handled it," he said, certainty ringing in his deep voice. "It's after ten. You better get to bed. Tomorrow is a work day."

"You can have either bedroom," she said.

"They're too far from yours. I'll take the sofa in here."

Erin's gaze went to the wine camel-back sofa. Hunter's long legs would hang over the side. She fit comfortably, but Hunter was at least six inches taller and broader. "It's too small."

"I've been in uncomfortable places before. Good night."

Dismissed, Erin said good night and started to her room. How were they going to stand being around each other when they couldn't say three words without one somehow annoying the other? Yet he hadn't let his annoyance stop him from doing his job.

Slowly, she opened the door. Cautiously, she entered, her

eyes searching every corner of the spacious room, flickering over the four-poster bed, the lingerie chest, her small writing desk, the mirrored dresser. Her searching gaze stopped.

The frightened face staring back at her told her she had to control her fear or risk once again becoming a woman who slept with all the lights on and jumped at the slightest noise.

In less than fifteen minutes Hunter had destroyed all the confidence and gains she had managed to salvage. When he had entered her house ahead of her with a drawn gun, it had shaken her confidence. Badly.

The possible consequences of what might have happened terrified her. She didn't want anyone hurt; she just wanted to get through the day without fear. That wasn't too much to ask. Having Hunter dogging her every step wasn't going to help.

Deep in thought, she undressed and took a long soothing bath. Until now, she hadn't truly let herself believe there was any real danger to herself.

She hadn't believed Scanlon wanted revenge so much that he would risk capture. She had almost convinced herself that her father and Hunter were overreacting. Hunter had effectively shown her otherwise.

Shoving her arms into her ivory silk robe, she tried to analyze Hunter. It was impossible. She didn't know enough about him. Apparently, he had done this sort of thing before.

Now his job included protecting her.

Restless, she left her room to get her nightly glass of juice before bedtime. Moonlight filtered through the sheer draperies on the far wall of the living room. Halfway across the room, a shadow moved. A choked cry erupted from her lips.

"It's me." Hunter switched on the brass lamp.

His shirt was off, revealing muscular shoulders and a sprinkling of hair on a wide chest. His jeans were unsnapped and unzipped. Her throat dried.

"Did you want something?"

Her head jerked up. She looked into eyes that were hard. "N . . . o"

He came toward her, in that slow predatory gait of his that

made her think of a beast stalking his prey, or a man coming to claim his woman. "Then why are you here?"

She swallowed the lump in her throat. "I . . . I was thirsty."

His lazy gaze ran the length of her. She felt hot, restless. "So thirsty that you forgot to put something on under your robe?"

Erin flushed and grabbed the quilted collar of the robe and pulled it securely around her throat. "I didn't think. I'm not used to anyone else being here."

If anything, his expression hardened. "It won't work, Ms. Cortland. I'm not going to do anything that will give you a reason to tell your father I got out of line."

Surprise widened her eyes. "That's ridiculous. We can't stand to be in the same room with each other."

"Lust has nothing to do with one person liking another," Hunter pointed out.

Anger flared in Erin's deep brown eyes. "So you already proved."

"Look, Ms. Cortland, I made a clumsy pass in Chicago, which I regret. Having me thrown out might seem like a good way of getting even."

"You think I'd stoop to something that low?"

"I think you'd do anything to try and convince yourself that Scanlon is halfway to Canada. As long as I'm here, you can't do that."

Being half-right didn't free him from being half-wrong. "You're the one half-dressed. Is that your normal attire for protecting your clients?"

He scowled. "I didn't expect you."

"Exactly," she said with growing heat. "You don't see me getting all hot and bothered by a naked chest. I'm sure you've seen women in much less, so why the accusation? Maybe you're the one who wants to leave?"

"Now, see here—"

"What's the matter, Hunter? You don't like your integrity questioned?" she asked.

"Once I commit to something I stay until it's finished."

''The same goes for me. I gave my father my word and I have no intention of going back on it . . . unless you continue with these witless accusations. It might surprise you, but I've been tempted by better.'' She flipped the collar of her robe down. ''This is my home. If you don't like the way I dress, don't look.''

Continuing to the kitchen, Erin poured her juice. Tempt him, her foot. She had more sense. What she'd really like to do was dump her juice on his head.

Chapter Three

Hunter watched Erin go into the kitchen and felt a grudging respect for her. She didn't back down. She gave as good as she got . . . with interest. Hell, he *had* overreacted.

The silken robe clinging to her body had sent him down for the count. He didn't think he had ever wanted anything so badly as to slide that robe slowly down her sleek body and reveal every lush curve. And she had stood there looking tempting and untouchable. He had taken his sexual frustration out on her.

But she could have left out that crack about being tempted by better.

He snapped his pants, pulled on his shirt, and walked into the kitchen. He wouldn't mind something to drink, himself.

Seeing her with the glass upturned, revealing the slender curve of her throat and the graceful flare of her wrist as the sleeve fell back from her arm, need shot through him. The muscles of his stomach clenched.

He wasn't aware of making a sound, but he must have, because she glanced up. She looked from the juice to his head, then smiled. The implication was clear. If he got out of line again he'd end up wearing orange juice.

Without a word, he returned to the living room. She passed him a short time later, humming.

Life was a bitch in cleats and she was doing double-time on his back. The thing was, he deserved every mark she inflicted on his sorry hide, Hunter thought as he stared at Erin's closed door. Although she had gone to her room thirty minutes earlier, light still spilled from beneath her door. She was probably having a tough time falling asleep. She had been through a lot today.

He wasn't helping.

She was going to have a hard enough time getting through this without his acting like a scorned lover. The trouble was he wanted her. Too much. He was frustrated and edgy as hell. But he could never have her. He didn't mix business with pleasure. He'd forgotten once and lived to regret it each day of his life.

His job was to protect Erin. If he'd followed through on the signals she'd sent him earlier, he'd be in bed with her now. He'd satisfy the hunger that gnawed at him, but he'd lose the edge he needed to be objective. He'd have his mind on losing himself in her moist heat and not on protecting her from the man who wanted to kill her.

Turning away from the door, Hunter flipped off the light and walked back over to the draped windows. Accent lights tried and failed to shine through the dense shrubbery. The spotlights in the trees shone on the flower beds below. The back of the house was just as poorly lit. Her parents' thoughts had been on enhancement, not protection from an escaped murderer.

Through a few phone calls, he'd already learned that her security company routed alarms to the police department. The response time averaged thirty minutes. The house sat too far back from the road for a passing car or a neighbor to hear her if she screamed for help. Scanlon couldn't have things more in his favor if he'd planned them.

In the morning Hunter would have to see about updating the

security for the house and trimming back some of the jungle. In the meantime, he needed to get some sleep.

But sleeping on the couch had proved impossible. He couldn't breathe without inhaling the soft, flowery fragrance he associated with Erin. The scent reminded him too much of what he couldn't have. He could imagine her curled up on the couch with a book. Or a man.

His jaw tightened. What was the matter with him? He enjoyed women, but they'd never stayed on his mind the way Erin did. She was an assignment. Nothing more.

He drew in a deep breath, then glanced back at the couch. He'd never get to sleep on the thing. That left one place. The floor.

He'd slept in worse places while he was on police assignment. Considering the ankle-deep thickness of her ivory carpet, it was probably more comfortable than his bed, anyway. It looked like he was going to find out.

Crossing the room, he picked up his jacket to use as a pillow, just as Erin's door opened. Backlight revealed the shapely curves of her body as she came toward him.

Her curly hair framed her beautiful face. Her skin was the color of dark honey. Delicate eyebrows arched over light-brown eyes that could melt a man's resistance at fifty feet. Hunter stood at less than fifteen, and she was getting closer by the second.

His fist clenched. She still didn't have anything on under that darn robe. His body hardened.

She stopped by the sofa. "Daddy wanted you to have these." Her arms opened. A pillow, a sheet, and a comforter fell. Indignation in each step, she returned to her room. The door closed with a crisp snap.

Hunter's mouth twitched into a grin. The lady wanted a piece of his hide. He walked over and picked up the bedding. The grin slid from his face. Goose down and Egyptian cotton.

His sheets were whatever had been cheap and on sale. They had so many fur balls on them that he sometimes felt as if he were sleeping on sand. Erin wouldn't use them for dust rags.

The outside of the house might be a bodyguard's nightmare, but the inside was a decorator's dream.

The rooms were bright and cheerful, and the color scheme of rich burgundy and muted shades of green and beige flowed effortlessly from one room to another. Her side chairs were covered in linen.

Nothing in his small, one-bedroom apartment was linen. Even if she hadn't been a client, she was out of his class. So why didn't his brain and his body agree?

Easy. His control around Erin was pitifully lacking. He didn't seem to be able to get it out of his head that sometimes when she looked at him, he knew she wanted him, too.

Temptation was a son-of-a-gun. As long as she was sending out mixed signals, things would be all right. But if she ever made up her mind she wanted him, they were both going to be in trouble.

He could only pray that, before that happened, the police would pick up Scanlon.

Tossing the floral tapestry pillows onto a chair, he spread the sheet on the couch. Lying down, he pulled the comforter up to his chin, then dragged the pillow under his head. He had Marcus to thank for making the night easier, and little else.

Sleep hadn't dimmed her anger.

Sitting on the sofa with his hands behind his head, Hunter watched Erin head for the kitchen for the second time. This trip, she had discarded the clinging robe for a tailored red suit. Varying lengths of lustrous pearls fell from her neck over the ascot tie of the white silk blouse. In her hand she carried her empty glass. On the previous trip it had been full of orange juice.

"Do you have any coffee?" he asked, watching the sway of her hips.

"No."

Was that satisfaction he heard in her too-cheerful reply? There was definitely a swagger to her walk. Hunter moved restlessly on the couch. Erin Cortland certainly knew how to pay a guy back.

He might have thought she had lied about the coffee, but he had already searched the kitchen and hadn't found any. An electric coffee maker, however, had given him a smidgen of hope.

"It's eight-thirty. We better leave if you want to be in your office by nine." Hunter stood and shoved his arms into his jacket. As soon as he had made sure Erin was safe, he was heading to his hotel room to get cleaned up and call Paul.

"Giving orders so early, Hunter?" Erin cooed on reentering the room. "Let's see how good you are at following them. I won't have my company disrupted or have you following me around. I thought about this most of the night and I think I have a solution we both can live with."

Hunter folded his arms. "Don't you think you should leave this up to me?"

She rolled her eyes. "You may be a security expert, but I'm not an idiot. Once I'm in my office on the eighth floor, the only way to get to me is by the elevator or the stairwell. If you'll station someone in each area in four-hour shifts, I can be free to see my clients and conduct business."

Hunter had to admit her plan had merit. Except for one thing. "Your father wants me with you."

Up went her chin. "My father will agree if you will." She extended her hand. "Do we have a deal?"

His gaze never left her face. Stubborn and intelligent. A dangerous combination in anyone, but especially in a woman who could turn your insides out. "What about when you move around the building?"

Her extended hand clenched, then relaxed. "I'll take the man in the outer office. Of course my secretary will have to know what's going on, but it will work. We'll only need a day or two before Scanlon is caught."

"So I get the night shift?"

Her hand clenched again, then she drew it to her side. "I

thought about that, also. I assume you know of a female security person who can stay here with me.''

She didn't want him around. It was what he'd thought he had wanted, too, until he'd seen the fear in her eyes last night.

Despite what she tried to make herself believe, Scanlon was out there somewhere. Hunter would bet his next paycheck on it. ''We'll see.''

She opened her mouth, only to be interrupted by the chime of the doorbell. Hunter whirled toward the sound. ''Are you expecting anyone?''

Erin frowned, then smiled. ''As a matter of fact, I am.''

Hunter grabbed her arm as she started for the door. Wide brown eyes stared up at him. He ignored them, and the spurt of awareness that zipped through his fingertips. ''Ask who it is first.''

''I know who it is.''

''The person standing on the other side of the door doesn't have to be the one you're expecting,'' Hunter told her.

''Who is it?'' Erin asked.

''Erin, it's Quinn. Open the door,'' came the male voice.

She threw an irritated glance at Hunter. ''Thanks for making me feel silly.''

''I'm not going to apologize for being cautious,'' Hunter told her, his voice dark. ''Forget for one second that Scanlon may be out there, and that could be the chance he's waiting for.'' Releasing her arm, he nodded toward the door. ''Your account executive is waiting.''

Erin didn't move. ''How do you know about Quinn?''

''I called your father this morning and he filled me in on some of the employees.''

''My staff has nothing to do with this.''

''I had to know if Scanlon could use any of them to get to you,'' Hunter told her. ''Your father puts your safety ahead of everything.''

''Erin, what's the matter? It's cold out here!'' Quinn shouted.

She glanced toward the door, then back at Hunter. ''Who exactly did you discuss?''

"Everyone in upper management."

Anger tightened her lips.

"Erin!"

"We haven't finished with this discussion, by a long shot, Hunter." Stiff-backed, she walked to the door.

Hunter shook his head. Add tenacious to the list.

Quinn Mathis, his shoulders hunched in an olive wool topcoat, rushed inside the marble foyer as soon as Erin flipped the deadbolt and opened the door.

"Good morning, Quinn. Sorry to keep you waiting."

His grin showed perfect white teeth. "You're well worth the wait. You look sensational, as usual." He pulled off his hand-sewn olive suede gloves and stuffed them inside his coat pocket. "For a minute I thought you weren't going to let me in."

Her smiled slipped a notch. "Sorry."

"You know I'd forgive you anything." He slipped off his coat and tossed the expensive garment casually over his left arm.

With an effort, Erin kept her smile in place. Now was not the time for Quinn to begin his pursuit of her again. Especially with Hunter nearby. She had known Quinn since kindergarten. Friendship was all there could ever be between them. But no matter how many times she told him, he'd have occasional relapses. Not enough, really, to annoy her, and Quinn seemed to know it. "You promised."

His teasing grin widened. "Sorry. You make a man forget."

She knew an exception. Unconsciously, Erin looked toward Hunter.

Quinn's gaze followed. The smile froze on his copper-toned face. "Who's he?"

"A guest," Erin stated simply. If she told Quinn about Scanlon, he'd hover over her like a mother hen. He was sweet, but he tended to overcompensate where she was concerned. He had always been that way. He had never thought her ex-husband was right for her. However, in that he'd been right. "Quinn Mathis, meet Jake Hunter."

Both men gave the briefest of nods, but their eyes openly

assessed the other. They sized each other up like two males in the wild measuring their opponent's ability and skill before fighting over the female.

Erin glanced between the two men and wanted to kick both of them. Each was acting as if the other was poaching on his private property. ''Please have a seat and I'll get my things.''

Quinn started toward the couch, then stopped abruptly on seeing the neatly folded bedding on top of the pillow. His accusing gaze zeroed in on Hunter, from his morning beard to his wrinkled blue shirt. ''What's going on here?''

''If what you're thinking was right, I wouldn't have slept on the couch.''

Erin gasped and threw a warning glare at Hunter. ''I've had enough of this. Both of you are here on company business. Quinn, if you'd prefer canceling our date for breakfast at Fontaine's, we can do it later in the week.''

''No. We need to start working on ideas if we're going to get that account,'' he hastily assured her, then glanced at Hunter. ''I just didn't expect anyone here.''

''I know, but my personal life is my own.'' She slipped on her cashmere coat before either man could help her, then picked up her briefcase. ''Hunter, I'll meet you in the office in an hour. We can finalize our decisions about the arrangements we were discussing at that time.''

Hunter crossed his arms. ''That won't be necessary. The instructions from your father were very specific.''

''Surely you aren't suggesting you accompany us?'' Erin asked in disbelief. ''You can see that it won't be necessary this morning.''

''Nope, I wasn't suggesting,'' Hunter replied pointedly.

Quinn's mood brightened. ''Good, because the restaurant has a strict dress code.''

This time it was Hunter who gave Quinn a thorough once-over. Nothing on the other man's athletic body came off the rack. His coat slung casually over his arm and his six-button wool serge suit cost more than some people made in a month.

Hunter didn't know Quinn, but he had done some searching on his laptop computer this morning after talking with Marcus.

Mathis's family had been leading figures in Austin's society until his father's finances had taken a nose-dive about two years before. Bad investments in the stock market had wiped out the family fortune. Declaring bankruptcy had saved little. Besides money, the family had lost its social standing. His parents had moved to Houston, but Quinn had stayed.

Hunter studied the younger man. He had the lean, hungry appearance of a man eager to be on top again. He had the picture-pretty looks, the charm, to get there. Judging from the way he was dressed, he liked to indulge himself in the finer things of life. A definite wannabee.

''Why don't I just test the dress code when Erin and I meet you there?'' Hunter questioned.

Quinn bristled. ''Erin said she didn't want you with us.''

''I'm sure she'll change her mind.'' Hunter's gaze fixed on Erin. ''You haven't forgotten the discussion with your father last night, have you?''

She bowed to the inevitable. ''Quinn, we'll go to Fontaine's later on in the week. Hunter and I will meet you at Mama's Place. He and I have further business to discuss and we might as well get some of it out of the way.''

For a moment Quinn looked as if he might object, but all he said was, ''Are you sure?''

She flashed him a dazzling smile. ''I am, and thank you. You don't know how much it means, knowing I can always count on you.''

Pleasure swept across Quinn's face. ''I'll always be there for you. I'll see you at the restaurant.''

He had barely closed the door behind him before Hunter said, ''I think Mathis is trying to fill more than the vice-president's position.''

She started to ask how he knew about the vacancy, then remembered his conversation with her father. ''What's that supposed to mean?''

''Nothing,'' Hunter said, and pulled the car keys out of his pocket. "We better get going. We wouldn't want to keep Mathis waiting."

Hunter was almost feeling mellow. He had enjoyed his breakfast and his three cups of coffee. He didn't even mind Quinn's occasional glare when he thought Erin wasn't looking. Whatever their relationship, it wasn't romantic. Neither was sending out any of the signals lovers gave. He was just another man in her probably long list of adoring men.

Wielding that much power over influential men was another kind of power. Even in the short time he had known her, he had realized she liked being in control. She wasn't going to let any man, not even an escaped murderer, make her hand over that control easily. She certainly didn't appear to have lost her appetite. She had put away enough food to satisfy a trucker.

She glanced up to see him watching her. "You have something to say?"

He almost smiled. "You always eat like that?"

"I enjoy good food."

"Obviously you haven't known Erin long," Quinn announced, a pleased smile on his face.

Watching Erin's white teeth close over a link sausage, Hunter replied, "Sometimes you'd rather do other things than eat."

Erin choked and glared at Hunter. Unrepentant, he handed her his untouched glass of juice. She snatched it from him and drank half the contents. "I can certainly think of a few things I'd like to do to you."

"I'm sure you could," Hunter said lazily. "In the meantime, if you're finished, we need to get to your office. You're overdue to call your father."

"Oh, my goodness." She glanced at the thin gold watch on her wrist. Nine-thirty-five. When she and her father had talked this morning, she hadn't remembered her breakfast appointment with Quinn. The entire conversation had revolved around Hunter.

When she realized she wouldn't get anywhere in her effort to have Hunter replaced, she'd assured her father she'd call once she reached the office. Her secretary would think she was at Fontaine's, and if her father called and she wasn't there . . .

Frantically, she glanced around for a waiter or a pay phone. Her cellular was in her briefcase in Hunter's car.

"At the entrance, on the right," Hunter supplied as he stood and reached for her chair.

Erin didn't bother asking him how he knew what she wanted or how he knew where the phone was in a restaurant he'd said he had never visited. She grabbed her purse.

As soon as she was upright, gentle fingers closed around her upper arm. One look at Hunter's expressionless face and she knew telling him he didn't need to go with her was pointless.

For a wild moment she wanted to. She didn't want the restrictions his presence imposed. She wanted her life and her freedom back. She didn't want to be constantly reminded that a man wanted her dead.

"Mr. Cortland is waiting."

Erin headed for the lobby. The most important thing now was to call her father.

"Hey, what's going on?" Quinn asked. He jumped up from his chair to follow them. "First, we have to sit in the back, now this."

"Quinn, please," Erin said as he caught up with them. At the pay phone she opened her purse for a quarter. The jingle of a coin against metal brought her head up. Hunter held the receiver out to her. Quick. Perceptive. Wasn't there anything he didn't think of? "Thank you."

Handing her the receiver, Hunter moved in front of Erin and inclined his head toward the cashier. "If I were you, Mathis, I'd worry more about that anxious-looking lady at the cash register. I do believe she thinks we're planning on leaving without paying the bill."

"That's ridiculous. They know us here by name," Quinn said with a hint of superiority.

"Then why did she call the security guard over?" Hunter asked mildly.

"What?" Quinn whirled. The cashier, their waiter, and a security guard were watching them closely. Quinn glanced toward Erin. All he could see behind Hunter was a hint of red as Erin shifted while talking on the phone. "Why are you standing so close to her?"

Hunter smiled.

Quinn's lips thinned. "I'm getting to the bottom of this, and then I want some answers from you."

Hairs on the back of Hunter's neck prickled as Quinn approached the counter and the cashier handed him the newspaper. Suspicion and fear were in the employees' eyes as their gaze scurried from Hunter to the paper clutched in Quinn's hands.

Hunter already knew what the newspaper contained. He had hoped for Erin to have her privacy a little longer, but if the horrified look on Quinn's face was any indication, it wasn't going to happen.

Hunter subtly shifted until he had a view of the entrance of the restaurant and of the dining room. *Come on, Mr. Cortland, get off the phone.*

"Daddy wants to talk with you."

Left-handed Hunter took the receiver, his broad shoulder blocking Erin from being seen from the lobby. Since they were in a corner, she'd have to ask him to move or brush past him to get by. Since she wasn't particularly fond of doing either, he knew she'd stay.

"Hunter." Then: "I know. I'll take care of everything. Now, we need to get going." Hunter hung up the phone, grabbed Erin with the same hand, and started for the front door.

As expected, Erin dug in her heels. "Wait. We can't just leave Quinn."

Hunter stared down into her stubborn face and knew he had two choices: explain or drag her from the restaurant. He jerked his head toward Quinn, reading the newspaper, and the intent employees and customers surrounding him. They now numbered six.

"Unless you want to be grilled on your feelings about Scanlon's escape and go through a rehash of the robbery, I suggest you move it."

She glanced in the direction he indicated. Her hands shook. "I thought I had more time."

He hated hearing the vulnerability in her voice, hated his inability to do anything about it. "Come on." This time she followed without protest.

"Erin, wait," Quinn called.

Hunter didn't slow his pace until he was outside. Quickly he scanned the parking lot, then started for his car, parked tail first.

"Did . . . did the newspaper mention Scanlon's threats?" Erin asked in a strained whisper.

"Yes." He opened the passenger door. The slight pressure he exerted to help her inside the car was met with resistance. "What is it now?"

"Did they make it sound as if my life is in danger?"

Hunter noted her voice was stronger, the trembling gone. The lady had guts. "The newspaper wants to sell newspapers. The reporter who wrote the story knows that. It can't do it without controversy and innuendoes. You should remember that from the last time."

"I'll never forget."

"Come on, get—" Hunter spun around at the sound of fast-approaching footsteps. The lines of his mouth tightened on seeing Quinn with a newspaper in his fist.

"Erin, wait. There's something you should know," Quinn told her as he came to a halt.

She bit her lip, then looked away from the newspaper.

"We're leaving," Hunter said.

Ignoring Hunter, Quinn caught Erin's free arm. "You can't leave until I tell you something."

"Take your hand off her."

The deadly menace in Hunter's voice brought Erin's and

Quinn's startled gazes to him. Unclamping his fingers, Quinn took a step backward. His eyes were wary, watchful. "I don't know what's with you and I don't care, but Erin needs to know she's in danger."

"If you'd really take the time to look at her, you'd know she already knows," Hunter snarled. "What she doesn't need is you giving her a blow-by-blow rundown of the newspaper article."

Quinn was instantly contrite on seeing Erin's strained features. "I'm sorry, Erin. I didn't think. I was just so worried about you. You know how much I care about you."

"It's all right, Quinn," Erin said, then turned to get into Hunter's car. She was bending over when she heard a squeal of brakes. Automatically she straightened and looked around. An older-model sedan with tinted windows sped past them. Two loud pops sounded.

Shots!

With a cry of terror, Erin flung herself into Hunter's arms. Quinn ducked down beside the car.

"It's a backfire," Hunter told her.

Her body went rigid against his. Arms that had gone around his neck withdrew. Stiff with dignity, she stepped away. "Sorry."

Her voice was a strained whisper. Hunter heard it and it cut through him like jagged glass.

"For a moment I thought it was a gunshot," Quinn admitted, nervously brushing his coat off.

Hunter heard Quinn, but his eyes never left Erin. She needed to be comforted, reassured. She needed to be held. Her snooty account executive was too busy trying to hide his own embarrassment.

When Erin had reached for Hunter, Quinn had been ducking for cover. He'd put his own safety above Erin's.

And Hunter was too afraid to give Erin the comfort she needed. "Are you all right?"

"Yes." She got into the car. Hunter looked at her, head bowed, hands clasped tightly in her lap. He wanted to say something, anything, to ease her fear and, if he wasn't mistaken, her embarrassment. "You had every right to act the way you did."

Her head lifted, but she said nothing. Cursing his inability to help her, he closed the door. When he pulled off, he saw Quinn in the rear-view mirror, leaning against his car. Hunter felt no sympathy for the man. His concern for Erin was all an act. Hunter hoped she wasn't fooled by Mathis's suave, solicitous manner.

"For all my talk, I'm a coward," Erin said at last.

Hunter's grip on the steering wheel relaxed. "Death isn't real to a lot of people unless it's staring them in the face."

"I . . . I know. I thought . . ." Her voice trailed off.

"It doesn't get any easier."

"You sound as if you're speaking from experience."

"I am."

"Were you a policeman or something?"

"Policeman."

"Where?"

Hunter threw a look at Erin as he stopped for a traffic light. She had calmed down considerably, but she wasn't ready to listen to her own thoughts. He didn't like talking about his past, but then he didn't like the frightened look on Erin's face, either.

"Chicago." He knew what the next question would be. "I was on the force for eight years. The last five as a detective. I met Paul when I went out to investigate a burglary at his house."

She shifted toward Hunter. "You're the one who told him he was lucky the thieves didn't take everything that wasn't bolted down."

"Yeah." Hunter took a turn. He smiled at the memory. "Not the most diplomatic thing to say to an influential man who had just lost fifty thousand dollars in rare coins. Paul just looked at me. I thought I'd be in the chief's office before the day was out."

"Uncle Paul isn't vindictive. Next to Daddy, he's one of the sweetest men I know," Erin defended.

Hunter noted the defensive sparkle in her eyes. "He's shrewd, cunning, and tenacious. I'll reserve my opinion on sweet, unless he's around Grace. His eyes still light up when he sees her."

"They have the same kind of love my parents had. The forever kind. No one should settle for less."

Flipping on his signal, Hunter turned into the underground parking lot of Cortland Innovations. He wasn't touching that one. His parents hadn't had it, and few of his friends had grabbed the brass ring for life. "Where should I park?"

"Straight ahead by the elevator. My name is on the wall."

Hunter pulled into the next empty space. "Why don't we change your routine for a couple of days?"

"He could be watching, couldn't he?"

"I'm paid always to remember he might be," Hunter said simply.

"And I try to forget." She glanced around the crowded parking garage. "But you already warned me against that, didn't you?"

"It's my job."

"Of course. Shall we go in?"

Somehow her politeness irritated him. What did she want from him? To let her think Scanlon had forgotten about her? That he was heading in the opposite direction? Hunter couldn't let that happen. Paul wasn't given to panic. He believed Scanlon was coming back, and that was good enough for Hunter.

Grabbing her attaché case from the back seat, Hunter got out of the car, then helped Erin out. Her gaze darted around the garage as soon as she stood. "I'm here," he reminded her.

Woeful eyes lifted. "Only I wish you didn't have to be."

"Come on." He started for the elevator. Her words caused his gut to clench. She was frightened. She needed the warmth of another caring human. It couldn't be him.

They were both silent as they rode the elevator to the eighth floor. As soon as the door opened and they stepped off they were greeted by two burly men in dark business suits.

"Everything OK?" Hunter asked.

"Yes, sir," they echoed one another.

"Erin Cortland, meet Mike Stanley and Chuck Powell, two of the best men in our Chicago office."

Greetings were exchanged. Erin looked up at Hunter. "Does this mean you accept my plan?"

"We'll talk in your office."

The three men followed Erin down the gray-carpeted hallway lined with photographs of famous account spokespersons, past her watchful secretary, and finally into her spacious corner office. "Well?"

His lips twitched at her impatience. "They'll be here until I return."

"Where are you going?"

"To my hotel room to shower and change. If I'm going to blend in, I can't do it the way I'm dressed."

"Then you plan on coming back?"

"I'm coming back."

Relief: he read it as easily as he could read his name. And she'd never admit it. He spoke to the two men. "You have your orders."

"Yes, sir."

He started from the room. His name caught him reaching for the door.

"Hunter?"

He looked over his shoulder. Erin hadn't moved from her position. "Yes?"

"You won't be long, will you?"

"I won't be long." He opened the door, then closed it behind him. He only took long enough to introduce himself to the secretary and tell her the two men would be in the outer office with her until further notice. If she had questions, she was to ask Mr. Cortland. Erin was not to be bothered.

"Yes, sir. I read the paper."

Nodding, Hunter headed for the elevator. He met Quinn in the hallway. Both men gave the briefest of nods. Stepping onto the elevator, Hunter jabbed *G,* half wondering if Erin might be interested in a buttoned-down selfish snob like Quinn. Then he berated himself for doing so.

Erin was a client and therefore off limits. He knew that better than anyone. He hadn't listened before, and another woman had paid the ultimate price.

Getting out of the elevator, he headed for his car, making a mental note to assign a guard to the parking garage. The opening of his door and the ringing of his car phone coincided. Sliding into his seat, he picked it up.

''Hunter here.''

In less than fifteen seconds he was out of the car again, running back to the elevator. He barely held his impatience at stops on the second and fifth floors.

On the fifth floor all the passengers got off. The woman about to step on took one look at Hunter and changed her mind. As the door closed, he jabbed *eight.*

As soon as there was enough of an opening, Hunter emerged. Long, impatient strides carried him down the hall into Erin's outer office. The two security guards stood as he entered.

''There's been a change of plans. Check out the parking garage and have my car waiting by the elevator in three minutes. Eighth car on the third row to the left. Blue Mustang.'' He flipped the key. Stanley caught it. They were both out of the door in seconds.

Hunter entered Erin's office and saw Quinn standing close behind her, looking over her shoulder.

His gaze jerked upward. Outrage distorted his features. ''How dare you burst into Erin's office without knocking or being announced.''

Hunter's gaze never left Erin's. ''I need to speak to you alone.''

''Now see here. I've just about had enough out of you.'' Quinn rounded Erin's desk. ''Who do you think you are?''

''Believe me, you don't want to push it.''

''Quinn, we'll go over these plans later.''

Snatching the folder from atop the desk, he stormed out of the room.

Erin slowly came to her feet. ''What . . . what is it? Is Daddy all right?''

''There's no easy way to say this. Judge Hughes was found murdered thirty minutes ago.''

Chapter Four

A strangled cry erupted from Erin's lips. ''My God.'' Stunned, she sagged in her seat.

Hunter rounded the desk and pulled a distraught Erin into his arms. ''I'm here. Nothing is going to happen to you. You hear me? Nothing,'' he promised, praying that he was right.

Clutching his jacket, she buried her face against his chest. Her body trembled.

''I'm here.'' His strong hand sweeping up and down her back, he whispered reassurance to her over and over.

''What . . . what happened?''

''Hit and run near his home while he was jogging.''

Her head lifted; terror vied with hope. ''Then we don't know if . . . if it was Scanlon?''

''We don't know that it wasn't, either.''

Erin flinched. At that moment, Hunter wanted very badly to have just one minute alone with the man who had done this to her.

''Come on. Your father is going to want to see you once he hears about this.''

''He doesn't know?''

Hunter shook his head. "Grimes wanted to notify me first. Your secretary told him I had just left."

"I don't want Daddy involved in this." Trembling hands clenched and unclenched on the smooth suede of Hunter's jacket.

"You're his daughter."

"That's why I want him kept out of this as much as possible. I'm all he has left," she said, willing Hunter to understand.

"All the more reason to call."

Erin briefly shut her eyes. Knowing Hunter was right didn't make what she had to do any easier. Unsteady fingers uncurled. Somehow she made herself leave the comforting warmth of Hunter's arms.

"I'll call him." She picked up the phone, then put it down. Her hands were shaking. She clutched them together to still them. The effort was futile.

"There's no shame in being afraid," Hunter said softly.

She shook her head blindly. "I don't want Daddy to see me like this. I don't want him worried."

"Once he hears what happened, you won't have any choice. He'll come to you, if necessary," Hunter said grimly. "It would be better for him if he was told while you were with him."

Beseeching eyes lifted. "I wish he didn't have to know, but you're right. I want to be there when he hears." Turning away, she went to put on her coat.

"Sometimes you can't protect those you care about."

His gritty voice was filled with such desolation that Erin glanced back at him. His expression was as emotionless as usual. Must be her imagination. Nothing much probably bothered Jake Hunter.

"Come on." His arm around her waist, he ushered her out of her office.

The front door of Marcus Cortland's home opened as soon as Jake helped Erin out of his car. One look at the housekeeper's concerned face and Erin knew someone had already told her father.

"Hello, Georgia. Where's Dad?"

"In his study, Ms. Cortland," the elderly woman said. "He and a police officer are waiting for you."

Erin touched the frightened woman's thin shoulder in reassurance, then headed for the study. Two steps inside the room, she saw her father pacing in front of the fireplace.

"Daddy." He looked up. Fear stared back at her. They met halfway across the room. She went into her father's arms without hesitation.

"Baby." His voice sounded thick.

"I'm fine, Daddy," she soothed. "Really. You shouldn't worry."

Marcus Cortland hugged her harder. "I know."

She wished she could have spared him this. He shouldn't have to go through any more misery. "Daddy, why don't you sit down?"

He finally loosened his hold and studied her face. "I love you."

Her smile trembled. "I love you too, Daddy."

His face grim, Marcus fleetingly touched her cheek. "Why don't you go on up to your room and lie down while I talk with Detective Grimes and Hunter."

"Pardon me, Mr. Cortland, but I think she needs to stay," Hunter interjected. "Ms. Cortland can handle the truth and she needs to know what she's up against."

"I disagree." Detective Grimes stepped forward. He nodded to Erin, then spoke directly to her father. "We have nothing concrete to connect Scanlon to the judge's death. It's unnecessary to frighten Ms. Cortland."

"Then why the call and why are you here?" Hunter asked roughly.

"Chief Tolliver," Grimes retorted through clenched teeth.

Hunter studied the smooth-shaven face of the young officer and understood all too well. The former police officer recalled the annoyance of being given directives that you totally disagreed with by your superior. No matter; you had to follow them, regardless. ''How long have you been a detective?''

Grimes's sandy head abruptly lifted and his green eyes narrowed. ''That has nothing to do with this case.''

The defensive statement gave Hunter his answer. ''Obviously you haven't been around long enough to learn how the system works. Chief Tolliver has. The police screwed this one up when a convicted murderer was allowed to escape.''

''The Austin police didn't allow Scanlon to escape,'' the detective said defensively.

''To the public, the police is the police,'' Hunter pointed out calmly. ''And now they're going to want to know if the death of a respected judge has any connection to Scanlon's escape. To know if they're safe.''

Annoyance crossed Grimes's face. ''I keep telling you that we found nothing at the scene of the crime to connect Scanlon with the judge's death.''

Hunter lifted his eyes heavenward. ''Did you expect him to leave you a calling card? No one can be sure of anything at the moment. We're going on speculation. You choose to believe Scanlon is still in the Huntsville area, don't you?''

''Scanlon has no reason to return,'' Grimes said curtly, obviously tired of repeating himself.

''Revenge is a powerful reason,'' Hunter replied with blunt impatience. ''Without Ms. Cortland's testimony, Scanlon would be a free man and, joke or not, the Desperadoes might have reconsidered. From what I've heard, they admire ruthlessness and cruelty.''

Erin whimpered.

''Nothing is certain,'' Detective Grimes protested.

''You hit the nail on the head. Nothing is certain except Scanlon is free and no fool. He proved that when he escaped.'' Hunter ran his hand across his hair. ''You're all excited because he got rid of the truck you had the license plate to. But we both know he wouldn't have done that unless he had another car picked out.''

The detective bristled. ''Every stolen car or forced entry in the area is being thoroughly investigated. There are year-round signs posted in the Huntsville area warning people not to pick up hitchhikers. Police departments in the surrounding cities have been notified. A team of dogs has been out since early morning.''

''And he's still free,'' Hunter tossed out.

His body rigid, the policeman faced Marcus and Erin. ''We'll get him. In the meantime, the patrol car in your neighborhood has been alerted.''

Hunter snorted. ''So he'll pass twice instead of once. Perhaps shine a high-beam light through the forest in Ms. Cortland's front yard.''

Marcus Cortland frowned. ''Erin, perhaps you should move back in here.''

''No, Daddy. I'm staying in my house,'' she said firmly, thankful her voice was steadier than her legs. ''Hunter is there.''

''Stirring up trouble,'' Detective Grimes muttered.

''My daughter is alive,'' Marcus said with heat. ''He can stir up as much trouble as he pleases. He has my full support, and that carries a lot of weight in this state.''

''Yes, sir.''

Hunter was pleased that the young policeman had sounded more annoyed than surly or defensive. Although Grimes needed to get his head out of the sand, he was a valuable link to information Hunter needed. ''Mr. Cortland, why don't you sit Ms. Cortland down while Detective Grimes fills us in.''

Erin sank into the wing chair by the fireplace, her father's hand still clasped in hers. She didn't want to hear this. She wanted to pretend the judge's death was an accident. An unfortunate accident that had no connection with her.

''Here.''

She glanced up. Hunter was in front of her, a crystal tumbler a fourth full of clear liquid in his hand. When she didn't move, he placed one of her hands then the other around the glass.

''I . . . I don't want anything.''

''It's just water.''

Her hands closed around the glass. With an unconscious

grace, he moved to stand beside the chair across from her. His gaze settled on her.

He watched her with piercing black eyes that were meant to disturb as much as they comforted. He wanted her left with no illusions of safety. She was going to have to hear how one of the leading citizens in the city had died, and know that she might be next.

By the time Detective Grimes was finished, Erin was glad she had something in her hands. She hadn't needed the water as much as she had needed something to keep her hands occupied. Thankfully, the glass was only a fourth full, or she might have spilled it everywhere.

She glanced up at Hunter, a short distance away, and knew he had purposefully not filled the glass for that very reason. He seemed to think of everything and to know her better than anyone. She was too keyed up and anxious to worry about it anymore. She simply accepted what he was.

Shortly after Detective Grimes had given her the basic details, Hunter looked at the two men and jerked his dark head in a direction away from Erin. After patting her hand, her father followed Hunter and Grimes.

Now the three were out of her hearing distance and deep in conversation, which was fine with her. Hunter had sensed she was at her limit. His objective wasn't to frighten her, but to make her believe.

Once he was assured he had accomplished that, he had left her to find what inner peace she could. The task was difficult, at best, with the three of them only a short distance away, and her father listening to all the unthinkable details she hadn't wanted him to hear.

Every so often Marcus would look at Hunter, as if for confirmation of something Detective Grimes had said. For whatever reason, her father seemed to have completely accepted Hunter as her guardian. It was just as obvious, from his harried expression, that the policeman wished Hunter was in another state.

* * *

''We already started questioning Judge Hughes's neighbors and the residents where the accident occurred. As far as I know, we haven't come up with anything,'' Detective Grimes said, his tone impatient.

''What about the jogger whose dog found the judge's body in the creek bed?'' Marcus asked.

''Didn't see or hear anything. He's a retired car salesman who usually goes jogging around seven each morning. He stayed in until around eight-thirty because of the early-morning fog.''

''I wish the judge had stayed in,'' Marcus announced solemnly.

The young detective nodded. ''The fog cut visibility drastically. We've had a slew of accidents on the freeways this morning for that very reason.''

''The timing of the judge's death bothers me,'' Hunter said. ''Visibility was poor, not zero. From the distance you say he was thrown, the car had to be traveling pretty fast. Most motorists aren't that reckless in a residential neighborhood.''

''Yes, but remember there's less than fifty feet of concrete over the bridge. Then it's grass again. Most joggers don't like to break their stride or change their route. My guess is he was coming across the bridge in the street when he was struck,'' the policeman pointed out. ''Wearing ear phones, he probably never knew what hit him. It's a possibility the driver didn't see him because he was wearing gray sweats. After hitting him, the driver panicked.''

''He might have a point, Hunter. We have one of the finest athletic clubs in the country, with jogging trails around a small lake, but residents still jog in the street,'' Marcus said, his exasperation obvious.

Detective Grimes perked up at the possibility of an ally. ''The driver might have thought he hit an animal or something.''

''Except for one thing,'' Hunter said. ''You said there were no skid marks. Hitting anything that fast will cause a vehicle to veer, if only for seconds. The natural instinct is to apply brakes . . . unless you were expecting the impact.''

Detective Grimes looked crestfallen, Marcus alarmed.

''With all the accidents from the fog, it's going to make finding a car with front-end damage almost impossible,'' Hunter said.

''The glass fragments from a headlight may be of some help,'' Grimes said.

Hunter didn't hold out much hope for that, but he decided to keep his opinion to himself. ''If anything else comes up, let me know. No matter when, call me.''

Marcus took his cue from Hunter. ''Thank you again, Detective Grimes. I appreciate your efforts.''

''Yes, sir.''

Marcus saw the policeman to the door, then came back to Hunter. ''I'm glad you're here.''

Hunter glanced at Erin: eyes closed, her head back against the leather wing chair. Both hands were still closed around the glass propped on her thigh. ''Your daughter might disagree with you.''

Marcus smiled. ''You're progressing. She'll accept you guarding her over moving back in with me.''

''Only because she doesn't want you involved in this.'' Hunter stuffed his hands into his pockets. ''She's just as protective of you as you are of her.''

''I know. She's the best part of Charlotte and me.''

Hunter grunted. ''You were both stubborn, huh?''

''As Louisiana mules,'' Marcus confirmed. ''The hardest time in our marriage was building our first home. From landscape to wallpaper, we were at odds. You ever been married, Hunter?''

''No.''

''Engaged?''

Hunter lifted a brow. Marcus looked up at him with the innocence of a baby. A baby cougar. ''My business and marriage wouldn't work.''

''Maybe you haven't met the right woman.''

Hunter didn't like the way the conversation was going. He didn't know what was going on in Marcus Cortland's mind, and Hunter didn't plan on finding out. ''About the landscape. It's too easy for a man to conceal himself.''

Marcus's jovial expression vanished. ''Chop down every last tree and shrub if you have to.''

''The trees can stay, with some improved lighting. Ms. Cortland said you and your wife planted them.''

The tension eased from Marcus's round face. ''We did. Had some of our best arguments over where they should go. But, if Charlotte were here, she'd take an ax to them herself to protect Erin. Then she'd go after Scanlon.''

Hunter laid his hand on the older man's shoulder. ''I'll keep her safe. You have my word on it.''

''Hunter, do you think it was Scanlon?'' Marcus asked slowly.

He wasn't going to let her father or Erin hide from the possible truth. ''There's nothing I can put my finger on, but I'm suspicious of coincidences.'' Hunter rubbed the back of his neck. ''To survive in the streets alone for as long as he did took cunning and ingenuity.''

Marcus's lips drew together in a straight line. ''He'll use it to try and hurt my baby, won't he?''

Hunter's face hardened. ''He'll have to go through me first.''

''If you two are finished whispering about me, I'm ready to go back to the office.'' Erin stood and placed the glass on the small Chesterfield table by the chair. ''I only told Nancy to cancel my morning appointments.''

Marcus stared at his daughter in disbelief. ''You can't be serious.''

''I am. I just can't sit here thinking about what happened to . . . to the judge. I'm needed back at my office.'' Erin knew her words sounded cold and unfeeling, but she was unable to do anything about it.

''The office can get along without you for a day,'' Marcus told her.

''Maybe it could if we had a vice-president, but we don't,'' Erin reminded him, very much aware that Hunter stood silent and watchful.

''Then choose one of the three candidates.''

''Dad—''

''Choose and stay home until this mess is over.''

''I can't possibly make a decision with all this going on,'' Erin countered, and ran a distracted hand through her curls.

''You're willing to make one regarding your safety.'' Hunter's eyes narrowed angrily.

''Because I know the facts and have thought things through,'' she reasoned. ''Now can we please just go?''

''It's almost noon. When had you planned on eating?'' Hunter asked.

''I couldn't . . . I'm not hungry.'' Erin shivered.

''I am,'' Hunter said. ''If you'll remember, you ate most of my breakfast.''

Indignation lifted her head. ''I drank your orange juice.''

Hunter faced Marcus. ''What's for lunch?''

''I'll call the kitchen and see.'' Marcus turned to his desk.

''Please tell Georgia to prepare for two, because I won't be here,'' Erin informed her father. ''If Hunter won't take me I'll call a cab.''

Hunter's voice was deadly quiet when he spoke. ''You're not leaving this house unless I'm with you.''

Erin shivered at the coldness in his voice. ''I'm going, with or without you.''

''You promised to accept Hunter and do as he asked,'' Marcus reminded her.

''If you'll remember, I said I'd follow his orders—within reason. I feel it's unreasonable for me to slink off some place and hide.'' She cast a swift look at Hunter. His face wasn't reassuring. ''I did ask him to come with me.''

''I'll be happy to, in the morning. I need to implement certain security measures at your home before nightfall.'' A dark eyebrow arched. "Some of your swamp has to go, and I thought you might want to be there so I won't cut down the wrong things."

"No one touches my mother's azalea bushes."

"Then you'd better be there, because I grew up in Chicago. One bush is like another to me."

Erin's eyes narrowed. "I don't believe you, Hunter."

He frowned. "I promise I grew up on the South side of Chicago."

"Not that." She waved her hand impatiently. "You're too observant and too intelligent not to be able to distinguish the differences between things."

He pinned her with a look. "Until one night seven months ago in Chicago, I might have agreed with you."

Erin's breath caught.

"Weren't you in Chicago about that time, Erin?" her father questioned.

"Y . . . yes."

A frown marched across Marcus's brow. "As I recall, unlike usual, you didn't enjoy your visit."

"Daddy, I thought you were going to see about lunch." Erin reminded him.

"Oh, yes." Marcus hurried to his desk.

A lean brown hand on Erin's arm prevented her from following. Accepting the inevitable, she looked up into Hunter's face and waited for the question he was sure to ask.

"What made this visit different?"

"As you said, it's in the past."

"Then it was because of me."

"We both made a mistake. Let it go at that."

His eyes narrowed. His voice dropped to a husky whisper as his gaze lowered to her lips. "One thing I didn't make a mistake about."

Erin felt heat in the pit of her stomach, felt her body respond. Her nipples actually tingled. No, Lord. He hadn't made a mistake about their strong attractions to each other.

His touch, his kiss, the overpowering sensations he created

within her were like nothing she had ever experienced. It was like being caught up in the eye of a hurricane. She had felt helpless, but exhilarated.

He stepped back, the aloofness of his gaze once again shutting her out. "Your father is waiting."

All through lunch Erin tried to find her equilibrium again. She envied Hunter's ability to hide his emotions. Sitting across from her, he acted as if he'd never made her remember the power and the passion of the kiss they shared in Chicago. Now she couldn't forget.

He called to her in ways no other man ever had. She was as confused by it as she had ever been by anything in her life.

"If you're about finished, Ms. Cortland, we should be going." Hunter forked his last bite of pecan pie into his mouth.

Marcus set his coffee cup down. "Why don't you call her Erin, and me Marcus?"

"It wouldn't be professional," Hunter said.

"Dad has a point." Erin sipped her iced tea and studied the reticent man across from her. "It's going to sound strange around the office if you don't. The office is very relaxed."

"She's right." Marcus smiled. "But darn if I can think of calling you any other name but Hunter."

Erin made a face. "A few have crossed my mind."

Marcus laughed.

Hunter placed his linen napkin on the tablecloth. "If you don't mind, I'd rather not hear them." He stood. "We have to go."

Erin noted he didn't say her name and she felt a tiny pang of disappointment. Standing, she hugged her father. "Take care, and don't worry. I'll call before I go to bed tonight."

The door to the dining room opened and Georgia came in with something in a big brown grocery bag. "Shrimp gumbo for dinner."

"Thank you, Georgia," Erin said, reaching for the bag.

Hunter reached it first. He hefted the bag, then frowned at its heavy weight. "You sure you cooked enough?"

Georgia smiled, showing the wide gap in her front teeth. "You can't just make a little gumbo. Everybody knows that."

"He's from Chicago, Georgia," Erin explained, a smile of her own on her lips.

"That so?" Hands on her slim hips, the housekeeper gave him a thorough once-over. "Once you taste my gumbo, you'll be glad I made that big pot."

Marcus smiled indulgently. "Georgia's not modest."

"After eating her baked ham and squash, I can see why," Hunter said honestly.

The woman beamed. "Wait until you taste some of my specialties."

Erin rolled her eyes. Another woman who has fallen under Hunter's spell.

"I'm looking forward to it. In the meantime, we'd better get going." His elbow nudged Erin in the small of her back.

Marcus followed them to the foyer. "You're sure you can get everything in place by nightfall?"

"Positive. *If* we get going."

"I can take a hint." Opening the front door, he stood aside. "Take care of my baby."

"You have my word."

Kissing her father lightly on the cheek, Erin went down the steps to Hunter's car. Her thoughts were contemplative. For a while, she had been able to forget about Scanlon but, as always, he was in her subconscious. Waiting.

Her life was changing and there was nothing she could do about it. She was a victim again, vulnerable, but thanks to Hunter she didn't feel helpless or alone.

She didn't have to be strong all the time. He had seen her terror, and understood. He hadn't thought less of her, as she had once thought of herself. No one outside her Victim Recovery group had been so cognizant of her feelings before. Her father had tried, but he didn't fully understand.

She frowned as Hunter took the off ramp of the freeway. Her puzzlement grew as he turned into the well-tended grounds of one of Austin's finest hotels.

He stopped under the canopy for valet parking. She glanced over at him.

"Until Scanlon is caught, I'm not leaving you."

Unexpectedly, her heart lurched, then she realized he meant not leaving her to change clothes as he had this morning. For a crazy moment, the way he had looked at her, the deep timbre of his voice, caused her to remember again the night they first met, remember the soul-shattering kiss, remember the supple flex of muscles beneath her fingertips, remember the hot thrust of his tongue.

She shivered as need raked slowly over her. A need she only felt with Hunter, a need she wasn't sure she could combat or control. Her body had had its first taste of passion and wanted more. Much more.

"Erin?"

She jerked out of her musing and looked straight into Hunter's emotionless eyes. Not a flicker of desire glowed in their black depths.

Swinging her legs out of the car, she stepped onto the curb, heard the attendant close her door, and tried to get her erratic emotions under control. Hunter had probably been trying to distract her in her father's study and she had been too inept to see it for what it was.

That was why he had handled lunch so well. He simply didn't feel what she felt. She was an assignment, nothing more.

Grasping Erin's arm, Hunter led her into the hotel and to the bank of elevators on the far side of the elegant lobby. He had seen the unguarded desire in Erin's eyes, and cursed fate. Somehow he knew she was remembering their kiss, remembering their bodies straining to get closer, remembering the heat, the passion.

The memory had ruined him for other women and given him

some of the worst nights of his life. Any woman who could sink her claws into a man with a single kiss was worth taking a wide berth around even if she wasn't his client.

Erin Cortland was off limits.

He could only pray his mind would remember: his body had already forgotten.

Chapter Five

Hunter learned what an azalea bush looked like out of bloom, and a dozen more plant species that he could happily have lived his life without knowing the identity of. Erin pointed out each one and, more often than not, imparted some family history of when it was planted.

She and her parents had shared a lot of happy times together. He and his parents had shared nothing but a name and a house filled with material possessions that they both worked two jobs to pay for.

They had time for acquiring 'things', but never for their two children. He didn't remember one sports event or school function they had attended for either him or his older brother, Gregory. His brother, who lived in New York and worked for a brokerage firm, was just as driven as their parents had been.

Greg's kids were growing up without him, and his wife was getting that restless look. He was too intent on making money to notice he was losing his family. Talking to him didn't help. Hunter would just have to be there for him when the marriage fell apart.

Hunter had learned early that 'things' don't bring happiness.

He had a feeling, listening to Erin, that she and her family would have been rich if they'd stayed in the shanty Marcus was born in.

On his knees beside a four-foot hedge of Japanese boxwoods, he glanced sideways as he replaced a forty-watt bulb with a floodlight and noted Erin's pensive face. Throughout the afternoon she had remained by his side.

He hadn't wasted his breath to ask her to stay inside until he was ready for her to show him what she didn't want cut. He, of all people, knew the importance of having a semblance of control over one's life.

Scanlon's escape and Judge Hughes's death had shaken her control but, luckily, they hadn't completely destroyed it. She was still able to function.

At the moment, she was busy. More important, she was helping take responsibility for her safety. For someone as independent as Erin, that was important.

Standing, he helped her to her feet and looked over the yard. It was still a forest, but the feeling of denseness was gone. Lower tree branches had been cut, shrubbery shaped and pruned. The mountain of clippings being loaded into a half-ton dump truck was testament to that.

"You're sure that once the lights are on the yard won't look like Texas Stadium during a Cowboys game?" Erin asked, scanning the dual lights that were attached to each tree.

"Positive. I just made it more difficult for anyone to use the trees as covering." Hunter pointed to each side of the house beneath the overhang. "The motion detection lights on the sides of the house are another story. If someone activates them, the light is going to be pretty bright. Only trouble is, a small animal or a bird can do the same thing."

"How do you know which one it is?"

"By waiting, listening, and being prepared to see what happens next," Hunter informed her easily. "If it's nothing, the light will go out in ten minutes."

"If it doesn't?"

"I'll handle it."

Erin shivered, remembering Hunter entering her house with his gun drawn. "I see."

"I'm not a hot-dogger. I won't put your life or mine in jeopardy."

"I know. You're good at what you do," Erin admitted, clutching the empty container from one of the flood lights. "Obviously, you've done this before."

"I wouldn't be very much good to you if I hadn't," he said matter-of-factly.

"But you didn't want to be my bodyguard, did you?"

Solemn eyes turned from surveying the yard. "It's not something I like doing."

She bit her lip, wondering why she was pushing it. He was here. That was all that should matter. Still. "Especially not with me."

"Yes."

She'd asked for it. She just hadn't expected the sudden pang of sadness at his answer. She looked anyplace but at his face. "I see."

For a long time he merely looked at her. As if compelled, Erin lifted her head and faced him. Finally he spoke. "I don't think you do. Taking responsibility for someone else's life is not something I take lightly. If a maniac is determined enough and cunning enough, there's always a possibility he or she will find a way to get past your defenses."

His expression implacable, he stared down into her face with a compelling intensity. "No matter what, I have to be focused one hundred percent all the time. To let anything distract my concentration is to risk my client. If the other guy gets an edge, it won't be because I gave it to him."

A thought struck her. She looked up through a sweep of lashes, aware that she was being provocative, aware that that wasn't her style, but doing it anyway. "Do I distract you?"

There was a deliberate pause. Erin held her breath, waiting for his answer.

"Me and any other guy with a heartbeat," he finally muttered.

Before she had time to exhale and savor his admission, he was speaking again. ''Why don't you go inside and clean up? I want to check on everything and make sure the man your father sent over knows I want all the brush hauled away before dark.''

She blinked at the shift in conversation, then looked at the house. They had been inside a couple of times since they returned. She knew it was safe, but she just didn't want to be alone.''I'll pick up the rest of the empty light containers first.'' Unconsciously, she touched the brim of the Texas Rangers' baseball cap that was shielding her features.

''Keep your cap on.'' Once she gave him a nod, he walked toward the two men loading shrubbery onto the truck.

For a long moment, she simply watched the way Hunter moved when he walked, the easy grace, the underlying promise of power. He didn't scare her so much, now, as he confused her.

She admitted to herself that she had deliberately asked the question about her distracting him because she had been fishing for a compliment. She wanted to know if he felt anything more than simple lust.

In Hunter's usual irritating fashion, he had answered her question, yet left her feeling more confused than ever. ''Any man with a heartbeat.'' The problem was, she had difficulty developing a relationship past that point. Sure, men were attracted to her, but so far none had elicited more than a mild interest on her part.

Until the night she met Hunter.

He had awakened a sensual stirring within her that she had never felt before. A curious quickening of her body that left her on edge and restless. Now that he was around her, the feeling was growing stronger, almost urgent. She sensed, with him, that it was finally possible to experience passion's promise.

As if Hunter were aware that she was watching him, he glanced over his shoulder. Caught staring, she waved. She was surprised to see him wave back, even more surprised to feel a smile lifting the corners of her lips.

Trying to tell herself it was silly to be disappointed that he hadn't smiled back, she tugged on her baseball cap and began tossing the empty cardboard holders for the light bulbs into a large trash bag. Hunter was protecting her; that was enough. If she wanted more, that was her problem.

Finished, she took the plastic trash sack to the truck and tossed it inside. Seeing that the men didn't need her help, she strolled back to the porch. A frown worked its way across her face. Something was different.

Realization came when she neared the steps. It was the quietness after the sawing, drilling, and hammering that the electrician, the alarm-company technician, and the gardener had made, most of the afternoon.

All of the men had been waiting in clearly marked trucks when she and Hunter had arrived. In a matter of minutes, Hunter had given them instructions and they had scattered in every direction.

After checking on the man installing sensors on her bedroom windows, Hunter had headed for the front door. Erin had been a step behind him.

Hunter had stopped her before she set one foot on the front porch. He had turned those hard eyes on her. She was already preparing an argument to go in with him when he surprised her by telling her to get into her grungiest clothes and wear a cap. She hadn't wasted time asking why. She didn't want to be alone. She felt safe with Hunter.

It wasn't until after she had been outside for a while that she figured out why he had asked her to dress the way he had. He didn't want her easily recognized. She glanced down at the faded jeans she had forgotten she owned and felt like smiling again. He'd certainly succeeded. In more ways than one.

The yard looked better than it had in the past year. More the way her parents had kept it. Her regular yardman had retired and his replacement hadn't done any more than she told him, keep the grass cut and weed the flower bed.

The flower beds and azalea bushes had once been her mother's pride. It would be two more months before the azaleas showed their profusion of colors again. She had already talked to the gardener her father had sent over about planting tulips next week. The yard was going to be beautiful and lush again.

And she was going to be here to see it. Scanlon wasn't going to end her life.

She watched the men climb back in the dump truck and slowly back out of the driveway. The truck had barely pulled out of the driveway when a black BMW turned in. She recognized both the driver and the speeding car.

Coat swirling in the crisp breeze, Quinn slammed out of the luxury sedan and rushed to her. Grasping hands pulled her against his chest and into his arms before she could do more than stand. "I came as soon as I heard the horrible news report on the radio. No wonder you left the office. You should have called." His voice was an odd mixture of censure and concern.

"Quinn, I can't breathe," Erin told him, her words muffled, her face mashed against his top coat.

His head, resting against the top of her head, didn't budge. "You must be terrified with Scanlon free and Judge Hughes murdered."

"Erin doesn't frighten as easily as some people."

Quinn jerked around at the sound of the cool voice filled with disdain. Surprise quickly turned to irritation. "Your job is to protect her, not to interfere in her private conversations."

"Who told you that?" Erin asked, taking the opportunity to back up a few paces.

"I finally figured things out when I heard about the judge." Quinn shot Hunter a condescending look, then turned to Erin. "But it looks like you have the wrong man for the job."

Puzzled, Erin frowned. "What are you talking about?"

Quinn was only too happy to give her a reply. "I could have been Scanlon, just then, and he would have been caught flatfooted. Get rid of him and hire someone else."

Erin suppressed her vexation. She had seen Hunter whirl, his right hand reaching for the small of his back, when Quinn's car barreled down the driveway. "Quinn, I appreciate your coming over but, as you can see, I'm fine."

"I'm staying as long as you need me."

She barely kept her composure. Quinn was an old friend. He had lost more than just money as a result of his family's financial problems. He had lost friends.

He'd had to swallow his pride and ask her for a job instead of running his own firm. He tended to be overprotective, because she was one of the few people who had remained his friend. He didn't like to share.

"Thank you, but that won't be necessary. Hunter is here."

"That's exactly what I mean." His condescending gaze tracked from Hunter's bare head to his scuffed boots. "You don't know anything about this man."

"I know all I need to know." Lightly taking Quinn's arm, she led him toward his car. "Thank you for coming over."

His reluctance to leave her evident, he glared over his shoulder at Hunter. "If you're sure."

"I am." Erin gave Quinn a slight tug to get him moving faster. "See you in the morning. We'll have to catch up on lost time to nail down a presentation for Fontaine's."

Quinn's mood brightened. "I have some ideas that I think you'll like."

"You always do," Erin said.

"See you in the morning." Quinn practically strutted to his car.

Hunter stepped off the porch as soon as Quinn's car was out of sight. "I'll be in shortly. Why don't you go rest, and I'll warm up the gumbo when I come in."

Erin stuck her hands in her pockets. "Sorry about Quinn. He has a tendency to be overexuberant."

Hunter's face remained impassive. "Go on in. I won't be long."

Erin didn't move. Instead, she tried to see through the inflexible mask he used so easily. "Hunter, I don't know if it means anything, but I know if it had been Scanlon he wouldn't have gotten anywhere near me."

"Go inside. I'll be in shortly."

Not a flicker of emotion crossed his face. Feeling oddly let down by his lack of response, she opened the door and went inside. Her confidence in him hadn't meant anything. Why should it? She meant nothing to him.

Being attracted to someone wasn't the same as caring for someone. If she was going to be able to end their time together emotionally unscathed, she mustn't confuse the two again.

In her bedroom, she slipped out of her clothes and into the shower. The most compelling man she had ever met was also one of the most difficult to understand.

Hunter was an enigma, a man who didn't fit into any mold she knew. He could make her uneasy, but she couldn't think of anyone else she'd rather have with her.

After growing up watching powerful men defer to her father, it was refreshing to see someone who did not. Especially a man who was not rich or influential in her father's world, but someone who was so sure of himself that nothing bothered him.

Least of all the boss's daughter.

Grimacing, Erin shut off the water and stepped out of the glass enclosure. Therein lay her problem. While most men courted her favor because of who she was, Hunter ignored her for the same reason.

Her problem.

Pulling on a pair of butterscotch-colored leggings and a taupe, mid-thigh turtleneck sweater, she went into the kitchen to heat up the gumbo for dinner. Hunter was already there, his back to her, freshly showered. Water still glistened in his dark hair and dampened a couple of spots on his blue shirt.

The urge to blot the moisture away was so strong that she had to take a deep breath to stop herself. Instead she laced her hands together and watched the play of muscles in his broad shoulders, the cupping of his jeans on his hips as he bent over to adjust the flame under the gumbo.

Now, *that* was a distraction.

Suddenly, he straightened and turned. Cool black eyes swept her in one encompassing sweep. Her body heated, tingled.

He shifted his attention back to the pot. "Almost ready."

"I . . . I could have done that," she said, her voice oddly shaky.

"No problem. You were taking a long time in the shower."

She flushed guiltily. "I was thinking."

Hard, ebony eyes came back to her. "Scanlon won't get to you."

Fear swept through her. Not for herself, but for Hunter. He stood between her and the man who could be out there somewhere waiting to kill her. "I don't want you hurt."

The force and the intensity of her words surprised her as much as they surprised Hunter. "Neither one of us is going to get hurt. But my stomach is hollow after clearing the front yard, so hustle up and fix the salad. Bread is in the oven and the gumbo is almost ready."

"And you talk about how much I eat?" Erin grumbled good-naturedly as she opened the refrigerator. "And don't think I didn't catch you ordering me—" Her words abruptly ceased as the bright beam of the motion detector lit up the kitchen window.

"Erin, it's all right," Hunter said, a moment before he laid a hand on her shoulder and searched her wide, terror-filled eyes. "Remember I told you they might come on."

She swallowed, the terror receding. "I know. It's just that for a moment I forgot."

"A person can tell you something a thousand times, but until you actually experience it for yourself you won't know how you'll react," he said. "It's natural to be a little jumpy. Don't beat yourself over the head. You don't have to be strong all the time."

The softness in his eyes, so unexpected and so desired, was almost her undoing. To keep from reaching out to it, she picked up the lettuce. If she let herself be lulled into accepting Hunter's strength, she'd forget how to depend on her own.

"You better check the bread."

* * *

The motion lights came on three more times within the next couple of hours. Each time, they turned off on their own. Although Hunter had told her not to be alarmed, she noticed an almost imperceptible alertness about him each time.

Although she tried to keep working on an ad campaign for a cosmetics company, she just couldn't think clearly. The thought that Scanlon could be lurking outside, that he might have had something to do with Judge Hughes's murder, was never too far from her mind.

"You want to talk?"

Her head jerked up. From across the room by the fireplace, Hunter watched her with his all-seeing eyes.

"About what?"

"Whatever has kept you from turning the page for the last hour," he pointed out.

He saw too much. Slowly, she closed the file and stood. "Thanks, but I think I'll turn in."

"If you change your mind, I'm here."

"You're a coward." Erin didn't back away from the truth this time. Her bottom lip tucked between her teeth, she stared at her closed bedroom door. Through the door was her juice, but Hunter was also out there.

Perhaps it was for the best that she was around him as little as possible. Being around Hunter, delving into her mixed emotions about him, wasn't going to get her anywhere. She had enough on her mind without adding a man to it. She'd just have to be thirsty.

"Erin."

She sprang up from the bed. "Yes?"

"Your juice."

Hesitant steps took her to the door. She glanced from the full glass of orange juice to Hunter. "Thank you."

"You're welcome. Good night."

"Good night, Hunter." She closed the door and sat back down on her bed, a small smile playing around her mouth. She hadn't missed how Hunter's hot gaze had swept over her when she opened the door. He might say it was to make sure she was all right, but she knew better.

Maybe having Hunter on her mind was exactly what she needed. With the thought swirling around in her head, she sipped her juice and stared at the closed bedroom door.

"Judge Dan Hughes's body was found by a jog—"

Erin came awake at once, her body tensing, her mind absorbing the droning words of the newscaster with growing dread. With a muffled cry, she rolled toward the edge of the bed, her hand blindly reaching for the push button to shut off the radio.

"The police deny a link to convicted murderer, Harry Scan—"

Her palm came downward sharply. The small radio skidded toward the edge of the nightstand. She grabbed for it and hit the heavy brass lamp instead. Radio and lamp hit the floor with a loud crash.

"After his sentence, Harry Scanlon also threatened prominent socialite and businesswoman—"

Erin scrambled out of bed and finally hit the "off" button, but not before she heard her name.

Her bedroom door burst open. Erin shivered, as much from the lethal promise in Hunter's dark eyes as from the sight of him with a gun in his hand. His gaze made a sweeping arc of the room before coming to rest on her.

Air stalled in her lungs. "I . . . I knocked the radio off. Sorry."

Sticking his gun into the waistband of his gray slacks, he crossed to her. "Leave it, before you cut yourself," he ordered, bending down to pick up the shattered remains of a porcelain bud vase.

He smelled like spring and moved like the sinuous shifting of shadows.

His large, capable hands paused. His head lifted. His probing gaze settled on her. "Sure you're all right?"

"Yes." She had been caught staring again. Hastily, she reached for a piece of the vase.

"You better get dressed."

Erin's entire body went taut. She had forgotten she was in her nightgown. Heat moved from her neck up her face. Crouched in front of him in her knee-length nightgown, she didn't know if it would be more prudent to act blase or run for cover. Indecision kept her still.

Looking at the top of Hunter's dark head again, she knew it wouldn't matter.

Dropping the piece of the vase into the small wastebasket he held, she pushed to her feet and walked into the bathroom. When she came out, she was going to take a cue from him. Strictly business.

How did you resist a woman who looked at you as if you were the embodiment of her most private and erotic dreams?

Hunter didn't know the answer to his question, but he was damned sure going to find the answer. He was going to keep his hands in his pockets, his pants zipped, and his mind on the job.

But, Lord have mercy, Erin wasn't helping.

On the seat next to him, as he drove to her office, her lavender wool skirt rode up enticingly over the honeyed smoothness of her long legs. They were a temptation he didn't need in his present state. Long legs like that could wrap around a man's waist and lead him straight to the gates of heaven.

Gripping the steering wheel, Hunter shifted uncomfortably in his seat. He might have had a better chance of resisting if it hadn't been for what happened this morning.

After he'd rushed into her bedroom and gotten his heart out of his throat, he'd looked at her again, really looked at her. He had almost lost it. All she had been wearing under her short silk gown was her glorious skin. At the time, he'd felt like a pervert for having seen her that way.

Yet the image kept returning. Every time he thought of her crouched before him, he wanted to drop to his knees before her and—

"It's OK. You know?"

Hunter's head whipped around. "What?"

Her lavender-gloved hand motioned toward the radio. "I'm fine now."

Tension eased. His guilt didn't. "We're almost at your office." He zipped through a signal light on yellow, saw the Cortland building, and cursed.

Erin brought her gaze from the side window and focused on Hunter, then looked in the direction he was staring. Several people were in front of the building. Reporters.

"Don't worry; they can't come into a private building. We'll miss them by parking underground." Hunter drove past a newly appointed security guard at the entrance of the parking garage.

A frown marched across the smoothness of Erin's brow at the sight of another uniformed guard at the entrance to the elevator. "I didn't want it to come to this. I didn't want to involve my employees."

"You didn't." Parking, Hunter unbuckled his seatbelt. "Blame Scanlon."

Her hands clenched in her lap. It was a long moment before she lifted her head. "You think it was him, don't you?"

There was no need for Hunter to ask what she was talking about. Except for that brief time in the bedroom this morning, her eyes had been haunted ever since he told her about the judge's death. They still were. "Instinct tells me yes."

"There are a lot of police officers looking for him." Her gloved fingers picked at the gold clasp on her purse.

She had enough to deal with without hearing him tell her that the police were overworked and underpaid. The case would get more attention than most because the judge was who he was, but arrests took time. "They'll get him."

Nodding, she unbuckled her seat belt and reached for her door handle. ''Always wait for me,'' Hunter said, and then he wanted to curse again when he saw the trembling in her hand.

Getting out, he scanned the area and signaled the guard. Opening her door, he helped Erin out of the car and walked by her side to the elevator. She neither looked to the left or to the right. He jabbed *eight.*

One single finger of a lavender-gloved hand pushed *one.*

Hunter looked from the elevator panel to Erin. ''What are you doing?''

''Facing the fears I can,'' she said softly.

''They'll be on you like a pack of wolves.''

She looked at him with calmness she was far from feeling. ''Then isn't it fortunate that I have a man called Hunter with me?''

The door opened and she stepped out, Hunter by her side. She went directly toward the double glass doors, feeling the stares of every person in the lobby and everyone crowded outside in the doorway.

Her stomach churned; her hands were sweaty inside her gloves.

''You're sure?'' Hunter asked, clasping her elbow.

''No, but I'm going to do it anyway,'' she told him. ''Let them in.''

Hunter caught the attention of the guard by the door. ''Open up.''

The door opened. The pack surged in, their eyes gleaming, their lips bared over teeth that were ready to tear and shred. They would show no mercy.

Chapter Six

''When did you learn of Judge Hughes's death?''

''Have you lost confidence in the Austin Police Department?''

''How do you feel about Harry Scanlon's escape?''

The questions struck hard and fast, like tiny stinging darts. She had no shield against them, no way of answering the questions, nor did she intend to answer them. She was going to follow her own agenda. She had learned the hard way that it was best to give a statement to the media, to appease them, rather than issue a 'no comment.'

The pack was hungry and seemed impossible to control. Throwing them something to sink their teeth into would at least pacify them for a little while.

Erin held up her hand. The pack quieted. Microphones were pushed into her face, flashbulbs went off. The bright light for a TV camera enveloped her, then the camera zoomed in on her face to capture the most minute expressions, to be replayed and speculated on over and over until the next big TV news story.

Hunter's fingers flexed on her arm, his impatience showing

in the rigid line of his body next to hers. He'd have them for breakfast if she'd let him. His strength somehow became hers.

In a steady voice, she began to speak. "I respected and admired Judge Hughes, and, like the rest of the city and state, will mourn the senseless death of a man whose dedication to the criminal justice system was well known. His integrity was of the highest caliber. I'm sure the police are doing everything they can to bring the guilty person responsible for his death to justice."

She paused, hoping to put as much distance as possible between the judge's death and Scanlon's escape. "I have every confidence in the quick recapture of Harry Scanlon by the police. Thank you."

Erin had half turned toward the elevator when a female reporter rushed forward and asked the question Erin had dreaded. "Do you believe Scanlon was responsible for Judge Hughes's death and that you're next?"

There was a stunned moment of absolute silence, then the other reporters took up the cry. They crowded around Erin and Hunter, their eyes alert, their ears seeming almost to twitch with expectation. Hunter's hand on her arm was the only thing that steadied her and kept the fear out of her eyes.

Two security guards moved in front of Erin, blocking her from the reporters. *Hunter's doing.*

Erin might have let him take care of things for her, but she had learned early to fight her own battles. As the daughter of Marcus and Charlotte Cortland, a lot of social doors were open to her, but the business ones were a lot harder to step through.

She'd done it, though, because she had been self-assured enough, and, yes, arrogant enough, to think she was as qualified and as capable as anyone else. She hadn't graduated at the top of her class for nothing. Eventually she showed the skeptics that she had inherited more from her father than his eyes and skin color. Now it was time to remind the press, as well.

The female reporter from the TV station barely repressed her glee. Her sparkling eyes had nothing to do with the reflection of the lights. She wasn't after a story: she was after ratings, and she didn't care at whose expense she got them. Now the rest of the pack scented fresh blood, and they were closing in for the kill. If Erin turned her back on them, she might as well get ready for the avalanche of speculations and innuendoes that were sure to follow.

"Please let go of my arm and ask the guards to step back," Erin said calmly.

Hunter glanced at Erin's face and did as requested. As soon as she was free and the men had moved, she walked to the reporter. The smirk slid from the other woman's perfectly made-up face.

"What I believe isn't important. The tragic thing is that a decent man is dead and a convicted murderer is free. A murderer who has already taken two small children's parents. In your eagerness for a story, I hope you will leave *them* to whatever peace they have found."

Spinning on her heels, Erin walked to the elevator. Inside, she punched *eight.* Hunter was right behind her.

"That she-wolf will think twice before she tries to advance her career at your expense again."

"She made me angry," Erin said, still fuming.

"So I noticed."

Erin looked at him and noted the smile tugging at the corner of his mouth. She wondered what it would be like if he really laughed. "She got off easy."

He frowned. "You think so?"

"She had to deal with me instead of you." The elevator doors slid open, and Erin didn't slow her pace until she stood in front of her secretary.

"Good morning, Nancy. I believe you know Mr. Hunter; he'll be with me today. If there are any calls for him, please put them through immediately."

"Yes, Ms. Cortland," the secretary said. "Good morning, Mr. Hunter."

"Morning," Hunter responded.

"Please bring in my revised schedule and let's see if I can

catch up.'' With that she was through the door into her office. Nancy quickly followed.

During the day Hunter easily came to understand why Marcus had handed over his business to his daughter. Hunter had expected the intelligence; he hadn't expected the tenacity or the energy. She never seemed to stop. She went from project to project with admirable ease.

Cortland was a ''full service'' advertising agency that included marketing. And in all phases of the business, from concept to finished presentation, Erin was involved. She didn't take that responsibility lightly.

As time passed, employees came and went, their curious gaze shifting to him. She introduced him as ''Mr. Hunter,'' then went about her business as if he weren't there. If she had to go to another department, he went with her.

He could have been bored out of his mind, but he discovered he found the whole process interesting. Watching the creative side of advertising and marketing was fascinating.

The employees were a congenial, supportive group of men and women. Their respect and concern for Erin was obvious. He knew Erin was probably getting tired of being asked if she was ''all right,'' but she kept her smile in place and thanked them for asking.

Mid-afternoon, the one person Hunter had wanted to talk with entered Erin's office. Quinn threw a dismissive glance in Hunter's direction, then continued to Erin's desk. From the bits and pieces of conversation he heard, he determined that they were discussing the Fontaine account.

From Erin's occasional nods and Quinn's happy expression, Hunter could see that she liked what she was hearing. Quinn was becoming more animated; he rounded the desk and leaned over Erin to point out something in the folder he had brought with him.

Hunter wanted to jerk the other man away from her. The urge had nothing to do with his job, but something suspiciously close to possessiveness. He didn't like the feeling. He had never been possessive of anything in his life.

He pushed up from the chair and went to stand by the window.

"Hunter?"

He glanced over his shoulder to meet Erin's questioning gaze.

"Bored, or restless?"

"Neither. Go back to work."

After a pause, she smiled and did as requested. The smile shouldn't have made him feel a strange unfurling of power and warmth, but it did. Ruthlessly, he clamped down on the emotion. Erin wasn't for him.

Several minutes later, Hunter heard Quinn leaving.

"I'll be back in a minute." He caught up with Quinn in the hallway.

"Mathis, I'd like to talk with you."

"I can't imagine anything we need to talk about." The younger man kept walking.

"That's where you're wrong." Hunter stepped in front of the agitated man, then glanced around to ensure that they wouldn't be overheard and to see that he had an unobstructed view of the entrance to Nancy's office. "From now on, keep your opinions and fears to yourself."

Belligerence shone in Quinn's eyes. "I don't have to listen to you."

"We both know someone you do have to listen to," Hunter told him easily.

Quinn's bravado faded. "Marcus knows how I feel about Erin."

Hunter's smile wasn't comforting. "If it came down to Erin's peace of mind or your feelings, we both know there would be no contest."

"You've made your point," Quinn said through clenched teeth.

"I hope you mean it, because this is the last time we're going to have this conversation. Because if we have to have it again, once Marcus finishes, it'll be on my terms,'' Hunter said, his voice full of menacing promise.

Eyes wide and fearful, Quinn took a step backwards.

''Call the next time before you come over.'' Leaving a furious Quinn, Hunter slipped back into Erin's office. She was watching him when he opened the door, unspoken questions in her brown eyes. ''I just needed to check on something. Everything's fine.''

He watched the fear recede, watched her go back to work. Taking a seat across the room, he sat down and continued to watch her, something he was finding himself doing more for pleasure than he was as part of his job.

As long as he took it no further, they were both safe. Simply put, he enjoyed looking at her. Whether she was pensive, as she was now, or ready to take on anyone who stood in her way, she was the most fascinating woman he had ever met.

It wasn't just her sensual beauty, though that was what had first attracted him to her; it was the woman beneath. Strong. Loyal. Fiercely protective of those she loved. Courageous.

His mouth twitched. Stubborn, too.

She tapped a pen against her lips, then stuck it into her mouth. He sucked in his breath and turned to gaze out the window on the other side of the room.

Around Erin, he remembered he was a man first and her bodyguard second. A dangerous situation.

''I have a confession to make.''

Hunter glanced up from the laptop computer he was working on and straight into Erin's troubled brown eyes. The campaign she had been studying for the cosmetics firm lay closed on the den sofa beside her.

She had been restless since the conversation she had had with her father just before they left her office. That was three hours ago. Hunter had thought at the time she had run into another dead end in trying to get rid of him. It had bothered him then and, in the three hours since, the mild disappointment hadn't eased.

He assumed that, as the night wore on, she'd relax and accept the fact that he was staying. It hadn't happened. Even after putting in ten hours at work, she was still revved up. Her gaze was alert, if a bit uneasy. She sat, stiff-backed, across from him.

Hunter shut down the system. He had a feeling this was going to take time and concentration. "What is it?"

Erin's hands clenched and unclenched her navy-blue slacks. "You're not going to like it."

"That may be, but you won't know for sure until you tell me what it is," Hunter said reasonably.

"I would have told you before, but you made me so angry I forgot." Her plum-colored lips pursed in annoyance.

"I see. So, whatever it is, it's my fault," Hunter offered.

Erin opened her mouth, then snapped it shut. She screwed up her face. "No, I'm responsible for my own behavior."

Hunter smiled. She sounded like an elementary-school student being told to repeat a rule she had just broken. "Does this oversight have something to do with the conversation you had with Marcus before you left work?"

Her eyes widened, then skirted away. "Yes."

"Then you might as well confess. I told him I'd give him a call later on tonight."

"I know." She stood. "It's really not so bad when you think about it. It's practically funny."

"Then why don't you tell me so we both can have a good laugh," Hunter said.

Instead of answering, Erin started out of the room. Hunter instinctively followed. She grasped one end of the glass-and-cherry cocktail table in front of the sofa he slept on in the living room. "I need your help."

A frown darted across his dark face. She couldn't want to rearrange furniture at this time of night. "Erin, can't it wait until tomorrow?"

"No."

Hunter helped her move the table. As soon as it was settled, she went to the sofa and removed the tapestry pillows, then the three cushions. Before the last one was stacked neatly on the wing chair, Hunter knew.

The sofa he had slept cramped on for two nights was a sleep sofa.

Hands in pockets, Erin stared at the wide expanse of queen-sized comfort she had just revealed. "You have every right to be upset."

"One question?"

Erin steeled herself. She wasn't letting Hunter's soft voice lull her. "You're entitled."

"If your father hadn't found out, where would I be sleeping tonight?"

His words sent a shaft of heat surging through her. She controlled it with the same ruthlessness with which she sought to control her fears. "I would have told you," she admitted with only a wisp of huskiness in her voice.

With his muscular arms folded across his tan-shirted chest, he studied her for a long moment, then: "Why tonight?"

"Because it's the first night I haven't been consumed with fighting my own fears long enough to think of someone else." Her confession surprised her as much as it did Hunter.

His arms came to his side. His expression softened. "You're entitled."

Seeing him relax and hearing her words repeated to her eased some of the tension within her. "I don't like being afraid."

"Or admitting to those fears," he said softly. "Somehow you've connected fear with control. You seem to think the only time you can be in control is when you aren't afraid. Fear can be as healthy as any other emotion, and as useful."

Erin wanted to deny the first part of his statement, but couldn't. "For me, they are connected."

"You don't have to have physical scars to be a victim." Hunter said tightly. "The emotional scars can be just as shattering. You have every right to feel powerless and afraid. You did your part, and the system let you down by allowing Scanlon to escape. Don't beat yourself over the head because you need a night light on to go to sleep.''

Her stricken eyes widened. ''How—?''

''There's a faint light under your door each night, but the lamp was off by this morning. If the lamp had been on you wouldn't have knocked off the radio.''

His perception somehow angered her. ''So, I sleep with a night light on. You don't know what it is to have your life turned upside down and your confidence shaken.''

''Yes, I do,'' he answered, his face taut and grim. ''More than you know.''

The admission hurled between them brought her up short. She heard the regret, the anger, and the guilt in his voice. Her own anger vanished. ''Is that why you left the police department?''

''Yes.''

The word was clipped, final. There would be no discussion. He had shut her out. She understood. Some things were difficult to accept or to discuss. She wasn't ready to lay bare her soul and, judging from the fury she had glimpsed earlier in his black eyes, neither was he.

''Did you talk with Detective Grimes today?''

''I called while you were in the bedroom, changing.'' Once again Hunter's face was remote. ''He had nothing new to report.''

Erin hadn't thought so. If nothing else, Hunter, unlike everyone else, didn't keep things from her. ''Is that good or bad?''

''It's hard to say.'' He sighed and rammed both hands into the pockets of his jeans. ''The best guess is that Scanlon's holed up someplace, since there have been no reports of anyone seeing him.''

Erin bit her lip. ''Where? Austin or Huntsville?''

Hunter kept his gaze steady. ''No one knows for sure. There were five auto thefts in the Huntsville area within ten hours of Scanlon's escape. Two of the cars are still missing.''

''If . . . if one of the car thieves was Scanlon, he had enough time to drive to Austin and . . .'' Her voice trailed off.

"Yes."

Erin's legs trembled. She sagged on the edge of the mattress, desperately trying to deny what was in Hunter's face, his rigid stance. "But he would have to have known where the judge lived."

"He was listed. All Scanlon had to do was look in the phone directory."

She felt chilled to her bones. Her worried gaze lifted. "My parents were listed in the phone book. The main library has all the old directories."

Hunter hunkered down in front of her and took her icy hands in his. "You're giving him too much credit. First, he'd have to know you lived in your parents' house. Second, those directories aren't kept out, and to get one he'd have to ask. He's not going to risk it."

"Then why the security?" she asked.

"I like being prepared," he said simply.

Hands clasped, staring down into his jet black eyes, Erin's terror, which had almost overwhelmed her, slowly withdrew. The judge had gone on blind faith; Hunter prepared for every eventuality. He assumed the worst and guarded against it.

Her Daddy and Paul had been right in their estimation of Hunter's skills. If anyone could keep her safe, it was the powerfully built man holding her hands. She had tried to erect a barrier against leaning on his strength, and had failed miserably.

Perhaps that was why she was able to let her guard down. With him, she didn't have to pretend. "I'll get your bedding."

"I can take care of it." Withdrawing his hands, he pushed himself up to his imposing height and stepped back. "Go get your juice."

Erin made a face and headed for the kitchen. He was also the only one who gave her orders. Even her father tried reasoning with her. Strange: Hunter's autocratic manner didn't bother her as much as it had two days ago.

What did bother her was the guilt and rage that had flickered across his face when she asked about the police department.

While Hunter took care of other people, who took care of him? Had someone been there for him when he needed it?

Reentering the living room, she saw him making up the sofa bed. He glanced up, and she was captured by the intensity of his eyes, dark and compelling. The rest of his features were just as captivating, with his sensual lower lip and his strong jaw.

He was easily one of the most self-sufficient men she had ever met. Yet she wondered and she worried, because he was also one of the most adept at hiding his feelings.

Hands braced on his hips, he asked, ''Something bothering you?''

''Yes, but I'll have to work it out for myself. Good night, Hunter.''

''Night.'' He tossed a pillow on the bed. ''Leave the lamp on until you're ready to turn it off.''

Erin paused. No one had given her permission to show her fears except her recovery group . . . until Hunter. She had sustained only a bump on the head from the steering wheel, so people were quick to tell her how lucky she was. Hunter knew it wasn't that simple.

He knew how quickly life could be taken.

Nodding, she continued to her bedroom and softly closed the door. The bedside lamp was already on. The light stood like a silent sentinel, keeping her nightmares at bay.

She wished she was strong enough to sleep in complete darkness. She wasn't. She accepted that hard truth and waited for the guilt that always came with the knowledge.

This time, it never came.

Instead, she remembered Hunter's words, his easy acceptance of her fears. He was a complicated man. He looked hard, but, underneath, he was sensitive and caring. It would take a lifetime to figure him out.

Going to her lingerie chest, she took out a nightgown. A long flannel one that covered her from head to toe. She wasn't taking any more chances that he'd catch her again in a revealing nightgown. Not that he would let himself notice for more than a second.

He wouldn't even unbend enough to call her by her first name. He just turned those magnetic eyes on her, demanding she look at him, and she always did.

Pulling her sweater over her head, she wondered why his refusal to call her by name disturbed her, and why she dreaded the thought that he never would.

Chapter Seven

Seeing the department heads already seated around the conference table sent Erin's simmering temper a couple of degrees higher. She prided herself on being punctual and demanded the same from those working for her. There were no reasons for keeping a client waiting, only excuses.

This morning she had learned that there were reasons.

Erin's reason for being late was shadowing her every movement. She had been thinking so much about him last night that she had forgotten to set her alarm. She had finally awakened on her own, twenty-seven minutes later than usual. Frantically, she had jumped out of bed, grabbed her robe, and gone to tell Hunter to get ready.

He was already dressed and calmly eating breakfast. He had looked up and asked if she was ready for hers.

"Why didn't you wake me up?"

He shrugged broad shoulders. "You needed your sleep more. I called and told Nancy and your father you were going to be late."

"What!" She couldn't believe his audacity. "You had no right to do anything of the kind. I'm behind as it is."

''Since you don't want breakfast, you better get dressed.'' He checked his watch. ''You just have time to make the creative session scheduled for nine-thirty.''

Contenting herself with a withering look, she had rushed to get ready. She had grabbed the easiest things to put on, cuffed tobacco-colored pants and a bronze metallic crew-neck sweater. It had been sheer luck to find the scarf that went with the sweater. When she had rushed back out, Hunter had been waiting by the back door.

He had driven in silence while she used the mirror on her visor to put on her make up. Mascara and liner were impossible. She settled for lipstick and a few swipes of her powder puff. Once she had glanced around while applying her lipstick, and directly into Hunter's hungry black eyes. Her stomach felt as if she had taken a fifteen-story freefall in an elevator.

The light had changed and he had sped off. Quietly she had put the lipstick away. Her hands were trembling too badly to apply it. The knowledge shot her annoyance to another level. So what if he was the most fascinating man she had ever met? He was also the most irritating. He wasn't right for her.

Once they'd arrived at her office, they had gone directly to the conference room. Hunter had taken a post by the door and assumed his position, with arms folded, ankles crossed, eyelids hooded. Placing her briefcase on the table, she shrugged off the trench coat that matched her pants and tossed it over the back of her chair.

More than one eyebrow went up. Hunter's fault again. She always wore a jacket. This morning she had forgotten it in her rush to leave. The most casual things she wore at the office were coordinates . . . with a jacket. Sending Hunter another glare, she called the meeting to order.

''Good morning, everyone. I apologize for keeping you waiting.''

''Erin, you still have two minutes to spare,'' noted Connie Bledsoe, her amber-colored face wreathed in a grin. ''Nancy told us you were on your way.''

Erin flicked another glance at Hunter. He leaned against the matte-gray wall by the door. He must have called while she was dressing. Was there nothing he didn't think of?

Bringing her attention back to the meeting, she said, ''As you know, Mystique Cosmetics is looking for an innovative way to market its hot new shades of lipstick.''

As soon as the words left her mouth, she remembered the way Hunter had looked at her lips in the car. Her stomach had that freefalling sensation again. With her hands pressed against the smooth mahogany of the conference table, she forced herself to continue. ''We've been asked to submit a concept. Any ideas?''

Connie sat up straighter in her chair. Slim, attractive, in her early fifties, she had a wry sense of humor. She had been the creative director at Cortland for three years. She was also one of the three in-house candidates for the vice-president's position. ''How about we do a play on the name Mystique? Whether in print or on film, to varying degrees, the concept would reinforce the manufacturer's familiarity.''

''I'm listening,'' Erin said, glad she could finally sit down.

''Scene opens in complete darkness. Then white smoke billows to fill the entire frame. Out of the smoke a curvaceous female figure emerges. She remains in the shadows. She raises her hand. The tube of lipstick is clearly defined. She applies the lipstick and a voice-over says, ''Why use anything else?'' Scene fades to black with the logo slanted across the screen in bold red script.''

''Opinions,'' Erin requested. She liked the idea. It was simple, yet effective. Still, she always liked to be open and flexible.

''I like it for print, but I think we need a man for the film,'' suggested Bob Peters, the graphic artist. ''Research shows women want to see a man.''

''I disagree,'' Connie said. ''Why state the obvious? The target audience already knows they use lipstick to attract a man, to make themselves look and feel better, or as a moisturizer. The teenagers and women we want to attract will only care about the first two reasons.''

''Then Bob is on target,'' Quinn said as he leaned back in

his chair and crossed his arms. ''Show the woman capturing the man she wants and the consumer is twice as likely to buy the product.''

Connie twirled her chair around until she faced Hunter. ''Showing the man shifts the focus. Unless it's the right kind of man.''

Erin, and every woman, looked at Hunter. He hadn't moved from the position he had taken on entering the room. As in her father's study, he looked as if the entire process bored him.

Yet, he still exuded a kind of dangerous, raw masculinity. The absence of a tie with his well-cut gray blazer and black slacks indicated that he would conform only to a point. He wouldn't be easy for a woman to catch or to keep. Taming was out of the question. But it would be well worth the effort if she succeeded.

''Mr. Hunter, what do you notice first about a woman?'' Connie asked. ''Her face? Her body? Her lipstick? The way she walks? What piques your interest?''

''Why ask him?'' Quinn questioned, his derision barely held in check. ''He doesn't know anything about advertising.''

''Maybe not, but I bet my Rolex he knows a lot about women,'' Connie quipped.

Erin felt her face flush and hoped no one noticed. Connie's Rolex was safe on her wrist.

''Mr. Hunter, I realize I've put you on the spot, but I really would like your opinion,'' Connie persisted.

He lifted a dark brow. ''You may not like it.''

''I'm prepared for that.''

''The answer to your question depends on the woman.'' Hunter came away from the wall. ''It also depends on how she applies the lipstick and what her body language is saying while she's putting it on. You look at her mouth and imagine its hot clinging softness on your mouth, your body, your—''

''I think that's enough,'' Erin interrupted, her face warm again. She raised her hand to pluck at her sweater, noticed Quinn's eyes trained on her, and adjusted the scarf around her neck instead.

Connie fanned herself with her hand. ''I agree.'' She wheeled around in her chair and faced Erin. ''I think a man in the ad would work, but only with the right kind of man, as I said before. A man with a kind of animal magnetism that comes across in print or on film.''

''You can't be suggesting we use *him.''* Quinn blurted.

Bob scratched his scraggly beard. ''He certainly has something.''

''An attitude,'' offered the art director, Sally Carsons. Stylish in pearls and an off-white Chanel suit, Sally had an eye for details and an instinct for what the public wanted. She had been with Cortland for ten years and was the third candidate for the vice-president's position. ''If we could give the impression that a woman could tame the untamable, a man like Hunter, the lipstick would walk out the door.''

Erin didn't know why, but she didn't like them talking about Hunter as if he were an inanimate object, or the idea of his being ogled by thousands of women. ''If we need a model, Hunter won't be it,'' she told them crisply.

All eyes swung to her. Heat climbed up her neck. She had sounded shrewish and mean-spirited. What was the matter with her?

''I quite agree,'' Quinn said in the ensuing silence. ''We need a professional. He can't handle the job he's been assigned.''

This time, the silence was so thick Erin actually felt she had difficulty drawing in air. She hadn't told anyone in the company except her secretary that Hunter was her bodyguard, but since he followed her everywhere, it wasn't hard to figure. And now Quinn had just slammed him.

Judging by Hunter's emotionless face, the remark hadn't bothered him. To Erin, it made the situation worse.

''You misunderstood me, Quinn. I meant Hunter has a prior obligation. One that he's proven to my father's and my satisfaction that he's more than capable of handling.''

Quinn slouched in his chair.

Once that was out of the way, her hardest task lay ahead. Hands clenched in her lap, Erin made herself meet Hunter's gaze. ''Of course, if he wishes to consider Sally's suggestion, other arrangements can be made.''

''As you said, I have a prior obligation.''

Erin let out a breath she hadn't known she was holding. ''As you wish.'' She turned to the art director. ''Since you have a clear picture of what the male model should look like, why don't you handle getting in touch with the model agencies, and see what they can come up with.''

''Whomever we get, he won't be as good as Hunter,'' Connie mumbled.

Erin said nothing. She felt the same way.

Hunter was annoyed. It had been building since this morning when Erin had accused him of taking too much on himself for letting her sleep. The meeting in the board room hadn't helped.

''Prior obligations.''

Every time he thought of Erin saying those two words he wanted to . . . He wasn't sure what he wanted to do to Erin. That was a lie. He knew perfectly well what he wanted to do with her and to her. None of it had anything to do with his job, and everything to do with being a man and her a woman.

Sitting on the side of his sofa bed, his head in his hand, Hunter was as restless and as edgy as he had ever been. He wanted a woman he couldn't have, a woman who was out of his league.

But there were those rare occasions like this morning in the car when she had looked up from putting on her lipstick, when he was sure all he had to do was make the move. He couldn't. He remembered all too well what had happened the last time he did his thinking with the wrong part of his anatomy.

A woman had paid the ultimate price.

He should have known better than to get caught up in the moment. He had seen too many people in dangerous situations mistake heightened emotions for love—and regret their lapses afterwards. You're so charged up: all your senses are alive, and common sense takes a back seat.

Yet he had walked into the same trap.

Erin wasn't going to pay for his stupidity. But it was becoming harder and harder to ignore her. Muttering an expletive, he pushed to his feet and went to the kitchen. Maybe a glass of water would cool him down.

A small night-light with a tulip-shaped cover showed the way. Erin probably hadn't noticed. He had installed them last night after she had gone to bed. This morning she had only been aware of being late. His mouth twisted. Tonight she had gone straight to her room after dinner. He hadn't seen her since.

He was reaching for the refrigerator when a light blinked, then went out. He whirled. The light was one of the ones that remained on all night at the corner of the garage and cast a dim shadow into the kitchen window. Hunter was moving back to the living room when the second light blinked out.

Light bulbs didn't flicker out . . . unless they were being unscrewed.

Grabbing his gun from beneath the pillow, he went into Erin's room without knocking. Curled up in a tight ball, she was asleep in the middle of the queen-sized bed.

His encompassing gaze took in the room in one swift glance and saw everything in place, and he stuck his gun in the back of his jeans. Silently, he crossed to her.

With one hand he shook her awake. The other picked up the phone and dialed 911. Erin awoke at the same time the 911 operator came on the line.

Fear widened her eyes. Clutching the bedspread, she sat up in bed and listened as Jake gave the information that there was a possible intruder.

"Is . . . is Scan—"

The alarm screamed.

"Lock the door and stay here." Jake was on his feet and running. Whoever it was had to be coming in through the door on the side of the garage. The thought came to him that the intruder must want to get inside pretty bad to ignore the motion lights and the alarm.

Scanlon.

The name reverberated in his ear. He slipped off the safety of the .38. With his gun raised, he slowly slid his left foot into the kitchen. A noise sounded behind him.

He whirled. Erin gave a startled shriek, her hands covering her mouth. Hunter's curse was crude and explicit. "Don't you ever listen?"

"You . . . you can't go out there."

"I don't have time for this," Hunter said roughly.

"Wait for the police."

"Go to your room."

A car engine spluttered in the garage.

"Now!" he growled, his eyes cold and bleak.

With a whimpered moan, Erin took one then another step backward.

Blotting out the image of Erin's terrified face, Hunter turned toward the garage. He had to concentrate on taking care of whoever it was out there. The intruder was either trying to steal one of the cars or trying to lure him into coming outside.

His hand was a scant inch from the doorknob when he heard the smooth rumble of Erin's Mercedes coming to life. He didn't wait any longer; he opened the door.

The man in the driver's seat saw Hunter, revved the engine, and zoomed backward. The car died before the hood cleared the garage. Before the thief could restart the engine, Hunter walked up and tapped the barrel of his .38 against the window pane.

"Sure you want to do this?"

Wide-eyed, the would-be thief slowly lifted his hands from the steering wheel. "Wise decision," Hunter said, and he opened the door.

Tall, pimple-faced, and belligerent, the teenager got out of the car. "If my foot hadn't slipped off the clutch you wouldn't have caught me."

Hunter shook his head at the stupidity of youth. "A Benz is fast, but it can't outrun a bullet."

The scraggly dressed youth blanched. His hands lifted a little higher.

"Exactly. Now, try to find the common sense some adult tried to teach you, and don't move." Hunter stepped back a few feet and yelled. "Erin. It's all right."

"H . . . hunter." Her voice wobbled.

"Everything is OK. It's just a kid trying to steal your car. I'll hold him until the police arrive. Stay inside." He went back to the teenager. "Assume the position against the back of the car. I'm sure you know it."

By the time Erin watched the last of the three police cars leave, she was almost light-headed with relief. The teenager who had tried to steal her car had thought it was a big joke that so many cars had come for him. Apparently, he hadn't known anything more about the occupants of the house than that someone drove a late-model Mercedes. It seemed rather ironic to her that she had traded in her Porsche for the Mercedes because its sturdiness made her feel safer.

The only way she had gotten that and every other bit of information was by listening with the back door cracked open. After Hunter had told her it was just a car thief, she had gone to her room and gotten dressed. She had thought the police would want to talk with her because it was her house. She never got the chance to find out.

Hunter stopped her before she stepped one foot in the garage. He had called 911, caught the thief, so her presence was unnecessary. Detective Grimes, sounding tired and disgruntled, had come inside briefly to assure her they didn't need her statement. Since she had defied Hunter once, she didn't push the issue.

She contented herself with eavesdropping. Once in a while she'd catch Hunter's hard glare in her direction. As usual, he didn't miss a thing. He was sharp, and he had scared her half to death. She was scared *for* him.

She now had a better understanding of the seemingly erratic behavior of frightened parents who cried, then fussed, then hugged a child when the child scared them.

Hunter wasn't a child.

He was a man. A man who called to her, and made her want what couldn't be. He wasn't going to let anything, including her, distract him from doing his job. And she wasn't sure if she really wanted to push the issue.

She had a feeling an affair with Hunter would either take her to the height of ecstasy or the depths of despair. With him, there'd be no in-between.

The garage door came down.

Erin spun and took off running for her room. She had just gotten into bed and pulled the covers up when the door opened.

She should have locked the door. "Hunter, I'm really tired."

Tall, dark, and powerful, he stalked to her. Calloused hands clamped around her upper forearms and drew her out of bed until she was at eye level with him, her feet dangling over the floor.

"Hunter—"

"Be quiet! You could have gotten yourself killed tonight," he announced angrily.

"I stayed in—"

"Not then," he exploded, cutting her off once again. "Coming after me when I told you to stay in your room. I could have—" He abruptly stopped, as if he couldn't bear the thought of completing his sentence.

"I wasn't afraid." At his expression of disbelief, she rushed on to explain. "I mean, I was scared, but not of you harming me."

"Accidents happen. I pointed my gun at you. If you ever do something like that again, I'll turn you over my knee." His gaze drilled into her.

"I didn't want you going outside," she explained. "It was too dangerous."

A muscle leaped in his jaw. "I can take care of myself. Don't you ever do something so stupid again." When she didn't respond, he jerked her closer. "Is that clear?"

"Yes," she said, willing to agree to anything for him to release her. The heat and the hardness of his body pressed against her caused an ache to unfurl deep within her. To her increased dismay, her nipples puckered. ''Y . . . you can put me down now.''

His hands clenched as if he planned to keep her dangling. ''Don't defy me again.'' Releasing her, he left the room. The door snapped shut.

His hands and body trembling badly, Hunter leaned against the door. He drew in a great gulp of air, then another one. There was anger, yes, but there was also desire raging in his blood.

He had made a mistake, going into Erin's room. A greater one by putting his hands on her and pulling her to him. Her skin was too soft, her scent too alluring. Somewhere between fear for her safety and anger at her stubbornness, lust had snuck up on him.

He remembered too well what her lips tasted like, how her body could soften against his, the pebble hardness of her nipples against his chest.

Drawing in another deep breath, Hunter went back to the sofa bed and sat on the edge, only to get up again. Sleep was impossible until his body calmed. That might take the rest of the night.

He headed for the kitchen and a glass of juice. Erin was going to drive him out of his mind.

But he'd fight the devil himself to stay by her side and keep her safe.

Chapter Eight

Hunter hadn't forgiven her.

Erin saw it in the not-so-subtle way he kept his broad shoulder turned away from her, heard it in the clipped monosyllabic answers he gave . . . if she pressed him.

The same way she had pressed him to play tonk. She had thought playing cards would loosen him up and make him more reasonable about what she wanted to ask. She had wasted her time.

Hunter slouched in his straight-backed chair at the small game table in the den. If his body were any looser he'd slide onto the floor. Trouble was, his mind remained an impenetrable wall to any friendly overtures she made.

He was beating the stuffing out of her with the same effortless ease he did everything else. Anyone else would show some reaction after winning eleven straight games.

His face was an inscrutable mask, with the same expression he had worn since this morning. His manners were coolly polite. But she couldn't shake the impression that beneath the cool surface was a tightly controlled anger dangerously close to exploding.

She might have thought she was imagining things, if her employees today hadn't kept looking over their shoulders at Hunter's brooding presence. A couple of the women who usually lingered to try and attract his attention opted to come back later. Those brave enough to stay had beat a fast exit as soon as their business was concluded. After lunch, not a single person entered her office.

She knew how they felt. It was like being confronted with a dangerous animal, with nothing standing between the two of you except prayer. Looking into Hunter's dark eyes, you knew prayer wouldn't help if he decided to come after you.

Somehow the thought didn't intimidate her as much as it had that morning. Hunter was keenly intelligent. He wouldn't harm anyone without a reason. He was angry on her behalf, but she knew he'd do everything within his power to protect her. It was a knowledge, despite her best efforts not to, that she drew on more and more as time passed.

Grimacing, she watched him pick up the card she had just thrown down, put it in his hand, then disc another card.

She pulled from the deck. It was a useless ten of hearts. She threw it back out. Again Hunter picked it up.

He was going to win again. And he had warmed up about as much as a polar bear sitting on a glacier.

Half-heartedly, she pulled from the deck as she recalled the blazing intensity of his black eyes and the iron grip of his hands around her arms last night. She wished his emotions could be someplace in between cool and furious.

''Passionate'' popped into her mind. If ever there was a man who could inspire passion, it was Hunter. It would be like the man, dark and dangerous and a little wild. Just as their first and only kiss had been. Her hand trembled slightly as she discarded the card she had just picked up.

Hunter picked it up and spread. ''Tonk.'' He announced it with about as much enthusiasm as a man might say that he was about to cut his toenails. His dark gaze lifted to her, silently asking if she had had enough.

''Shuffle the cards.''

For a moment something indiscernible flickered in his ebony eyes, then it was gone. His large hand swept the cards up.

Erin discarded her plan of lulling Hunter into a good mood. She'd have to face this issue head-on. He wasn't going to like what she was about to say, but at least she wasn't in this by herself.

If she had learned anything from her four days with Hunter as her living shadow, it was that he respected Marcus Cortland and her godfather, Paul Morris. The only way she could win the coming argument was to have them on her side.

"Hunter, do you have a tux?"

"No."

"It wouldn't be difficult to rent one."

"Is there a specific reason for that question?" he asked, his attention on the five cards he was dealing to each of them. "Or are you trying to make conversation?"

With difficulty Erin kept the smile on her face. "There is a benefit tomorrow night at Mildred and John King's home and I'd like to go."

"No." Sweeping up his cards, he gazed at them dispassionately.

"It's a worthwhile affair," Erin told him. "Some of Austin's elite society will be there. The mayor included."

"You won't."

The smile slid from her face. "I wouldn't bet on it. Daddy is agreeable."

Slouched in his chair, he looked over the top of his cards. "After last night, I'd think you'd want to stay close to home."

"That's exactly why I intend to go," she told him, warming to her topic. "Several non-profit organizations will reap the benefits of the affair. One of them I particularly admire. Victim Recovery."

Finally he laid the cards aside and studied her closely. "Did your admiration begin before or after the robbery?"

"After," she admitted.

Hunter picked up his cards, discarded one, then pulled one

from the deck. ''Then they will understand more than anyone why you won't be there.''

''They might, but I won't,'' Erin said with feeling. ''I am not hiding in this house another day. Scanlon took enough from me.''

His black eyes lifted, narrowed. ''If you aren't careful, he can take a lot more.''

She flinched, but kept her gaze steady. ''That thought is never far from my mind. That's why I'm going tomorrow night.'' She leaned forward in her chair, wanting him to understand. ''You saw how close my father and I are, but even with his support I had a difficult time getting my life back to normal. For those without resources or strong support, I can see where it would be almost impossible.

''People in my recovery group were the only ones who truly understood what it was like to be carefree one minute, ready to take on anything, and the next minute plunged into your worst nightmare. Only you're not asleep.''

Hunter knew the feeling. He had been a cocky so-and-so who thought he had it all figured out. He never doubted his ability. And he had been deadly wrong. He had learned the hard way that you can't control all situations. Life took unexpected turns sometimes. He wouldn't forget again, or let Erin.

''Just because it wasn't Scanlon last night doesn't mean he's not out there,'' he warned.

''But it wasn't, and you took care of the car thief,'' she reminded him, unnecessarily.

He scowled across the table at her. ''But it could have been.'' Didn't she understand that there was always a possibility that he wouldn't be quick enough, fast enough? That gut-wrenching thought kept him awake at night. ''Send them a check.''

''You still don't understand.'' Restless, she stood, then paced beside the table. ''It's not just about money. It's learning to live without fear. Each time one of the members in our group has a little victory, like going to the grocery store alone or going into a dark room or, yes, sleeping with the lights off, it's like we all share in it. Because it means there's hope for those who haven't reached that point."

His expression hardened. "So you're going to make yourself a target so your group will feel better about themselves."

"Hunter, I'll feel better about myself, too. I'll be in control. I won't feel so powerless." Her hand tunneled through her hair. "You say Scanlon is out there. I don't know. I do know I can't hide forever. That gives him too much power and too much control over my life."

"If I say no?"

Somehow she made herself meet his angry gaze. "Then I'll go without you. Daddy realizes how important this is to me and so does Paul. I think it's their way of making up for not being able to help me. It wasn't their fault. I needed someone who understood what I had been through, someone who has walked in hell and come out unscathed."

"You're making a mistake."

Her chin lifted. Determination shone in her light brown eyes. "I'm going, Hunter. With you, I hope, but without you if I have to."

Hunter came out of the chair in one controlled rush. He crossed the den in seconds, jerked up the receiver, and jabbed the automatic key to dial Marcus's number. Marcus picked up the phone on the third ring.

"It's too dangerous for her to go," Hunter told Marcus as soon as he came on the line.

"You'll be with her," Marcus said.

Calloused fingers bit into the receiver. "Nothing is ever foolproof, Marcus."

There was a long silence. When Marcus spoke again, his voice was less sure. "It's by invitation only, and the Kings always have extra security on the premises for their large social gatherings. This benefit is very important to her, Hunter."

"Important enough to risk her safety?"

"Not to me, but it is to Erin. She's a grown woman, and I've pushed her all I can," Marcus told him. "She has it in her head that, if she doesn't attend this thing tomorrow night, she'll have let Scanlon take something else from her. I'll do anything to see that that doesn't happen.

"I don't want to see her the way she was in the first weeks following the robbery. I could have lost her, Hunter. Each time we looked at each other, we both were confronted with the possibility. I was a mirror of her pain and she was mine."

Hunter's stomach clenched. He knew all too well what Marcus was talking about. He had left the Chicago Police Department for similar reasons. But where Marcus had felt fear, Hunter had been consumed with guilt. Both could lead to a wrong decision. "Scanlon is out there. Don't ask me how I know; I just do."

"She's dug in her heels on this one, Hunter. Since it's for an organization that helped my baby regain her independence, I'll go with her wishes on this," Marcus told him. "The best I can do is get in touch with John and Mildred and let them know why you'll be there and ask them to check security measures with you."

"That may not be enough," Hunter said grimly. "If her name is published in the papers, Scanlon will know where to look."

"I've already spoken to John and Mildred about that."

Realizing he wasn't getting anywhere with Marcus, Hunter said goodbye and hung up. Next he dialed his partner's private number. Less than two minutes later he hung up the phone again.

Erin's hands were locked together to keep them from trembling. She didn't have to ask if they had backed her up. Her ears were still ringing from the loud clang when Hunter had hung up the phone with Paul. Hunter was too furious for anything else.

His black eyes swung to her with lethal precision. "How did you get them to agree?"

"I simply told them the truth. It was important that I regain some control of my life. Besides that, I've been good. But I can't take much more of my movements being curtailed," she informed him. "Either I get out of the house or I might make things more difficult for you."

Hands on his hips, Hunter snorted. "You don't call this difficult?"

"I call it negotiations," she said sweetly.

"I call it blackmail," Hunter snarled. "Well, I'm laying a few ground rules. You stay by my side all night, in my sight. If I say we leave, we leave. No questions."

"It's a deal." She started from the den, then turned, smiling. "Don't forget to see about a tux. Mildred King is a stickler for formality."

"I think you're making a mistake."

Her smile faded. "I have to go, Hunter. Please try to understand."

"I'll never understand why you'd want to put your life in danger," he said angrily.

"Hunter, I want to live. This is not some whim," she said, trying to keep her voice calm. "But I want my life to be the way it was before I stopped to use the ATM machine. Do you know I haven't been able to use one since? Sometimes I see one and get nauseous."

"This isn't the way, Erin." He looked hard and unapproachable.

Erin knew he looked that way because he was worried about her. "Maybe not for you, but it is for me. It'll be all right. Please, try to understand."

She wanted his acceptance. The thought splintered through Hunter. Looking at him with those liquid brown eyes of hers that could turn him on faster than lightning, how could she expect him to accept her putting her life in danger?

Then he noticed something else: the slight smudges beneath her eyes, and the tenseness around her mouth, that hadn't been there four days ago.

Living in fear changed people. It could either make you stronger or weaker. Erin chose to use it to make her stronger. He could either help her or hinder her by standing in her way.

"I hate ties," he finally answered.

The tension around her mouth eased. ''So I noticed. You haven't worn one yet to the office.''

Wry amusement lifted the corners of his mouth. ''In my Chicago office, I keep one in my desk for the rare occasions when Grace stops by. She says it looks more professional.''

Erin laughed, a rich sound that was as smooth as it was enticing. ''She's mild compared to Mildred. But both throw a fun party. Who knows, you might have fun.''

''At least we both know it won't end the same way.''

Erin's eyes widened. Her sharp intake of breath cut across the small space separating them.

Hunter knew she was recalling the night on the balcony. But was her memory of their heated kiss, or of his callous remark? ''This time you won't have to worry about me getting out of line.''

Something like disappointment flickered in her eyes. ''No, of course not. Good night, Hunter.''

''Night.'' He watched her retreat from him as fast as possible without running. Keep running, Erin, he thought. Because if you ever stop we're going to make the biggest mistake of our lives.

The charity benefit brought out the elite of Austin's society, just as Erin had said it would. There was enough wealth in the elegant fifty-foot ballroom to fund several non-profit organizations for the next few years. The trick was to see that the prospect became a reality. That was where Erin came in.

Hunter, in a black tux, had barely removed the heavy satin cape from around Erin's bare shoulders before she was off across the room to greet their host and hostess. Her long gold skirt shimmered and rustled with each impatient movement. After a brief introduction, she was moving again. Hunter followed in her wake.

Since then, she had been a constant swirl of motion in incandescent gold satin. She seemed to have an uncanny knack for knowing just when to mention Victim Recovery and when to ask for a hefty donation. To those insensitive enough to dig for details about Erin's having been a victim herself, her answer was always straightforward.

"I'm still learning to face my fears. It's a battle I hope you never have to fight. Please help me help others who were thrust into a life-altering situation that was not of their own choosing."

She spoke the words with such sincerity and courage that most of the people tucked their heads in embarrassment for probing. Then they made up for it by promising a sizable donation. With each passing minute Hunter found himself more inordinately proud of her. He just wished she had waited until after Scanlon was caught.

Tugging at the starched collar of his white pleated shirt, he barely kept the scowl from his face as Erin tucked another check into her small gold bag then looked around the room for another prospect. "Can't you stand still for ten minutes?"

Smiling, she looked up at him through a sweep of lush lashes. "You wouldn't want me to waste the mellow effect the combination of band and all the good food is having on the guests, would you?"

"From all the checks you've got tucked into your bag, I'd say we can take a few minutes off to enjoy some of the food I haven't gotten within fifteen feet of," he told her.

"I suppose we could take a small break." She eyed him critically. "If you stop frowning and stop tugging at that tie."

Hunter ran another long finger around his collar, then he gave up. "I told you I don't like ties."

"That's an understatement," Erin said. "You'd think it was a noose or something."

"Feels like one." Hunter glanced down at Erin, then away. He wished she had worn something other than the strapless bustier covered in metallic golden sequins and beads. From his height, every time he turned to say something to her, his gaze somehow managed to find the golden brown swell of her lush breasts.

"You certainly are grumpy," Erin told him. "Maybe some food will help."

''Yeah, maybe it will.'' Taking her arm, he headed across the crowded room. Hunter spotted Quinn making his way to them, and he instinctively tightened his hold on Erin.

Questioning brown eyes looked up at him. ''What is it?''

''Good evening, Erin. You look sensational,'' Quinn said, his gaze warm.

Hunter flexed his right fist when he saw Quinn's gaze flicker to the swell of Erin's breasts. ''Excuse us, Mathis. We were about to get something to eat.''

Quinn, dressed in a tailored black tux, frowned. ''Erin, I was hoping you'd dance with me.''

''I'd love—''

''No.''

Two pairs of startled eyes swung to Hunter. Erin spoke first. ''I beg your pardon?''

''Ground rules, remember?'' Hunter said.

Her eyes widened. ''Surely you didn't mean that literally.''

''That's exactly what I meant,'' he told her. ''By my side and in my sight.''

Quinn bristled. ''That's ridiculous. You're exceeding your authority.''

Hunter lifted a dark brow. ''That's not for you to say, Mathis. Besides, at least I have some. You don't have any.''

The other man stiffened, then spun on his well-shod heels and stalked away.

Frowning, Erin turned on Hunter. ''You didn't have to be so rude to him.''

Hunter's face tightened. ''But it's all right for him to say whatever he wants to me?''

''I didn't say that,'' Erin told him.

''You didn't have to.'' Taking her arm, he headed for the tables of food.

''Hunter, you aren't having a good time?'' Marcus asked as he stopped before them sometime later.

''I'm not here to have a good time.''

"Well, that's no reason for me not to have one," Erin complained. "You won't even let me dance. You can see the dance floor from here."

"You agreed. By my side," he said, not sure if it was concern for her safety or an unknown possessiveness that made him keep her by his side.

"Do you dance, Hunter?"

"Sometimes."

"Then you dance with her," Marcus said.

"That's all right, Dad," Erin said hurriedly.

"Nonsense. You love to dance. It's the perfect solution." He glanced between the two stiff-backed people. "You talked me into letting you come tonight; I want you to have a good time. This may be the last chance you get out for a while."

Erin blanched. "Have you heard something?"

"No, I haven't. I didn't mean to upset you." Her father caught her shaking hands in his. "It's just that I know how independent you are and I wanted you to have a little of it back."

"Thanks, Daddy."

"Now, you and Hunter get on the dance floor. I want to see a smile on both of your faces."

"That bad, huh?" Erin asked.

"Only Quinn looks sadder."

Erin sent Hunter a disgruntled look. "Hunter wouldn't let me dance with him, either."

"You knew the ground rules when we came," Hunter responded.

"Something tells me you follow rules only if they suit you."

"You're right." Taking her hand, he walked with her onto the dance floor and drew her into his arms. Their bodies and their steps fit perfectly.

Erin tucked her head beneath his chin and relaxed into his strong arms. The dance was the same, yet so different from the last one. Instead of the heat and urgency, it was filled with expectancy.

"Are you asleep?"

She smiled. ''No. You dance well.''

''You're pretty good yourself.'' Pulling her closer, he twirled her around the floor; each seemed lost in their own thoughts.

The music stopped. Reluctantly they drew apart. Their gazes met, held. She remembered their first dance, remembered the kiss, and wondered if he remembered, as well.

''I'll always regret my bad behavior,'' Jake murmured. For once his eyes were unguarded.

''It's in the past,'' she said, and walked away before she could ask something foolish like whether he regretted the kiss they had shared, as well. Jake wasn't for her.

They were almost back to the place where Marcus waited for them when someone lightly touched her arm. She turned to see Mildred King.

''Excuse me, Erin; I'd like you to meet some of the major contributors to tonight's gala.''

''Of course,'' Erin said.

Mildred's gaze went hesitantly to Hunter. ''They wanted to meet you privately. You know some of the donors want anonymity.''

Erin glanced up into Hunter's eyes, asking him without words to agree. Mildred knew all about his purpose for being there.

''Where are they?'' Hunter asked.

''Just across the room,'' Mildred said.

His dark gaze pinned Erin. ''If you get out of my sight for more than ten seconds, I'm coming for you and then we're leaving.''

''Oh, dear,'' Mildred said softly.

''Is there a problem, Mrs. King?'' Hunter inquired, watching the woman's hand nervously flutter over her diamond-and-sapphire necklace.

''Why, no,'' she quickly assured him. ''Come, Erin. We don't want to keep them waiting.''

Hunter watched them leave, a strange uneasiness prickling him. Mrs. King glanced back, her gaze worried. Hunter moved after them. Something wasn't right. He cut Erin's time in half. Five seconds was all she had.

"Hunter, where is Erin going?" Marcus asked as he walked over to him.

"With Mrs. King to meet some of the donors," Hunter answered, never taking his gaze from Erin.

"Good. I wanted to tell you this without Erin around."

Hearing the urgency in Marcus's voice, Hunter glanced back at him. "What is it?"

"While you were dancing, I learned the co-chairman was on a local talk show this morning. When asked some of the people attending and the organizations to benefit, she mentioned Erin's name and Victim Recovery."

Hunter barely bit back something harsh and explicit. His head came up and around. He saw the red blaze of Mildred's gown near the door to the ballroom, but not the shimmering gold of Erin's gown, nor her face.

His gut clenched. Erin was gone.

Chapter Nine

Erin slipped out the front door of the Kings' home and glanced around the brightly lit front yard. Late-model cars and a couple of sports utility vehicles lined the sides of the quiet residential street.

A tall, slender man in a police uniform stopped in front of the walkway, glanced her way and nodded. The erratic pounding of her heart slowed. She wasn't alone.

Standing beneath one of the twin gleaming brass porch lights on either side of the recessed double doors, Erin nodded to the watchful security guard, then took the bricked path around to the back of the house.

The garden room in the back of the Kings' two-story Colonial home was Erin's destination. Quinn was there waiting for her. With Mildred's help, he had arranged for a private dinner. Via the intercom they would be able to hear and dance to the music piped from the ballroom.

Mildred had thought it was very romantic until she had had to face Hunter. By the time they had gotten out of his range of hearing, the self-assured socialite was actually wringing her hands.

Seeing her distress, Erin had assured her hostess she could handle Hunter. So why was she rushing to tell Quinn this was a crazy idea? Easy. No one could ''handle'' Hunter. She knew that better than anyone.

Just as she knew that, if Quinn hadn't had such a hard time in the past few years, she would have ignored his request. In a way, he was testing her; in another, seeking reassurance that she wasn't going to turn her back on him as so many others had. She just wished he had found another way.

Pulling her cape closer, she paused. The lights in the glass-enclosed garden room were easily discernible. The pathway leading to it was not. Uncertainty kept her immobile.

She had walked this path on several occasions, and she remembered accent lights being interspersed with the lush border of monkey grass. Neither were visible now. Furtively, she glanced around, then quickly chastised herself.

''Erin, don't be such a coward,'' she muttered. This was just the kind of situation she had told Hunter recovering crime victims had to deal with. Spouting theory was much easier than putting it into practice.

Ten seconds.

Hunter's terse words acted as a prod to her back. Willing herself to loosen her grip on her cape, she started toward the garden room. She didn't have time for being a coward. Hunter was probably already looking for her.

He wasn't going to be happy when he couldn't locate her. He'd probably tie her to his side after to—

She froze. Her thoughts splintered as she heard a sound behind her. Slowly, she turned. ''I . . . is anyone there??''

Silence.

Her throat dried. ''Answer me. Hunter, is that—''

A twig snapped as if crushed beneath a heavy weight. A cry erupted from her throat as she jerked up her full-length skirt with both hands and ran toward the garden room.

Her cape slipped from her shoulders. Too panicky to notice, she continued her headlong flight.

Someone was behind her. She could feel him, hear his footsteps.

"Erin. Stop. Erin, it's Hunter."

She stumbled to a stop. By the time she had righted herself, Hunter was a step away. She flung herself against his chest. Her arms frantically circled his neck and held on.

"What the hell were you doing out here?"

She burrowed closer. The pounding beat of his heart was oddly reassuring. She didn't care how much he yelled and fussed at her.

Hunter had come for her. He wouldn't let anything happen to her. She was safe.

Hunter's anger died the second he felt Erin shudder, heard her jagged breathing. Hands that had held her forearms in fury pulled her to him with something close to desperation.

Hearing her scream had turned his blood cold. In all of his eight years in the police department nothing had compared to the overwhelming terror he felt on hearing that one petrified sound. Finding her cape on the ground had almost sent him to his knees.

He pushed her away from him. "Why did you scream?"

She shivered and tried without success to get closer to his comforting warmth again. "I . . . I thought I heard someone. I called and no one answered, then a twig snapped." She swallowed convulsively. "It must have been you. I guess you didn't hear me call your name."

The tension loosening in Hunter tightened again. He hadn't heard Erin call his name, only her scream. "Let's go inside." Pulling her closer to the protective shield of his body, he led her back along the walk. Without breaking his stride, he picked up her cape.

Rounding the corner of the house, they were met by the off-duty policeman and Marcus. Her father's worried gaze flickered from his obviously distraught daughter to the grim-faced man by her side. The two men exchanged a long look.

Fear flashed in Marcus's eyes, but all he said was, "Come on, baby. Let's go inside."

Erin looked at Hunter. ''I . . . I'm sorry. I didn't mean—'' She bit her lower lip.

''Go inside with your father. I'll be there in a minute.''

''Aren't you going with us?'' she asked.

''No,'' Hunter said. His voice was biting, and he was unable to control it.

Erin flinched, then turned away. After another glance at Hunter, Marcus followed her. Hunter watched them until the front door closed.

He turned to the policeman. ''Get a flashlight. I want to check something out.''

Less than five minutes later Hunter had the answer he had been searching for. It sent another cold chill through him. Taking out his handkerchief and a pen, he began to work.

Hunter was silent as he drove her home. Erin wasn't lulled into thinking he was through with her. His words when he had reentered the house to get her had been too precise. He was holding his temper with an iron will, but she had a feeling that, as soon as they were alone, he'd release it. Upon her.

Entering her house, she cut the alarm off, then reset it for on at home as soon as Hunter closed the door. Going to the living room, she took off her cape, sat on the couch, and waited.

She didn't have to wait long.

''Why were you outside?''

She had known the question was coming, just as she had known she couldn't tell him the truth. There was enough animosity between Quinn and Hunter without adding a reason for more.

Poor Mildred had looked worried and guilt-ridden when Hunter had come into the study, where Erin, Marcus, and the Kings were waiting, and announced without preamble that he was taking Erin home.

No one had said a word. Her father had looked relieved, Mr. King worried.

"I asked you a question, Erin." Impatiently, he jerked off his tie, then tossed his coat aside.

After all the times she had wanted him to say her name, now that he had, the word felt like a lash across her back. She had acted foolishly, in Hunter's mind. Her answer wasn't going to help. "I was going to meet someone."

"Was the prospect of meeting some man worth your life?" he asked, his words barely short of contempt.

"It wasn't that kind of meeting," she told him. "I don't sneak around nor do I sleep around. You should know that better than anyone."

A direct hit. Hunter's face hardened into a mask of fury. "Then why sneak off?"

She glanced away. "I had my reasons."

"This isn't a game. Maybe you need to remember that." Reaching into his coat pocket, he drew out his handkerchief. Lying on the white square of cloth were two thin brown cigarette butts.

Frowning, Erin looked from the slender brown stubs to Hunter. "I don't understand. What do those have to do with me?"

"I ran a profile on Scanlon the day after I took this job," Hunter told her. "These are his brand. I found them beneath a tree off the walkway where you lost your cape."

Erin's eyes widened. She couldn't look away from the cigarette butts. She began to shake. Her heart thundered in her chest. Finally, her horrified gaze lifted to Hunter.

"H . . . he was at the party?"

Hunter's hands fisted over the stubs. "Grimes is sending out a car to pick these up, to try and get fingerprints off them. I think if they get the right match it'll prove Scanlon is in Austin. The only problem is that it's a long process."

"I don't understand. I thought fingerprints were easily identifiable."

"They are if you have the right area printed on file. Then you have to have the exact area on the evidence to match them up."

He lifted his free hand to demonstrate. ''Although the front of the hand is covered with ridges, only the fingers and the palm are printed when someone is booked. The lab has to lift the prints from the butts, which could take anywhere from twenty-four to forty-eight hours, because paper takes a special process. Then, we have to hope for a match with the prints the police have on file for Scanlon.''

''So, if he shook out his cigarette, as I've seen some people do, then grasped it between his lips, they may not be able to match the prints,'' Erin reasoned.

''Yes,'' Hunter stated in frustration.

''Then we don't know for sure,'' Erin said. ''Someone else might have left them.''

''They could have, but the butts look fresh. There's something else.'' Rage, that he made no effort to hide, swept across Hunter's face. ''The lights along the walkway had been unscrewed.''

Realization hit Erin full force. Terror engulfed her. ''B . . . but he couldn't have known I'd be outside, or at the party.''

''This morning, the co-chairman told about a hundred thousand listeners on a popular TV program that you would be there. Your father only learned about it after you had disappeared.'' A muscle leaped in his jaw. ''From where I found the cigarettes, there was a clear view of the ballroom through the terrace doors. It's my guess he unscrewed the lights to escape detection, while waiting to get an opportunity to act.''

''And I gave him one,'' she said, her voice strained. ''H . . . he could h . . . have won tonight, couldn't he?''

Seeing her fear cut Hunter to the quick. He had never wanted this to happen. Ruthlessly, he shoved the handkerchief into his pocket. She needed to learn caution. He just hated to be the one who always had to teach her that lesson.

Hunter came down beside her, his large hands closing around her bare forearm. ''You're safe.''

Erin lifted her head. ''I feel safe with you.''

Her whispered words meant more to him than it was wise to admit. ''It's my job.''

Unshed tears glittered in her eyes. "Tonight he could have hurt you, too. I put both of us at risk. I'm sorry. So sorry."

The tears gliding down her smooth brown cheeks tore his heart. Without thought, he pulled her into his lap. His arms closed securely around her. "Don't cry, honey. It's all right."

"I was only going to be gone for a few minutes. I remembered that the pathway had always been lit, but after all my talk about courage, and knowing you were going to come looking for me, I went anyway." She shuddered. "At the time, I was trying to tell myself how brave I was."

His hand swept up and down her back in reassurance. "It's over."

"I knew you would come looking for me," she told him, burrowing closer, her arms trying to circle his waist, her face pressed against his shirt front.

"Shh. Don't cry. I won't let anything happen to either of us."

A memory pricked him. Another time. Another place. Another woman. Death.

No! His mind and body both rebelled against the memory. Erin would live. Nothing was going to harm her. As if he needed to reassure himself, his lips brushed against her cheek, her forehead, the corner of her lips.

Her lips parted naturally and sweetly. His tongue tenderly probed the recesses of her soft mouth.

Her whimper of passion shot through him like wildfire. *So long.* He had waited so long to taste her lips again. It was everything that he remembered, and so much more.

Sweet passion. Hot need.

Her skin was the velvet warmth that haunted his dreams. Smooth and fragrant. Soft and enticing.

His hand cupped the swell of her breast. It wasn't enough. He wanted to feel her nipple swell and pout for him. One long finger slipped inside the bustier. Heat and softness greeted him.

Hunter almost groaned. She was so soft, so giving. He could lose himself in such softness. . . .

His head abruptly lifted. Sanity returned, and with it anger at his disgusting lack of control. Erin, her eyes glazed with passion, lay half beneath him, one breast exposed. Erin was too vulnerable for this. He, of all people, knew how danger could easily turn into passion and death.

Rolling to his feet, he handed her her cape. "Sorry."

Although it was only a matter of seconds, it seemed to Hunter an eternity before she took the cape from his hand and covered her upper body.

Clutching the cape to her chest, Erin stared at Hunter. His rejection hurt as much as the coldness of his expression. For a while she had thought he cared. She had been a fool. Once he had wanted her passion. Now that she was a client, he didn't even want that.

Gathering the only defense she had left, her dignity, she headed toward her bedroom.

"Adrenalin is the most powerful aphrodisiac in the world," Hunter rasped. "We'd both regret it later."

Erin continued to her room and softly closed the door behind her. She leaned against it until her legs stopped shaking. Perhaps he was right.

Perhaps it was the wildness, the element of danger in Hunter that attracted her so. Never in her life had she reacted so strongly to a man.

Sighing, she pushed away from the door and went to get ready for bed. She had enough to think about besides a man who couldn't or wouldn't let himself think of her as just a woman. Her ego in that area had been dented enough without Hunter adding to the damage. He wasn't for her.

She was halfway across the room before she realized he had been wrong about one thing: the night had ended as their first night had. They had parted angrily after a kiss, and Erin had been left feeling empty.

Hunter protected her body, but he was wreaking havoc on her emotions.

* * *

She couldn't sleep.

Restlessly, Erin moved around in her bedroom, fluffing a pillow on the oversized chair, repositioning the ottoman in front of it, checking the dryness of the soil in her African violet. Brushing the dry soil away from her fingertips, she went to the bathroom for a glass of water and returned to give the dry plant a drink.

Finished, the glass clutched in her hand, she looked around for some other small task. Anything to keep her mind busy. Neither the hardback novel on her bed nor the spec sheets on the lipstick for Mystique on her desk had been able to keep her attention for more than a few minutes. Her mind always circled back to her problem.

A man wanted her dead.

And the only thing that kept him from accomplishing his goal was Hunter. Which meant Hunter was in as much danger as she was.

She hadn't wanted this. Had tried so desperately to believe Scanlon was miles away, that he hadn't anything to do with Judge Hughes's death.

Tonight Hunter had shown her something different. Her hand trembling, she set the glass atop her desk, then slowly went to the ottoman and sat on the edge of it. The cowardly part of her wanted to hate him for shattering her illusion; the other part of her, the part that fought to bring some normalcy to her life, knew he took no pleasure in making her face reality.

She understood that his rage hadn't been directed at her so much as it had been felt on her behalf. With understanding came acceptance; she couldn't hide from the truth any longer.

Somewhere in Austin, Scanlon was waiting for another chance.

"Erin, are you all right?"

The deep timbre of Hunter's voice danced along her ragged nerves, somehow soothing them. "Yes."

"May I come in?"

"Yes."

Her bedroom door slowly opened. Hunter's powerfully built

body almost filled the space. Dark eyes glittered in his intense face. Closing the door, he crossed the room. ''Trouble sleeping?''

''A little.'' Head bowed, she picked at the belt of her robe.

''Maybe you just need this.''

Slowly, her head lifted. For the first time, she noticed the glass of juice in his hand. A large, competent hand that made her lose reason.

She took the glass, careful not to touch his hand. ''Thank you. I'll be all right now. You better go get some sleep yourself.''

He turned. She had to clamp her teeth to keep from saying his name and calling him back. But instead of leaving, as she had expected, he drew the bedspread off the bed, came back to her, took the juice from her hands, then wrapped the covering around her.

Sitting in the oversized chair, he pulled her against him and settled her head on his broad shoulder. ''Go to sleep, Erin.''

She thought of protesting, then snuggled closer to him. She was scared. Hunter knew it. Denying the truth wouldn't help get her through the night. Hunter holding her would.

''Thank you,'' she whispered.

''The nights are always worse if you're alone.''

She angled her head up to see the rugged curve of his strong jaw. Something in his tone told her he was speaking from experience. ''Were you alone?''

His body tensed against hers. Erin held her breath, waiting, hoping he would share a glimpse of his past with her.

''Yes.''

She worked her arm out of the cocoon of covering, and lightly touched his cheek with her fingertips. There was nothing she could do or say to take away the bleakness she had heard in that one word. Only let him know that tonight neither one of them had to be alone.

''I'm glad you're here,'' she whispered.

His large hand closed around her smaller, fragile one, but he didn't put it under the cover as she expected. ''Go to sleep.''

Snuggling against him again, she closed her eyes. She was safe. Hunter was with her.

Hunter knew the exact moment Erin slid into sleep. He could release her hand. He didn't. Instead, he held her delicate hand against his chest and watched her sleep. She looked peaceful in the rose print flannel gown and robe. He prayed she was.

He hadn't known what her reaction would be to him when he came to her door. She had every right to be angry, after his crazy stunt of kissing her. Seeing her fighting fear and misery was worse than anything he had imagined. He could no more have kept from holding her than he could have kept from caring about her.

He had fought it as long as he could. In the stillness of the room, holding her, he could admit to himself how much she had grown to mean to him. And when this was over, he would have to walk away.

Erin wasn't for him. They came from two different worlds, lived in different parts of the country, shared nothing in common but an elemental awareness that sometimes singed the air they breathed.

And he was going to make sure he didn't forget. Marcus trusted Hunter with his daughter, Paul trusted Hunter with his goddaughter, Erin trusted him enough to go to sleep in his arms.

More than anything, Erin's complete trust in him touched him, as nothing else ever had. Because of that trust, he would make sure that, when he left, he'd leave her as she had been when he had first seen her.

Vitally alive and untouched by a man who could offer her nothing but heartache.

Erin slowly emerged from sleep, her body stretching, gliding over something warm and hard. Sooty eyelashes drifted upward. Hot onyx eyes stared down at her.

Hunter. She was half lying on his wide chest. Her robe hung off one shoulder. One of her legs was thrust intimately between his. The texture of his soft jeans scraped against her bare thigh.

Her first thought should have been embarrassment. She waited for it to hit. It didn't. She knew why, in the next breath. Lying in Hunter's arms felt too good for her to be embarrassed. Judging from the hard bulge against her thigh, he was feeling pretty good too.

She smiled.

Hunter grunted. In one powerful motion, he set her away from him, stood, and started from the room. "I'll go start breakfast."

Erin watched his long, purposeful strides from the room, and she lay down on the bed, still smiling. Hunter wasn't as unaffected by her as he had pretended. She had his number, and she wasn't going to be afraid any longer to risk trying to get him to admit his feelings.

If nothing else, the situation with Scanlon had made her realize that sometimes you had to go after what you wanted, to grasp as much happiness as you could, and not be afraid of the consequences. Tomorrow wasn't promised.

She wanted Hunter and she was going after him.

Throwing back the covers, she got out of bed and headed for the shower. *Look out, Hunter, I'm coming after you.*

Chapter Ten

Hunter couldn't believe it. Erin acted as if there had been nothing unusual about waking up half on top of him, with him as hard as a rock.

He shoved his hand across his head and tried to calm down. She had actually smiled at him. Trusting him was one thing, getting that close to a man who wanted her so badly that he was almost constantly aroused was something entirely different.

And she had smiled. Hunter scowled at the memory.

The ringing of the kitchen phone interrupted his dark thoughts. He jerked up the receiver. "Yeah," he answered, his irritation roughing his voice.

"Let me speak to Erin," came the terse request.

Hunter almost smiled. He crossed his legs at the ankles and leisurely hit the automatic button on the coffee maker. He *had* smiled when he found a can of coffee in the pantry while he was searching for a jar of jelly the day after he moved in.

"Did you hear me? I want to speak to Erin."

"I heard you, Mathis." Hunter had a pretty good idea who Erin had been going to meet the night before. Quinn had also been missing from the party. The high-strung account executive wasn't high on the list of people Hunter liked.

Not that he ever had been. Too smooth. Too much from Erin's world.

The sudden realization that he might be jealous caused Hunter to jerk upright. "She's getting dressed."

There was a long, telling silence on the line. "Erin is usually up by now. It's after nine."

"She'd have to be up to be getting dressed, wouldn't she," Hunter answered.

"You know what I meant," Quinn snapped.

Hunter had had enough of the man. "I'll tell her you called."

"You do that."

The phone clicked in Hunter's ear. With a frown moving across his dark brow, he replaced the receiver. He had taken entirely too much pleasure in annoying Mathis. But his stupid stunt last night could have gotten Erin killed. Hunter's face twisted into another scowl. Perhaps he needed to have another talk with Mathis.

The phone rang again just as Hunter reached for a coffee cup. If it was Mathis again, Hunter was going to singe his ears. "Yeah."

"Is everything all right, Hunter?"

Instantly contrite, Hunter settled against the cabinet again. "Sorry, Marcus. Everything is fine."

"How did Erin sleep last night?" he inquired. "I didn't like the way she looked when you took her home."

"About as well as could be expected," Hunter told the other man, trying to remember he was talking to Erin's father, and not remember how good it felt to have Erin's sleek length sprawled enticingly on top of his. "She's getting dressed now."

Marcus sighed. "Must have been a bad night. She's usually an early riser."

She's the one who had me rising, Hunter thought before he could stop himself. His jeans were getting snugger, and he shifted. "She managed to get some sleep."

"I'm glad to hear it." Marcus paused, then continued,

"There's something I think you should know. Mildred told me after you left with Erin that Quinn had talked her into getting a message to Erin to meet him in the garden room for a quiet dinner."

Hunter's irritation returned. Leave it up to a smooth talker like Mathis to think of something like that. Erin had probably thought it was romantic and had gone rushing off to meet him. "I guessed as much."

"Don't be upset with Erin. She's always had a soft spot in her heart for him since his family lost everything and so many people turned their backs on him," Marcus related.

"That sounds like her."

"He's the reason she's dragging her feet on naming the vice-president. She doesn't want to hurt him. He's great making deals, but he has absolutely no managerial skills," Marcus lamented. "Erin left him in charge of the office while she and the vice-president were out of town on a business trip and they came back to find the office in chaos. He's too dictatorial and too opinionated."

"So I noticed," Hunter said thinly. "But this time he went too far."

"I know. As soon as I hang up I'm giving him a call." Marcus's tone was tight. "I don't want a repeat of last night. Not that I think Erin would be so foolish again."

"She said she was coming directly back," Hunter defended, then scowled. Erin shouldn't have gone in the first place.

"She told me the same thing after we came back inside the Kings' home," Marcus said. "She didn't tell me the name, just said she didn't want the person waiting on her."

Hunter poured himself a cup of coffee. "She should stop thinking about other people and start putting herself first. The Victim Recovery group, and now Mathis. There's probably a lot more I don't know of."

"Offhand I could name several. However, I'm not sure thinking of herself first is in her nature. She takes after her mother in that regard," Marcus told him. "But I'll at least make sure

Quinn doesn't put her in a position where she has to make *that* decision again."

"I'll leave it up to you then."

Marcus chuckled. "Something tells me if I hadn't taken care of Quinn, you would have."

"The thought crossed my mind." Hunter took a sip of coffee.

"You always have her best interests at heart."

Uncomfortable with the compliment, Hunter set the cup on the counter. Yeah, he had her best interests at heart, and he had been about five seconds from sliding into her this morning. "You want to come over for breakfast?" He needed a buffer.

"No thank you. I've already eaten, but how about this afternoon?" Marcus asked. "I can have Georgia prepare something."

"Sounds good. The gumbo left in two days."

"She'll be pleased to hear it. See you around five. Goodbye, Hunter. Tell Erin I called."

"I will. Goodbye."

The phone had barely settled before it rang again. "Erin needs an answering service," Hunter muttered as he looked longingly at his coffee. "Hello."

"Hunter. It's Detective Grimes."

All hint of agitation left Hunter's face. "Did you get something already?"

"No. The lab's still working on it, but preliminary tests don't look good. He must have worn gloves."

"Son-of—"

"I know," Detective Grimes said. "It would have been nice one way or the other to make a positive ID."

"I know it was him," Hunter said coldly.

"So you keep insisting, but until you or the police can prove it we're back to where we started," Grimes said, his voice tired. "I'll keep you posted."

"Sounds like you've been up for a while," Hunter said.

"Unfortunately, murder never takes a holiday."

"I know." Hunter sipped his lukewarm coffee. "Nothing new with the Desperadoes?"

"A blank," Grimes admitted. "They're probably jumping with glee because we're coming up empty."

The cup hit the counter with a soft thud. "He's hiding someplace. Waiting."

"Where? We circulated his picture. It's been on the news. Still nothing," Grimes reminded him, then: "How's Ms. Cortland? Last night must have scared her."

"Erin's a fighter."

"We both know that can have its bad sides." Grimes sighed loudly. "You know it would make things easier all around for everyone, including Ms. Cortland, if she changed her mind and left town for a few days."

"If you think it's easy for her, think again," Hunter told the other man.

"Look, Hunter, let's put things out in the open. If Ms. Cortland was out of town, I'd have one less worry," Grimes said frankly. "I could stand one less worry."

"Getting leaned on, are you?" Hunter guessed. "You must be learning the hard truth about politics, power, and the police." Hunter's own lesson had come with a very high price tag. A human life. With more effort than usual, he pushed the dark memory to the back of his mind.

"You might say that. Well, will she go?"

"Hold on a minute; I'll ask her." Having heard Erin enter the kitchen, Hunter glanced over his shoulder and almost dropped the phone.

Erin, dressed in a sweater and blue jeans, leaned casually against the doorframe with her arms crossed beneath her breasts. The jeans clung like a second skin, the cropped knit long-sleeved pink sweater like a man's fantasy.

Hunter's body remembered all her softness against him that morning and acted with predictable swiftness. Clenching his teeth, he fought for a semblance of control.

"Grimes on the line," Hunter said, then cleared his throat to combat the squeakiness he'd heard. Squeakiness. Lord. He hadn't lost his cool with a woman since he was a freshman in high school. ''He wants to know if you've changed your mind about taking a trip out of town.''

Her calm expression didn't alter. ''Please tell Detective Grimes good morning for me, and that my answer is the same.''

''She said to say hello and she's staying.'' Hunter listened as the detective said one very explicit word, then added that he'd be in touch if anything developed.

''Thanks,'' Hunter said, and hung up the phone. Folding his arms, he crossed his legs at the ankles and watched Erin open the refrigerator and pour herself a tall glass of juice. Her hands were steady, she looked rested. But there was an indefinable sparkle in her brown eyes that hadn't been there before.

Catching him looking at her, she smiled and offered her glass. ''You want some?''

Hunter's body tightened. He looked closer at her beautiful face, the sparkling brown eyes. Had there been an invitation in her smooth voice? Or had he heard what he had dreaded and wished for for so long?

No. Erin wasn't the type to come on to a man. He lifted his cup. ''No thanks.''

She glanced around the bright kitchen. ''Where's breakfast?''

''The phone's been ringing so much I haven't had time to prepare it,'' Hunter complained as he opened the refrigerator door. ''Omelet coming up.''

''Any calls for me?'' she asked, and leaned against the counter by the stove.

Hunter's traitorous gaze slipped to the narrow band of honeyed flesh by her belly button before he could control the movement. Taking the coward's way out, he turned away from Erin instead of toward her as he cracked the eggs.

''You had two. One from Mathis,'' he told her, and couldn't resist a quick peek to see her reaction.

''And the other one?'' she inquired, bending over to get the omelet pan from the bottom of the cabinet. Faded denim cupped her soft bottom.

Hunter gulped. ''Your father. He's coming over for dinner.''

"That's nice." She placed the pan on the stove, then took out sweet butter, cheese, ham, and mushrooms. "I think you've whipped the eggs enough."

He glanced down at the beaten eggs. His mind had been completely on Erin. The omelet would probably be as tough as rubber and as tasteless. "I thought you didn't like jeans," he asked before he could stop himself.

Her exquisite face relaxed into another smile, this one more potent than the last. "I thought I might help Mr. Dawkins when he comes over. I was going to plant pots of budding tulips since I missed getting the bulbs into the ground in October."

Hunter eyed the clinging sweater, the exposed silken flesh, and thought *not in that sweater.* "What time is he coming?"

Erin finished cutting the ingredients. "Around ten."

"We better get breakfast so we'll be ready." Putting butter into the pan, he turned on the burner.

"You don't have to help."

"I could use the exercise," he said, angling the pan to coat the bottom.

Erin lifted a delicate brow. "And where I go, you go?"

He almost smiled. "You're finally learning."

Mr. Dawkins arrived, with a truckload of potted tulips, exactly at ten. At one minute past ten, Mike Stanley and Chuck Powell pulled up behind him. When she heard the vehicles, Erin lifted the curtain of the kitchen window. She frowned when she saw the two security men get out of a green sedan.

"You're leaving?" She didn't realize the dejection in her voice until she heard it aloud.

"No. I made a phone call while you were changing clothes," Hunter said, eyeing the maroon-and-gold Huston-Tillotson college sweatshirt she wore. "I want to make sure the front is covered while we're in the back."

"Oh," she mumbled, embarrassed.

"Come on, those tulips aren't going to plant themselves." Hunter started for the back door.

* * *

During the next hours, Erin did more bending, stooping, and reaching than in the most strenuous aerobics class she had ever attended. She enjoyed every minute of it. Gradually the bleak backyard was transformed into a colorful display of yellow and red.

She had been so pleased she had asked the gardener about plants for the several large empty pots around the pool. He had grinned, and off he had gone in his truck. He returned an hour later with several flats of pansies. They'd continue to bloom through the cold weather, until summer. By then, she could switch to begonias and impatiens to cascade down the sides of the pots.

The thought made her happy until she glanced up at Hunter, and read his mind as clearly as if he had spoken. By summer he would be gone. Fighting the misery the thought brought, she picked up a flat of the pansies and headed for the clay urn near the base of the waterfall.

"You don't do anything by half measure, do you?" Hunter asked as he took the tray of flowers from her.

"If you're going to commit to something, give it your best." Dropping to her knees, she began to loosen the dirt in the pot.

Hunkered down beside her, Hunter studied her pensive face. All day she had been as happy and carefree as a kid out on a holiday from school. He didn't like to see the shadows return to her eyes. "The Victim Recovery group teach you that?"

Her small spade paused for a moment. "No. Marriage."

Hunter had known she had been married. The idea that she had once belonged to another man bothered him. It wasn't rational, it wasn't professional, and there wasn't a thing he could do about it.

"What happened?" He was crossing the line, but he had already crossed it when he had allowed her to sleep in his arms and had enjoyed every torturous second.

She reached for a flower and put it in the small hole waiting for it. "I confused friendship with love and made us both unhappy. Since it lasted only a year and the experience left me disheartened, I took my maiden name back, since I didn't think I'd ever marry again.''

''Some man will come along and change your mind.'' Even as the words left his mouth he regretted that he wouldn't be that man.

She looked at him over her shoulder, her brown eyes direct. ''You might be right. Could you hand me some bone meal, please? It's over by the other plants.''

Hunter stared at her while she calmly planted flowers, and he wanted to stay and ask if she had anyone in mind. Mathis popped into his mind. Hunter's hands clenched.

''Is something wrong?'' she asked mildly, when he continued to stare at her.

''No.'' He pushed to his feet and stalked off. Erin was smarter than that. She might feel sorry for the man, but that didn't mean she wanted to marry him. But who?

Grabbing the bone meal, he started back, and stopped in his tracks at the musical sound of laughter. Erin, her head thrown back, was laughing at the antics of two squirrels chasing each other from branch to branch in the trees overhead.

The sound was captivating and alluring. Mathis was not getting her. Hunter realized he was being jealous and it was none of his concern, but his mind was made up nonetheless. The other man didn't deserve a vibrant woman like Erin and, if Hunter had his way, he wasn't going to get her.

''You should laugh more often.'' He kneeled down beside her and handed her the bag.

''There hasn't been much reason to in the past week.'' Shaking out the white granules, she thoroughly mixed them in the soil.

''That'll change soon. You'll have laughter every day.'' *And I won't be around to hear it.*

Sinking back on her heels, she turned to him. ''What about you, Hunter?''

A frown crossed his dark face. ''What are you talking about?''

"What would make you have days like this, days filled with sunshine and laughter and peace?"

You. He glanced out over the yard, away from the velvet warmth of her brown eyes, the lush softness of her lips. "I haven't thought about it much."

"Pity. You deserve what you give to others."

His head whipped back around. His expression was guarded.

"You gave me back the ability to enjoy a beautiful day and laugh again. Thank you." Her smile was filled with melancholy. "I wish I could do the same for you."

"It's my job," he said, as much for his benefit as hers. Neither could afford to forget.

"Yes, so you keep saying." She leaned up and began digging in the pot.

"I'll go get some more plants."

"I haven't finished planting half of these," she called.

"Never hurts to be prepared," Hunter said, and kept walking.

Erin lounged on the couch in the den with her feet tucked under her and flipped through a magazine. She wanted to hug herself with glee. She was gradually getting through his wall of indifference. She smiled, remembering how effusively he had greeted her father.

She'd quickly set Hunter back by dressing for dinner. She had on the slim black cotton-knit sheath that flattered her figure . . . if Hunter's covert glances were any indication.

She'd caught him once and he had scowled like the very devil. Smiling sweetly, she'd asked if there was something wrong with the stuffed peppers. She'd had the distinct impression that if her father hadn't been there, with an amused smile on his face, Hunter would have said something very different from his terse "no."

Since her father was a very perceptive man, she had no doubt he understood that the relationship between Hunter and her was changing. That he approved was obvious from his indulgent smile and easy manner.

Kissing her goodnight, he had whispered, ''Good luck. I think you'll need it.''

From the way Hunter had been practically glued to the TV set since her father left, it looked like Marcus had been right. She wasn't giving up. She didn't know where a relationship with him would lead, but she was going to find out. He would offer no guarantees. Neither did life.

The phone rang and he picked it up before the first ring ended. Too fast to have been paying any attention to the sitcom. Erin winced for the other person's ear. Hunter's terse greeting had the sharp bite of a whip.

He listened for a while longer, then hung up the phone and went back to watching the TV screen.

''Wrong number?''

''No one answered.''

Erin laid the magazine aside and put her feet on the floor. Although Hunter had resumed his sprawling position in the easy chair, she could sense the subtle change in his body. ''You said no one answered; do you think someone was there?''

''I heard the phone click just before I hung up.''

''That concerns you? I bet you're one of those people who has to know everyone who calls. I bet you had Caller ID the day after the service was offered.''

He finally looked at her. ''Anything I can't explain concerns me.''

''Anything?'' Erin asked, speculation in her voice.

''Anything.''

''You're a very cautious man, Hunter.''

''In my line of business, I've had to be,'' he said.

Lifting her legs onto the sofa again, she leaned back and placed her arms across the back. ''Which business would that be?''

Instead of answering, he got up from the chair and came to her. He spoke to her across the coffee table. ''You're playing a risky game, Erin.''

Powerful, dark, and dangerous, he stared down at her, his

face implacable. ''I don't know what you mean,'' she said, but her voice was breathy.

''Yes, you do, and I want it to stop.'' His gaze swept from her long, bare legs to her shapely breasts beneath the clinging knit. ''There's not going to be a repeat of last night.''

''Which part?'' she asked. ''The kiss, or you holding me while I went to sleep?''

His black eyes blazed. ''Go to bed, Erin, and if you forget your juice tonight don't expect me to bring it.''

Slowly she drew her arms down and stood. Her gaze was direct, despite the pounding of her heart. ''I'd never expect more from you, Hunter, than you're willing to give.''

''That doesn't mean I wouldn't expect it of myself,'' he said tightly.

''Then one of us has a problem, and I don't think it's me.''

''You have no idea what you're asking.'' He viciously shoved his hand across his head. ''It's the situation. You're grateful to me.''

''I might be grateful, but I'm not stupid,'' she tossed.

''People in life-threatening situations sometimes let their emotions get in the way of common sense,'' he told her.

''Who was she?'' she questioned. There had been more than irritation, there had been desperation in his voice.

Hunter's face went slack, then misery and guilt hardened his features. His eyes were as cold and lifeless as icicles.

''I'm sorry.'' She reached out to him and he jerked away. His rejection hurt worse than a physical blow. ''I won't bother you again.'' Turning, she went to her room.

Chapter Eleven

She didn't want to face him.

Erin leaned against the window of her bedroom and looked out over the backyard. The scene of budding and blooming flowers that had brought such peace to her less than twenty-four hours ago now offered none.

Hunter had apparently been involved with another woman and, from his desolate expression last night, the experience had scarred him very badly. She had tossed and turned most of the night, thinking about what might have happened. The one sure thing that kept returning was that the woman was no longer in his life.

Erin had been around Hunter long enough to know that he was honest and up front. He wasn't the type of man to have a woman on the side. He had to know mentioning another relationship would have been the one thing that would have stopped Erin from coming on to him. Yet he hadn't said anything.

Therefore, it stood to reason that the unknown woman was gone, but she was obviously not forgotten. Judging from all his self-directed anger and his efforts to keep Erin's and his relationship on a professional level, the woman had somehow interfered with his ability to do his job.

To a self-reliant and by-the-book man like Hunter, that must have been devastating. He'd do anything to keep himself from repeating that mistake again. He would guard his heart as valiantly and as relentlessly as he guarded Erin.

The phone on her nightstand rang. She ignored it, as she had the other times. She had called her father shortly after she woke up that morning. If anyone else was on the line, she didn't want to talk with them. She wasn't in the mood for witty conversation.

Sundays were usually her day of winding down after going to church and having dinner with her father. Later, in his study, they would discuss what had happened that week at work.

It was almost noon and she had yet to leave her room. Sighing, she leaned her forehead against the cool glass of the window pane. She was trying to put off the inevitable.

Seeing the bleakness in Hunter's midnight eyes and knowing she had put it there with her careless probing was tearing her apart. He had given her so much and, in her need for more, she had hurt him.

Lifting her head, she turned from the window and looked at the rumpled covers on the oversized chair. What sleep she had managed to get last night had been in the wide chair, with the bedspread she and Hunter had shared pulled up to her chin. The woodsy fragrance he wore lingered on the bedding. She had closed her eyes and made believe he was with her.

A poor substitute.

Erin glanced at the door. She couldn't put off facing him any longer. He'd knocked on the door when she had been talking on the phone to her father. Once assured that she was all right, he had left. That had been four hours ago. Sooner or later he'd return, and this time he wouldn't talk through the door.

He'd want to see with his own eyes that she was all right. No matter what his personal feelings were, he took his responsibilities seriously. And if she was going to be able to look back on last night with anything but shame and misery, she'd have to have the courage to face him first.

Leaving her room, she went in search of Hunter. She found him in the kitchen, standing at the stove. He glanced around. Her breath caught and then trembled out over her lips.

Hunter always did that to her. Took her breath away. "Good morning," she offered tentatively.

"Morning." Ebony eyes searched over her like invisible fingers. "You missed breakfast."

Such a normal conversation, when the situation wasn't normal at all. "I wasn't hungry."

A dark eyebrow lifted, but all he said was, "Then you should be hungry now. Grab a seat. Steaks coming up."

Thinking perhaps making her apology would be easier sitting down, she started for the chair. The sight of a purple pansy in a sleeve of foil and pink-colored plastic wrap on a breakfast tray stopped her in mid-stride. There had been several left over after she finished the clay pots.

Stunned, pleased beyond measure, her gaze lifted to Hunter. His back was to her.

Opening the door to the oven grill, he removed the steaks. "Marcus said you like yours medium. Mine has to be charred." Placing the beef on the plates, he set them on the table and finally looked at her.

His face, often remote and unreadable, was the same. But the eyes. Those compelling eyes of his were wary and watchful.

Erin picked up the flower with a hand that trembled. Her smile was just as unsteady and tremulous. "Thank you for forgiving me. I'm sorry."

"You didn't know. It happened a long time ago." He pulled out her chair. "We better eat before it gets cold."

Erin took her seat. Somehow the happiness of a moment ago had dimmed. He had forgiven her, but the topic remained off limits. Hunter was still keeping a part of himself from her, and until he decided differently there was no hope of them developing anything deeper.

She had to accept his decision and pray he'd change his mind. The alternative was too painful to think about.

The doorbell rang a little after seven that night. Casting a quick look at Erin, who was curled up on the living-room sofa asleep, Hunter went to the door. A flicker of the curtain showed Quinn Mathis.

Hunter opened the door. "Yes?"

"I'd like to see Erin," the other man said.

"She's asleep."

Hands deep in his pockets, Quinn tried to look anywhere but at Hunter's unrelenting face. "I'm sure she wouldn't mind if you woke her up. It's important."

Hunter couldn't believe the selfishness of the other man. "We'll be in the office tomorrow at nine."

"Look, I just want to tell her I'm sorry."

"Sorry for her, or because Marcus had a heart-to-heart with you?" Hunter asked.

Quinn flushed. "That had nothing to do with anything."

Hunter snorted. "And I'm the tooth fairy."

"Oh, I see now. You just want Erin for yourself." Quinn's condescending gaze tracked from Hunter's scuffed boots to his bulky black sweater. "She's out of your class. She may depend on you while Scanlon is free, but when it's over Marcus will write you a check and neither one of them will ever think twice about you again."

His statement was so close to Hunter's own thoughts about Erin that he had to grip the doorknob to keep from planting his fist in Mathis's smirking face. "This door is closing in two seconds. Stay at your own risk."

"Give her these, at least." Bending, Quinn picked up a beautiful bouquet of deep-red roses and baby's breath.

Hunter thought of the pansy he had put on Erin's tray and his gut clenched. *Out of his class* pounded in his ears. Taking the crystal vase with one hand, he closed the door with the other.

For a long time he stood in the foyer. He wanted to toss the roses out the back door. Putting the pansy on her tray had been impulsive and stupid. He had known she was feeling bad and hiding from him, and he had wanted to make her feel better.

Remembering her joy when she had been planting the flowers, he had gone outside and gotten one. A little improvisation, and he had thought it looked pretty good. Until now.

He put the roses on the side table. Erin could decide where she wanted them when she woke up, which didn't look like it would be any time soon. After they had cleaned up the kitchen, she had gotten a blanket and a pillow, curled up, and given him a sleepy smile. She was probably asleep by the time her lashes closed.

Since then he had sat there and just watched her. The light-blue blanket was pulled up to her chin, her knees bent. He might have thought she was cold, but he knew she liked to sleep that way.

So he watched her sleep, knowing that, when he went to bed, the memory of her curled up on the sofa would stay with him. Haunt him. He wouldn't get any more sleep than he had last night.

Erin stirred up old memories and guilt. This time it wouldn't end the same way. Erin would have her sunny days and her laughter.

Without her, he'd have none.

Between one moment and the next, Erin was awake. Something was wrong. Panic zipped through her as she sat up on the sofa.

Hunter was angry. The fury in his voice was hot and sizzling. Throwing back the blanket, she followed the sound of his voice.

''He's called here three times. I can't keep it from her much longer,'' he snapped impatiently. ''There must be some way to trace the calls faster and catch this creep before he leaves the pay phones. Put more police in the area.''

Impotent anger pushed him to his feet. ''What do you mean,

the calls could be a coincidence? You think some nut has called Erin three times from three different pay phones, for the fun of it? Grimes, take your head out of the sand, for God's sake. That phone exchange area is less than thirty minutes from here.''

There was a pause, then: ''No, I haven't asked her if someone has been calling her and hanging up without saying anything,'' he said tersely.

''No, they haven't.''

Hunter swung around. Surprise and rage registered on his dark brown face, then they were wiped away. ''Stand by the phone, Grimes, I'll call you back.'' He dropped the receiver into the cradle. ''How long have you been there?''

''Long enough,'' she said, fighting the chill sweeping over her. ''If he has my phone number, he knows where I live.''

''Not necessarily.'' Ebony eyes studied her.

''What do you mean?''

''From what I've heard and read in the report Grimes sent me, Scanlon is not the type to warn someone he's coming.''

''Then why the phone calls?''

''My guess is because he can't get to you any other way and he wants to rattle you into making a mistake however he can,'' Hunter told her.

Erin wrapped her arms around her body. ''Like I did at the party?''

''Yes.''

''That won't happen again.''

''I hope not.'' Hunter studied her closely. ''If he can shake your confidence in those around you, his chances improve.''

''My confidence in you was never an issue,'' she confessed.

''But you're independent and headstrong and used to calling the shots. I interfere with that,'' Hunter bluntly reminded her.

''And I want to live, to be able to continue,'' she told him with more calm than she felt.

Hunter's expression hardened. ''You will. How many people have your phone number?''

She moved to perch one hip on the edge of the sofa. ''A

select few. It was always unlisted, but after the robbery when the media began bothering me, I had it changed again.''

''How select?'' he questioned.

''My executives, my Soror sisters, my business club, my . . .'' her voice trailed off as realization dawned.

''That's what I thought. You have a lot of friends and you'd want to be there for everyone,'' he said, not unkindly.

''B . . . but how could he get the number?''

''The same way I did after the first suspicious phone call.'' Hunter folded his arms. ''You may have an unlisted number, but the co-chairman, Charlotte Anderson, who gave the TV interview, doesn't. She wasn't in, but her daughter was kind enough to look in her personal directory by the phone and give me your number after I mentioned I was a reporter with the *Austin Chronicle* and wanted to do an in-depth story on both of you.''

Erin tucked her lower lip between her teeth. ''Candace is only seventeen. She was trying to help.''

''I know. At least she was smart enough not to give out your home address.''

The knowledge sank into Erin like a soothing balm. Her arms, clutching her stomach, relaxed.

Lifting the receiver, Hunter punched the redial button. Grimes answered the phone before the first ring ended.

''Detective Grimes.''

''I'm back. She hasn't received any strange phone calls, and her unlisted phone number might as well be listed, with all the people who have the number.'' Hunter sighed. ''I'll keep in touch.'' He hung up the phone.

She took a step closer, her eyes watching his. ''Why didn't you tell me?''

''It was something you could do nothing about except worry.''

She frowned. ''But, before, you always wanted me to know everything.''

Hunter shoved his hands into his pockets. ''It was necessary for you to believe Scanlon was out there. Once you accepted the reality of that there was no need to worry you further.''

Lines of puzzlement disappeared from her forehead. ''You were trying to protect me,'' she said, her voice filled with awe.

''That's my job,'' he reminded her tightly.

Despite everything, Erin almost smiled at the tight-lipped way he had uttered that terse statement. ''Detective Grimes probably wishes it wasn't.''

The corner of Hunter's sensuous mouth twitched. ''That he does. He has the potential to become a good cop, if he'd stop being so factual.''

''You don't appear to be the type to let your emotions rule you overmuch, either.''

The hint of amusement disappeared. ''No, I'm not, but I've learned to trust my instincts, over the years.''

She tilted her head to one side, studying him openly. ''Ever been wrong?''

''Once or twice,'' he told her, his eyes piercing.

Erin remembered a balmy night in Chicago and a wild, passionate kiss. From the way he was watching her, she realized he was remembering it too. She tucked the information away and asked, ''Now your instincts tell you Scanlon is the one calling me.''

''Who else?''

''You don't think it could be a coincidence?''

''To a seasoned cop, there's no such thing as coincidence.''

Erin nodded her acceptance. She had total confidence in Hunter's ability. ''Have you told Daddy about the phone calls?''

''No.''

''Good, then please don't. I don't want him worried any more than he already is.'' She rose. ''I'm going to turn in.''

Hunter frowned. ''Just like that.''

''Just like that. He's on a pay phone trying to scare me. He won't get away with it,'' she said firmly.

''You're something else.'' Hunter shook his head.

''You thought I'd fall apart?'' she asked, her tone mildly disappointed.

"I didn't know what to think, except I didn't want to hand you any more grief," he answered honestly.

"You haven't. Like you once told me, this is Scanlon's doing."

The corners of his mouth twitched. "Now, you remember what I told you."

"I always remember everything you tell me," she said, her voice oddly breathless.

All traces of humor fled. Midnight eyes narrowed. "Good night."

"Good night." Turning, she went toward the bedroom. She stopped, seeing the roses, then rushed over to them. Her eyes wide, she lowered her head and inhaled their rich fragrance. "They're beautiful."

Hunter's familiar mask descended again. "Mathis brought them by."

"When?"

"A couple of hours ago while you were asleep." He inclined his head. "They're his way of apologizing."

Erin's eyes widened. "You know."

"Mildred got nervous and confessed to your father."

"Poor thing," Erin lamented. "She said she thought it was romantic, until she had to face you. I've seen Mildred stare down powerful politicians, and she practically crumbled after speaking to you."

"Smart woman. You should have taken a cue from her."

"I will from now on. Good night." She went down the hall to her bedroom.

"Aren't you going to take your flowers?"

"No, I thought I'd leave them there." Opening her door, she looked back at him. "I already have a flower." She entered her room, taking with her Hunter's bright flash of a smile.

Hunter wasn't smiling the next morning when Erin walked out of her bedroom, dressed and ready to go to work. No amount of reasoning on his part could change her mind. She just stood there, her chin set at a determined angle. In her stubborn mind, going to work wasn't giving Scanlon an edge: it was refusing to let fear rule her life.

Deciding after ten minutes that he was wasting his breath and getting perilously close to trying to shake some sense into her beautiful head, he had given up. But as the day advanced, his anger returned. She was taking facing her fears too far. While he admired her courage, his gut was in knots.

Scanlon was getting too close. The phone calls proved that.

To her credit, once in her office, Erin had followed his orders . . . until it was time to go home. She had balked, but good. The reason made Hunter grip his fist and let loose with more than a few choice, explicit words.

She had stood quietly in her office while he vented his frustration, then had walked over to him and said, ''I'll be safe with you.''

Hearing her say those words, seeing the surety of that statement in her serene brown eyes, tore at his heart and soul. She believed in him too damn much. There were always unforeseen circumstances that you couldn't take into account.

Telling Erin that did little good. Her complete assurance in his ability was humbling and terrifying.

So here he was, on 1st Street Bridge at 9:13 P.M., watching the film crew make the final preparations for shooting the Mystique lipstick promo commercial. Erin was going to give him his first gray hairs.

''You shouldn't be here.'' He practically snarled the words.

''Hunter, I told you I wouldn't take any chances,'' Erin told him.

''You're taking one now.'' He looked over the bridge to the boaters on the Colorado River below, then back to the spectators pressed against the orange-and-white barricades.

''I'm dressed as one of the technicians. He won't know me,'' Erin said, yanking her Dallas Cowboys Super Bowl XXX blue and white cap down over her eyes. ''Sally worked a miracle by finding a male model and getting us a permit to shoot this soon. It's now or never.''

Hunter's gaze swung back to the crowd, the policemen standing in front, then back to Erin. He could easily pick her out in a crowd. The proud way she carried herself, her voluptuous body, her exquisite face.

She started across the bridge. Hunter's hand flashed out and stopped her. "Where're you going?"

"I want to talk to the cameraman," Erin explained. "I want to make sure he's shooting from the right angle."

"Isn't Connie Bledsoe taking care of that?"

"Yes, but I just want to make sure."

His hand didn't loosen. "Do you always check behind her?"

"No, but this time there is another advertising company after the same account. We have to do it right the first time," she told him, patiently waiting for him to release her.

"It was her idea."

"But it's my company."

He stared down into Erin's stubborn face. Short of creating a scene and drawing more attention to her, there was nothing he could do. "All right, but I'm sticking close."

She smiled. "Never thought differently."

She went quickly to the producer. Hunter moved in front of her while she, Connie, and the stocky producer went over the scene again.

Hunter didn't see the problem. All it entailed was a woman walking out of the fog, applying lipstick, then turning toward a man. Child's play.

The child's play took ten takes before everyone was satisfied with the shoot. The woman hadn't been sensuous enough; the man hadn't looked dangerous enough. When one had it, the other didn't. Hunter had been grateful when the producer announced it was a wrap.

Connie, in a long black cape, walked over to where Erin and Hunter stood off to the side. Grinning, the creative director winked at Hunter. "I still think you would have been better. I bet you would have gotten it right in one take."

"We'll never know." Hunter scanned the bridge as the crew began packing up their equipment.

"If you ever change your mind, give me a call." The elegant woman eyed his powerful body. "You could sell anything from mouthwash to soft drinks. Sally thinks so, too."

"No doubt with my shirt off," he said, not bothering to keep the sarcasm out of his voice.

"It sells."

"When I take my shirt off, it won't be before a camera."

Her grin broadened to just short of a leer. "Lucky woman, whoever she is."

"Hunter, I thought you were in a hurry to leave," Erin said crisply.

Connie and Hunter both turned at the sharpness of her voice. The smile faded from Connie's face. "Sorry. You two go on. I'll make sure everything is taken care of here before I leave."

Erin had sounded like a jealous shrew. The look of understanding on Connie's face only made Erin feel worse. "No, I'm the one who is sorry. I guess I'm a little tired."

The older woman grabbed her hand. "You're entitled. I don't blame you one bit."

Not knowing if she wanted to delve deeper into the other woman's meaning, Erin walked toward the barricade. A silent Hunter fell into step beside her. At his car, she waited for him to unlock her door, then she slid inside and fastened her seat belt.

She was glad he didn't try to talk to her. What could she say? Sorry, I'm jealous.

Erin was jealous.

No matter how much he wanted to deny it, the knowledge stunned and pleased Hunter. Erin wasn't for him, but he'd be lying if he said it didn't soothe his ego to learn she didn't want other women coming on to him, even in jest.

Sure, the fact that he was protecting her had a lot to do with her feelings. He'd be a fool to act on her attraction, but it was gratifying to know about it. Maybe in the future he could look back on this assignment and not feel like someone had ripped out his heart.

Maybe, but not likely.

At the car, Hunter unlocked the passenger door for Erin, then went around to the driver's side. He got inside and pulled away from the curb. Out of habit, Hunter checked his rearview mirror. Halfway down the block behind him a car pulled out. A frown worked its way across his brow.

He and Erin, like the other people leaving the bridge, had come from the opposite direction. He would have seen anyone getting into their car. He hadn't. Therefore, the person or persons must already have been in their car.

Waiting.

Hunter eased to a stop at the signal light, leaving enough room to maneuver between his Mustang and the Maxima in front. He wasn't about to get boxed in if he was right and the car tried to pull up beside him.

The light changed. Keeping an eye on the black sedan, Hunter opted against the dark narrow side streets and headed for the freeway.

The car followed, keeping pace with the Mustang. When Hunter slowed, the car slowed. If he sped up, the car sped up. The sedan always stayed too far back for Hunter to read the license plate or tell anything about the driver.

Only one thing was certain. They were being followed.

Chapter Twelve

Hunter had two choices. He could call Grimes and hope it didn't take fifteen minutes to track the detective down, as it had with the phone calls, or he could take care of the matter himself.

The car following them moved up another car length.

"Brace yourself."

Turning from staring out the window, Erin frowned. "What?"

"Brace yourself," Hunter repeated tightly. "I'm going to ditch whoever is following us."

Erin tensed, then threw a frantic glance over her shoulder, even as she followed Hunter's directions. Hunter's gaze flickered over her. In the next instant, he stepped on the gas. The Mustang shot around the car in front of it, then another.

Hunter zig-zagged across two lanes of the freeway. A car horn blared angrily as he expertly crossed a third lane. His speed increased, instead of slowing. He took the off-ramp at seventy-five miles an hour.

Trembling, her heart beating erratically, Erin resisted the restraint of the seat belt and tried to look behind them. Glaring headlights of two fast-moving vehicles followed them off the freeway.

"D . . . did we lose him?"

Hunter's hard gaze cut to his side-view mirror before answering. "Yes."

Briefly shutting her eyes, Erin let out a shaky breath. The wild dash across the freeway had been nothing compared to the rising terror she had felt. While she had been feeling sorry for herself, Scanlon had made a move against her. If Hunter hadn't been alert, he might have succeeded.

"You all right?"

The concern in his voice only made her feel worse about her childish behavior on the bridge. "Yes. Thanks to you."

Turning her head, she looked at his stern profile. Once again, she wondered who worried about Hunter while he took care of others. "How about you?"

His surprised gaze jerked to her, then back to the road as he sped through a green signal light. "Fine."

She straightened in her seat. There were questions she wanted to ask, but she didn't want to distract Hunter. He might have eased her mind, but the alertness of his body showed that he was still thinking, still calculating. There was only one thing left to do: help him keep watch.

She wasn't surprised when, twenty minutes later, he took a different route to her house, then drove by the subdivision before circling around and coming in on the back street. He didn't leave anything to chance.

"Erin, he's not following us. I left him behind on the freeway," Hunter said as he maneuvered one of the winding curves on her street.

"I know. I'm just helping you keep watch." Since he had broken his silence and they were near her house, she decided it was all right to talk again. "How did you know someone was following us?"

He glanced over at her. "Despite it being a popular area, most of the people there tonight were either back at the shoot or strolling along the shore line. In the long walk down the hill I didn't see anyone get into the car that pulled out behind us."

Apprehension clutched at her. "He followed us from the office?"

"No," Hunter said with confidence. "I would have spotted him the same way I spotted him tonight."

"But if he didn't follow us, how did he know how to find me?"

"That's what I've been asking myself." Frustration edged his voice. "If I didn't know better, I'd think he had a connection inside."

Her body stiffened. "You can't be serious? No one on my staff would give out that kind of information."

"Calm down. I didn't say they had." He activated the garage-door opener and drove inside.

"Good, because my staff is loyal," she fumed, getting out of the car as soon as it stopped.

"People reveal things sometimes without meaning to," Hunter told her.

She eyed him standing in front of the back door. "Everyone can't be as guarded as you."

Something flashed in his gaze before he wiped it away and opened the door. The alarm sounded. Flipping on the light, Hunter crossed to the panel and punched in the four-digit code. "I'll lock up and set the alarm. Good night."

Seeing the closed look on his face made her want to cry. She had put it there. "Hunter—"

"I need to call Detective Grimes." Stepping past her, he closed the back door, then reactivated the inside alarm.

"You won't let me say I'm sorry."

"There's nothing to be sorry for. You only spoke the truth." He headed for the den.

Tugging off her cap in frustration, she followed him. "If it was the truth, it wouldn't bother either of us. It does."

"I have a call to make." He reached for the phone.

Erin moved it out of reach. Her eyes glinted with determination to see this through. "Does nothing get through to you?"

''Now is not the time for this.''

''I can't think of a better time than now.''

''You're upset. It's understandable.''

''Don't you dare try to patronize me. You're darn right I'm upset.'' Hands on slim hips, she glared at him. ''Normal people get upset. But you wouldn't know anything about that, would you?''

A muscle twitched in his jaw.

''Well, I'm sorry. I'm a normal person and when something bothers me, I have to let it out.'' She took a step closer. ''You bother me, Hunter. You bother me a great deal. It disturbs the hell out of me that you see me as a case and not as a woman, that I can't get through to you.''

Silence stretched across the room. Erin wouldn't have taken back the words if she could. Nothing. She started past him.

''You get to me too much,'' he said, as if the words were being dragged from him.

Her eyes softened. ''Hunter—''

''Scanlon is still out there.''

Erin continued walking closer to him until she felt the warmth of his body, smelled his woodsy cologne, felt the solid length of his muscled thighs. ''Are you trying to remind me, or yourself?''

''Both,'' he gritted out.

Erin smiled. ''Just checking.''

''This is not going to change things.''

The wattage of her smile increased. ''Wanna bet?''

''Go to bed, Erin.''

She tilted her head to one side, her heart jumping with gladness. ''Do you realize you're always ordering me to go to bed? I wonder why?''

His answer was his narrowed gaze.

''All right, Hunter. I'll be good. For now.'' Smiling, she left.

Fist clenched, Hunter watched her leave. He didn't need the distraction. Not now. But it was all too easy to picture Erin wearing the flowery gown and him sliding it off. Stalking across the room, he picked up the phone and dialed homicide.

Light flooded the living room. ''Sorry to disturb you, but I have to do this before I forget again.''

Lying on his sofa bed, Hunter watched Erin cross the living room in her flowered robe and satin slippers. Although he had heard her leave her room a few minutes earlier and go into the kitchen, he was still surprised to see her in the living room.

After the first night, when she had seen him with his shirt off and pants unzipped, she had never come out of her room again until morning once she said good night. ''Can't that wait until tomorrow?''

''No.'' Erin tilted the porcelain water can with a painted bouquet of wildflowers on the side.

Since he had little choice, Hunter sat up and observed Erin watering the half-dead fern on the stand by the bay window. His gaze was watchful. Apparently she wasn't handling having been followed in the car as well as he had thought she was. ''Looks like you're a little late.''

''This has happened before,'' she confided, breaking off several dead stems and putting them in the wastebasket. ''It'll come out again. You'll see.''

Hunter had his doubts on both issues: the flower's rejuvenation and his being there to see it. ''Yeah, well, good night.''

Instead of leaving, she set the can down and straightened a picture. ''This never hangs straight.''

''I'm cutting the light off in ten seconds.''

''I'll go put this up.'' She disappeared into the kitchen.

''Five seconds and counting,'' he called when she didn't reappear.

She came back into view, her arms folded around her chest awkwardly, then she plopped down on the love seat at the end of the sleep sofa. She didn't seem to be in any hurry to leave.

''Are you afraid he might have followed us home?'' Hunter questioned.

She shrugged. "Not really. I don't think you'd be relaxing in bed if you thought that."

Hunter arched a dark brow. Her astuteness was astounding. But she was wrong about one thing. He was hardly relaxing. His body was on full alert, all because of the woman across from him.

"Care to give me a hint as to what's bothering you?"

Drawing her knees up, she folded her arms across them and lowered her chin. "What made you want to become a policeman?"

Stalling. Erin was up to something. He recalled the benefit. "Is there some high-society party or a benefit coming up this weekend?"

She shrugged. "There are a couple of parties. I declined, but if you want to go I can call and uncancel."

He scowled. "I don't want to go."

"Then why did you ask?"

"Because you're stalling and up to something. The last time you did that you wanted to go someplace you knew I'd object to," he told her with feeling.

"Were you always this suspicious or did it occur after you became a policeman?"

"People like you make me suspicious."

Her head came up. "And what exactly is 'people like me'?"

"People who like to have their way."

She relaxed. "Don't you like having your way?"

He'd like to have his way with her, but he didn't think that was what she was talking about. "Sometimes."

She smiled. "Spoken like a true diplomat. Now stop doing what you accused me of and tell me why you wanted to be a policeman."

"I wanted to make a difference." The words sounded naive and corny now, but they were the truth, nonetheless.

"Somehow that doesn't surprise me."

He settled back against the couch. "Surprised my parents and older brother."

"What did they want you to do?"

"Anything to make money," Hunter said, the annoyance slipping through, even after all these years.

"What do they do?"

"My parents are part-owners of an import-export store at O'Hare and my brother is a stockbroker in New York."

"They should have known better," she said, tilting her head to one side. "You hate ties."

Hunter smiled. He hadn't meant to; it just slipped through. The usual response from people was stunned amazement, then the question of what had happened to him.

Her head came up again. "Hunter, are you actually smiling at me, or am I sleepwalking?"

"You caught me off guard," he admitted frankly.

She grinned. "Now I know I'm sleepwalking."

"Then you better get back to bed." He relaxed against the sofa.

"I'm not sleepy." Amusement slipped from her face. Her chin came back down to rest on her drawn-up knees.

"I am. The light goes off in two seconds."

"Go on. I'll just sit here for a while. I can see how to get to my room by the night-light." She leaned back in the chair. "Thank you again for buying them."

"You're welcome, and you're stalling again." He looked at the light switch near the door. "I don't wear pajama bottoms."

Erin's lower jaw dropped, then she snapped her mouth shut. "I won't look."

"How do I know I can trust you?" he asked.

"I've seen a male body before," she told him.

"You haven't seen mine."

She swallowed, her gaze unerringly going back over the wide, muscular chest. Seeing him without his shirt had almost made her forget about her plans. "Just be glad I'm not Connie."

Hunter grunted. "Point taken. She'd probably try to find a camera."

"She knows the market. We're lucky to have her."

"Is she going to get the vice-president's position?"

"That's confidential. I hope you'll let me interview them alone tomorrow."

Hunter jerked upright. "Surely you . . . No. You're staying home tomorrow."

"I'm not," she said. "You said he's trying to rattle me, and I won't let him succeed. He doesn't know where I live and, once I get inside either place, I'm safe."

"You have to get there," he reminded her, grimly.

"You'll see that I will."

Her blithe assurance pricked a nerve. "Dammit, Erin. I'm not without faults. I'm not all-seeing. Don't depend on me so much."

"I'm sorry. I didn't realize. I guess my putting all the responsibility on you isn't fair." She glanced away. "You can cut the light out now."

Looking at her huddled in the chair, Hunter wanted nothing more than to cross the room and pull her into his arms. He couldn't. He wouldn't let her go until he had made her his and, once he did that, he wasn't sure if he could ever let her go.

But neither could he let her go through this alone.

Throwing back the cover, he stood. Erin kept her gaze averted. She wasn't going to look. He scooped her up in his arms, glad he really was wearing pajama bottoms.

Wide, weary eyes stared at him, caught halfway between surprise and need. The need drew him as nothing else could. "I'll keep you safe."

She relaxed against him, her head pressed against his chest. "I know. I'm sorry."

His chin rested on top of her head. "I'm the one who's sorry. I shouldn't have blown up at you like I did."

"It's funny. At first I didn't want to depend on you, but somehow I didn't seem to be able to help myself." She angled her head up to look at him. "I feel safe with you, but if it bothers you maybe one of the other men could be with me during the day."

"I get night duty."

"Would that be so bad?" she asked, the desire plain in her eyes.

"Erin, don't. My control isn't very good at the moment."

"Good. I'd hate to be the only one feeling this way." Her lips touched his. Hunter's resistance melted like ice in a hot skillet. He pulled her to him with desperate urgency. She met him the same way. Heat and need, too long denied, flared between them.

They were lost in the taste and the growing hunger for each other. All their senses were sharpened and attuned. His urgent hand swept down her body, his palm cupping her hip to him, letting her feel his hard need. Instinctively, Erin adjusted to him.

Somehow they found themselves on the mattress and without the unbearable restrictions of clothes. Hunter drew her down, his hands and mouth everywhere on her hot, silken flesh. Erin had never felt so alive.

She fit perfectly into his arms. His greedy mouth closed hotly over her nipple and suckled. She arched into him, her fingers closing over his head, urging him closer. Passion and need and a deep unfilled ache coiled in her lower body.

His skin was wonderfully, maddeningly hot against her body, her searching hands. Each flex of muscle excited her and urged her to explore the resiliency of his flesh as he was exploring hers.

Her whispered plea for him to hurry, her breasts pressed against his chest as she nipped his shoulder almost shattered what little control he had left.

A rough, hungry sound erupted from his throat as he pressed her against the mattress. He moved her legs aside and entered. She was wet and tight and ready. Sheer pleasure spiraled through him.

The exquisite sensation of being filled so completely urged her hips upward. Her long legs wrapped around his waist. His thrusts were deep and powerful. She met each one, asking for more. He gave. Soon she felt herself spinning, reaching.

His hard mouth captured her cries of rapture and made them

his own. He surged into her moist, velvet softness one final time, his powerful body quivering. They both reached satisfaction at the same time.

Countless moments later, Erin surfaced. She sensed the instant Hunter became aware of what he had done. Without a word, he rolled over and lay by her side. She bit her lower lip to keep from crying out at the loss. Although their bodies touched, emotionally he was miles away and already building the wall back up to stand between them.

His retreat tore at her heart. "Please don't say you're sorry."

After a long moment, he turned and gently pulled her back into his arms. His hand stroked the smoothness of her naked back. "How can I be sorry for something so beautiful?"

She lifted hopeful eyes to him. "You felt it too?"

"I'm not *that* controlled."

Her smile trembled. "I . . . I never felt anything like this before. I had nothing to measure your response by."

"But you were married?" He frowned.

"We . . . we weren't very compatible." She buried her head against his chest. "It was my fault. I thought something was either wrong in my psyche or I was too caught up in business. I knew I was wrong on both counts the night I saw you in Chicago."

Strong fingers lifted her chin. "You literally took my breath away. I haven't been the same since."

"You mean you aren't usually this grouchy?" she teased.

"I mean I haven't touched another woman since you walked away from me."

"Hunter, I—"

"No promises," he interrupted. "No declarations."

"When this is over we'll just say good-bye and walk away," she said, trying to keep the misery out of her voice.

"Exactly. I shouldn't have made love to you," he admitted tightly. "But now that I have, I'm not sure I can keep my hands off you. Your father and Paul trusted me.

You're a client."

"I'm also a grown woman, in case you have forgotten."

Hunter grunted. "Does that feel as if any part of me has memory lapses?"

Erin felt the hard proof of his desire against her thigh and moved against it. "Guess not."

He frowned again. "Stop that."

Her hand took the place of her leg as her fingers lovingly measured his length. "Is that better?"

He answered with a groan. Removing her hand, he rolled over on top of her. He was deep inside her before she drew her next breath.

Hunter awoke with Erin sprawled half atop his body, her head beneath his chin. She was warm and soft and precious. She lay, trusting, in his arms. He wanted to shut out the world and keep her there. An impossible task. He knew. He had tried five years ago.

It hadn't worked then. It wouldn't work now. Reality always came back.

He shouldn't have made love to her, but he was through bemoaning it. She was the most exquisite, the most compelling, woman he had ever met. She was strong and courageous and loyal. She called to him as no other woman ever had. But their time together was fated to be short.

When he left, he didn't want her to remember him with regrets, only pleasure. His body stirred. He controlled his urge to wake her up by sliding inside her sleek warmth. Instead he shook her lightly by the shoulder, his voice rough to combat his arousal.

"Time to get up."

Resisting waking, Erin burrowed closer, murmuring his name. Her nipples brushed against his chest. Need sliced through him. He sucked in his breath. "Come on. Wake up."

Slowly lifting her head, she opened her eyes. A smile blossomed. "Good morning."

''Good morning,'' he muttered, trying to keep his mind off how beautiful she looked and off the arousing brush of her tempting body against his. ''I want to leave early, so you'd better get a move on,'' he said, his voice harsh and gritty with strain.

A small frown darted across her face because of his hard expression. She looked as if she wanted to say something; instead she sat up, holding the sheet to her naked breasts, and glanced around.

''Here.'' He held out her robe.

''Thanks.'' Slipping on the robe, she stood up and drew it securely around her.

''What's wrong?'' he asked. Why was she avoiding looking at him?

''Nothing. I better get dressed.'' She went down the hall before he could stop her.

Hunter shoved his hand across his head. It had started already. The awkardness. The hurt feelings because he hadn't done or said something she expected him to. He wasn't good at mornings after. Maybe that was why, in the past, he had preferred leaving after sexual encounters.

The thought had never entered his mind last night. Erin had felt good and right in his arms. And for the first time since he had left the police force, he hadn't been haunted by guilt and anger.

Only he hadn't been able to bring her the same sense of inner peace and well-being she had brought him. Somehow he had failed her. The thought unsettled him.

Getting up, he snatched his pajama bottoms from the floor. He put them on, then jerked the comforter off the bed. Something heavy thumped by his feet. He glanced down at the solid brass candlestick that usually sat on the mantle of the fireplace in the den.

Tossing the cover aside, he picked up the candlestick. A cold knot formed in his stomach. He stalked to Erin's bedroom and entered without knocking.

Standing in front of her lingerie chest, she glanced around when she heard the door open. ''Hunter, what is it?''

He lifted the candlestick. ''This was in the bed. Why?''

She shut the open drawer before speaking. ''You're not going to like my answer.''

His face fierce, he crossed to her. ''I already figured that out.''

Her chin lifted. ''You watch over me while I work, while I sleep, even when I'm upset with you. But who watches over you? I wanted to give you back a small measure of what your being here has given me. Then, if you needed help, I'd be there.''

Memories surfaced of another woman trying to protect him, and paying with her life. ''I don't need your help. I can take care of myself, and your interference would probably get both of us killed. Don't ever pull something stupid like this again. Do you understand?'' he said through clenched teeth.

''Yes.'' She stepped around him.

''Where are you going?''

She glanced back over her shoulder. ''To get dressed. I wouldn't want to interfere with your plans. At least I can do that right.''

Her stilted words sliced through him. The regrets had started already. Pain, not pleasure. Making love in a professional relationship changed everything. He should have remembered.

He hadn't, and now Erin was paying the price. His grip tightened on the candlestick as he left the room. At least she wouldn't have to pay the ultimate price, as Sondra had.

Erin would live.

Chapter Thirteen

Eyes closed, head bent, Erin stood under the shower and let the warm water pour down over her. She would not cry. She had faced disappointments before and gotten over them. She was old enough to know life didn't always work out the way one wanted it to.

She had known before she slept with Hunter that things might not work out between them. He was an intensely private and self-contained person. Trying to get through to him had been a long shot, at best. It wasn't his fault that he couldn't love her the way she loved him.

The realization of her love for him didn't surprise her. She wouldn't have wanted something more between them if it had only been a sexual attraction. What she felt for Hunter was deeper, stronger.

She loved him, and he had looked through her this morning as if she were a stranger. Fighting the growing lump in her throat, she shut off the water and reached for a giant bath towel.

Her fault. If she had made Hunter feel only a fraction of the overwhelming rightness and pleasure he had made her feel, this morning he would have awakened her with kisses or a smile, instead of orders to get dressed.

Her fault. She wasn't woman enough to interest him beyond the sexual encounter. Knowing that he hadn't been intimate with another woman since they met in Chicago only caused Erin greater pain. He had waited and she had disappointed him.

Finished drying, she lotioned and sprayed on her favorite perfume, then put on red lacy silk undergarments. She needed something to bolster her wounded pride, and she was feeling vulnerable enough to bolster it in any way she could.

The way she saw things, she could either admit she had made a horrible mistake or get Hunter to admit he had. Hunter would not go down easily. His reaction when she had tried to help him showed that. He was determined to follow his code of honor.

He'd fight any attempts at establishing a lasting relationship. If she wanted him, she'd have to be strong enough to let her pride take a back seat and go after him.

Because, without Hunter, she would never be completely happy again.

In that moment, she had the answer to her question. Pride would never hold her, never touch her, as Hunter had. Pride would leave her cold and wanting and lonely. It was in her nature to fight for what she wanted. She wanted Hunter. He could shout and pick fights, but she was going to keep after him until she wore down his resistance and he admitted he cared.

Thirty minutes later Erin entered the kitchen. Hunter was sitting at the table drinking coffee and reading the paper. His gaze lifted. His lips parted, but no words came out. He simply stared.

"Did I get dressed fast enough?" she asked sweetly.

His mouth snapped shut. The cup hit the saucer with a loud clink. "I thought you were going to the office."

She lifted a delicate brow. "What makes you think I'm not?"

His hot gaze swept from her red spiked heels to the hem of a form-fitting red jersey mini-dress, to the scooped neckline revealing the creamy swell of her breasts. His expression hardened. "No reason."

"Is that my juice and toast?"

"Yes."

"You take such good care of me." She wanted to pat him on the cheek when he winced. She'd get them both through this.

Instead of sitting, she leaned her hip against the table. She ate slowly, using her tongue to leisurely blot the moisture and crumbs from her mouth. Hunter never took his eyes from her until she finished. "I'm ready if you are."

"Where's your coat?" he asked, his voice husky.

"The weatherman says it's going to be another unseasonably warm day." She lifted her arms; the red dress rose up another inch. "The long sleeves will keep me warm enough if the weather changes."

"Wear one anyway." Getting up, he grabbed their plates and went to the sink.

"Somehow I thought you'd say that." Erin didn't smile until her back was to Hunter. Stubborn, impossible, adorable man.

Erin left the kitchen then came back wearing a red-belted swing coat the exact length of her dress and a pair of sunshades. "I didn't think a cap would go with this outfit."

Hunter's mouth tightened. Somehow the glasses and the coat only made her more alluring. He wanted to rip off both of them, and then slowly unzip her dress to reveal the woman beneath. The woman who had inflamed his senses last night. The woman he was trying hard not to touch again.

"Do I pass inspection?"

Her voice was a husky invitation. He ignored it, the same way he was trying to ignore the growing need in his lower body. "Let's go."

"You're so gracious," she told him. Turning to the control panel, she set the alarm. Finished, she brushed by Hunter as he held the back door open for her.

He inhaled the floral fragrance of her perfume and fought memories and desire. She was not going to get to him. He was stronger than that. Closing the door with more force than necessary, he got inside the car.

He started the engine, then reached for the gear shift. He touched something soft. He knew better than to look, but an irresistible urge compelled him to do so anyway. Erin's coat lay open against his hand. But what caused his mouth to become dry was the long, sleek, golden-brown length of her legs.

Memories struck him of those legs locked around his hips, urging him faster, deeper. Jerking his traitorous gaze away, he stepped on the gas. Tires squealed as he came out of the garage and hit the street. Erin was not going to get to him.

"My, my. We're in a hurry."

"My foot slipped," he said, then winced at the blatant lie. So what if he admitted to himself that he wanted her?

Since that night in Chicago, he'd never stopped wanting her, and he had held up.

Until last night!

A wisp of sound came to him. His hand clenched the steering wheel. It came again. For some reason Erin was crossing and uncrossing her legs, twisting and turning in her seat. He wished she'd keep still. All he had to do was last another fifteen minutes and they would be at her office.

"Is it working?"

"What?" Startled, he glanced at her.

"Leaving early." She glanced over her shoulder again, then straightened in her seat. "I've been trying to see if we're being followed. I can't tell."

"We're not," Hunter answered. At least he was sure about *that.* "Don't worry. Grimes assigned an unmarked police car to follow us today."

"I'm not worried." She checked her side-view mirror.

"Then why do you keep looking?"

"I told you. I wanted to see if I could see him."

"And I told you I could handle things," Hunter said, unable to keep the irritation out of his voice.

"I know." She frowned into the side-view mirror. "Which car is the police one?"

"Erin, aren't you listening to me?"

"I always listen to you, Hunter." She gave him her full attention. "Sometimes I wonder if you listen to me."

"What's that supposed to mean?"

"Just because we slept together, you don't owe me anything. We're both as free as we were last night, so you can relax and forget about it."

"Are you going to forget about it?"

"No, but I'm not the one beating myself over the head about it, either," she said frankly.

"You don't have to; I'm doing enough for the both of us." Downshifting the car, Hunter entered the parking garage of the Cortland building.

Erin waited until he pulled into a parking space and cut the engine before she spoke. "If you could undo last night, would you?"

"It shouldn't have happened."

"That's not what I asked."

Hunter had one—damning—answer. "No."

"Neither would I," she said softly. "Now, can we go in? I'm burning up in this coat."

Hunter decided to let her change the subject. There wasn't much more he could do with her at the moment.

Inside her office, Erin hung up her coat, then went behind her desk. From the tingling sensation down her spine, she knew Hunter watched every step. The dress flowed over her body like water. She wished she could take a peek at his face, but she didn't dare. It was a safe bet he wasn't pleased.

Sitting behind her desk, she checked her calendar for the day. She almost groaned. She had slated today to interview the three candidates for the vice-president's position. She wasn't looking forward to that. No matter how she phrased the reason for her decision, a close friend was going to be hurt.

"Trouble?"

Erin glanced up at Hunter sprawled in a chair across the room. It had taken her some hard work to try and look seductive. He did it effortlessly.

The herringbone sports coat, black slacks, and white shirt suited his dark, dangerous looks. He had an edge to him. He was just civilized enough to be in polite society, but he'd never conform.

Jake Hunter was his own man.

"I'm supposed to interview the candidates today for the vice-president's position," she told him, and leaned back in her chair.

"Putting it off won't make it easier on you, or the two losers."

She sent him a disgruntled look as she propped her arms on the desk. "I might have known that would be your attitude."

"Putting something off doesn't make it easier," Hunter said. "Mathis will get over losing."

She straightened abruptly. "How did . . . what makes you say that?"

Dark eyes narrowed. "I have my reasons."

"One of them is that you don't like Quinn . . . but he's been through a lot."

Hunter snorted and stood. "And he didn't learn one thing about how it felt being one of the have-nots. He's a rude, selfish, and conceited wannabee. He believes his charm and looks will get him through anything."

"He's a good account executive," Erin defended.

Hunter braced his hands on her desk. "I noticed you didn't say a good person."

"Why are you so hard on him? You give everyone else here a break except Quinn. Even you and Detective Grimes seem to have come to some sort of understanding. Why are you so hard on him?" she asked, rising to her feet.

Because he wants you, too. Because it's tearing me up inside to think he might one day have you.

Hunter bit back the answer. It wasn't like him to be the dog-in-the-manger type. But he had never wanted a woman as much as he wanted Erin. He was caught between desire and duty, a position he'd sworn never to be in again.

He straightened. "We just didn't click."

"Perhaps you should have tried harder."

"So it's my fault? Quinn is always the one wronged."

"I didn't mean it that way. I simply meant—"

"Save it. It doesn't matter." Hands in his pockets, he went to stand by the window, looking at the the tranquil waters of Lake Travis below.

"You're not having the last word on this." She came around the desk and went to him. "You're one of the most self-sufficient, most self-contained people I know. Quinn doesn't have your strength of character, nor your toughness. Nothing affects you for long."

"It doesn't, huh? Why don't we just see about that." Unrelenting hands jerked her to a wide chest. His mouth crashed down on hers. He expected resistance. He didn't get any. Erin met him with a power and passion to equal his own.

He couldn't seem to get enough of her taste, her scent. He dove deeper, trying to find some solid foundation in his spiralling world. He found none. Only a growing hunger he knew could be satisfied only one way.

He lifted his head and pushed her away from him. Both of them were breathing hard. "You're driving me crazy—you know that?"

"I . . . like I said, it's nice to know I'm not the only one feeling this way."

"This has got to stop."

"Kiss me one more time and we'll talk about it."

"Erin, be serious."

"I thought I was."

For the first time that day, Hunter felt like smiling. "What am I going to do with you?"

She grinned. "I bet we could think of something."

He frowned. "Erin—"

She placed her finger on his lips. "If you're going to start up again, I'd rather not hear it."

His hand captured hers. "Like I said, putting it off doesn't make it any easier."

"I also remember you telling me you've been wrong before."

His eyebrow lifted. "You have a very selective memory."

She smiled up at him. "What can I say? Women are smart that way."

Dropping her hand, he stepped back. "Go to work."

"Yes, boss."

Ebony eyes narrowed. "One day that mouth of yours is going to get you into trouble."

"I hope that's a promise."

Hunter's mouth fell open.

Erin grinned and went behind her desk. She didn't know what had gotten into her, but she liked it. She liked teasing Hunter, liked laughing with him. She was going to do everything in her power to make sure his assignment with her was permanent.

Hunter watched Erin, her head bent, her finger and thumb worrying the gold hoop in her ear, the other hand poised to flip a page on the report she was studying. She had strength, courage, and too much stubbornness. For whatever reason, she had decided she wanted him, and being around her was too dangerous for either of them.

There was only one way to change that. He had to find Scanlon.

"I'm assigning Powell to be with you today."

Surprise lifted her head. "Why?"

"I have some things to take care of," Hunter said. "He's a good man."

But he's not you, she wanted to say—but she couldn't. "How long will you be gone?"

"I'm not sure."

She picked up a gold pen that was on top of her desk. "I see."

Hunter jammed his hands into his pockets. She looked as if he was abandoning her. "Powell knows how to get in touch with me if something comes up."

"I'm sure I'll be fine."

He pulled his hand out of his pocket and went to the door. "Stay out of trouble."

"I'll do my best."

"See that you do. I'm going to ask Powell for a full report when I return."

Her eyes glittered. "Don't you dare."

"Then follow orders so I won't have to." He reached for the door knob.

"Hunter?"

"Yes?"

She bit her lower lip. "Does your leaving have anything to do with Scanlon?"

"Yes." One lie today was enough.

"You mind telling me why?"

"I'm going to look for him."

"I don't suppose it would do any good to ask you not to go."

"No."

"Then be careful. It's your turn to cook dinner."

"Call if you need me." The door closed behind him.

Almost immediately, Powell entered. The muscularly built security agent nodded, then positioned himself by the door.

"Is the other security guard with Hunter?"

"Mike is outside in the outer office. There are also people stationed in the lobby, elevator, and stairwell. You're quite safe," he informed her, obviously thinking that was her main concern.

"What about Hunter? Who's with him?"

He quickly learned differently. "Hunter didn't discuss his plans with me."

"But what if he needs help? Can't one of you go with him?"

Powell looked at her oddly. ''Hunter can take care of himself. And if one of us left our posts he'd have us for lunch.''

Erin sighed and tossed the pen aside. Powell was right on both counts. But there was such a thing as being too self-sufficient. ''If he comes back with one scratch on him, he'll have to answer to me.''

''Yes, Ms. Cortland.''

''You might as well sit down,'' Erin told him. ''Something tells me this is going to be a long day.''

Another dead end. Hunter emerged from the bar on Ninth Street with no more information than he had gone in with. No one admitted to seeing Scanlon; the cash incentive he'd offered hadn't helped.

Oh, they had tried to come up with some stories, but it wasn't difficult to tell they were lying. The shifting eyes, the nervous swallows, the agitated movements, were dead giveaways.

Hunter got into his car and drove down the street to the Star Club, another of the haunts of Scanlon's that Detective Grimes had reluctantly supplied Hunter with. Grimes was positive there was nothing new to be learned. Hunter wasn't so sure.

Scanlon couldn't have dropped off the face of the earth without money or help from someone. Hunter was determined to find out what he could.

The exterior of the Star Club was as dreary and run-down as the last bar. Scanlon might have wanted to hit the big time, but he had wallowed in the lowest places.

Inside, Hunter slipped onto a stool and ordered a beer in a bottle. Considering the surroundings, it was the only way to be sure he was getting what he ordered.

A long-neck finally appeared on the scarred surface. Hunter laid a ten on the counter. A grubby paw instantly swept it up.

''There's more where that came from if you can help me.''

The bill disappeared into an equally dirty apron pocket. The bartender's bald head gleamed as he looked around quickly to see who might have heard.

Greed. Hunter could almost smell it—among other things—on the big, burly man.

"I'm looking for Scanlon."

Disappointment soured his hard, lived-in face. "Like I told the police, I ain't seen him."

"You're sure?"

"Course I'm sure," he sneered. "Not likely I'd want to give up the hundred the other man offered if I didn't have to."

Hunter's antenna went off. "Can you describe the other man?"

The unkempt man's interest perked up. "What's in it for me?"

Another ten appeared on the bar. The bartender reached for the bill, but Hunter snatched it away. "Information first."

"He was a black man in a suit."

"Is that all?"

The bartender's greedy gaze went from Hunter to his hand, holding the money just out of reach. "Tall, good build, expensive suit."

"When did he come in?"

"The night after Scanlon escaped."

"What information did he want about Scanlon?"

"The same as you. Had I seen him."

"Has he been back since?"

Bushy eyebrows bunched. "That's a lot of questions for a ten."

"Maybe some of your regulars won't think that way."

"No," the bartender quickly answered.

Hunter released the money. It disappeared. "If he comes in again, call me, and you'll get that hundred you wanted." Handing the man his card with his mobile phone number, Hunter stood. "There's a fifty bonus if he's still here when I get here."

"He'll be here."

Hunter left the bar. He had no doubt the man would be there. In what condition was another matter. The bartender was greedy.

In his car, Hunter dialed Grimes's number. There was another player in the game. From what Hunter knew, Scanlon had no close associates who might fit the bartender's description, and that made Hunter uneasy. Someone else was looking for Scanlon; Scanlon was looking for Erin.

Hunter didn't like the new circumstances one bit. Something was wrong, and he was going to find out what.

Chapter Fourteen

Erin couldn't concentrate, a rarity for her in a planning session. More than once in the last half hour, she had caught her mind drifting. She had always prided herself on her ability to push everything aside and focus on the issue at hand. What happened in these meetings determined the direction for Cortland Innovations. It was imperative that she be at her best.

Today she wasn't.

From the puzzled, then knowing looks of the people sitting around the table, a few had figured out why. Hunter's glaring absence.

She missed him and she was worried. He had called Powell, a little after lunch. They had spoken briefly, then the conversation had ended.

Although she had been in her office when the call had come through, Hunter hadn't asked to speak to her. While a part of her understood the reason, it hadn't stopped the slight from hurting.

Hunter was trying to reestablish the distance between them. He had four men—that she knew of—watching over her. There was no reason to talk to her directly. Unless it was for his own personal need. He didn't want to admit to that need.

Yet, he was out there, someplace, trying to find a killer before the killer found her.

''Erin. Erin?''

Erin came out of her musing and looked straight into the worried face of Connie Bledsoe. ''Sorry, I missed what you said.''

''That's obvious,'' Connie said. ''Is everything all right?''

''Of course. I'm just a little tired,'' Erin said. From the sideways glances around the table, no one was convinced that was the full story. She had worked tired before and had never had any difficulty concentrating.

''Can I get you something?'' Quinn asked, his handsome face lined with concern.

''No, thank you.'' Erin forced a smile. ''Connie, you were saying?''

''Do you want to go with Quinn and me to present the prospectives to Mystique this afternoon?'' the creative director repeated.

Erin felt a surge of relief at the reprieve from having to make a decision on the vice-president's position today. Irritation followed. It wasn't like her to shirk her duty. Hunter's reprimand ringing in her ear wasn't helping.

''Yes, I would, but that would mean rescheduling the final interviews.''

''Can't be helped,'' Connie advised. ''Mystique's president called, and he wants to see what we have ASAP.''

''We've got to move on this today,'' Quinn told her. ''Besides, you know the best man for the job.''

''Or woman,'' Connie and Sally added, in unison.

Quinn leaned back in his chair and smiled.

Erin saw his look of utter confidence, and realized Hunter was right. Dragging her feet on this one had made things worse, not better. ''I apologize for the delay in naming the new vice-president. I plan to correct that oversight if the three candidates don't mind rescheduling their appointments for later this evening."

As she had anticipated, the three involved were only too eager to agree. "I'll see you in alpha order, as scheduled, as soon as I return from Mystique. What time is the appointment?"

Connie glanced at her Rolex. "Two-fifteen. Forty-five minutes from now."

"Sally, you know how these meetings go. I can call you when we leave Mystique or you can wait."

"I'll wait."

"Thank you." Erin glanced between Connie and Quinn. "I'd like to hear your strategies, and we can leave in twenty minutes."

Before either of them could speak, Powell spoke from the back of the conference room. "Ms. Cortland, may I please have a word with you?"

She frowned at the interruption. "Can't it wait? We're on a tight schedule here."

"No, ma'am."

"Bossy for a hireling, isn't he?" Quinn mumbled.

Erin heard the snide remark and frowned at Quinn. "Excuse me." Rising, she stepped outside the conference room. "Yes?"

"Hunter wants you to stay in the building unless he's with you."

Erin folded her arms. "He should have thought of that before he left."

"It wasn't on your schedule," he reminded her reasonably.

"It is now."

"Yes, ma'am." He pulled out his cellular phone. "Should I call Hunter and tell him?"

Her arms came to her sides. "He'd come back, wouldn't he?"

"Yes, ma'am."

"But he wouldn't be happy, would he?"

"He'd come."

Those two words said it all. Hunter took his responsibilities seriously. Although she'd like to go to Mystique, it wasn't necessary. The film was a solid piece of work. She had made sure of that by being present when it was made, thanks to Hunter. Connie and Quinn could do the rest.

What Hunter was doing was important to both of them. She had to let him do what he felt was best. "Put it away."

"Yes, ma'am." He slipped the phone back in his pocket.

"Out of curiosity, what would you have done if I'd tried to leave before Hunter got here?"

"Followed orders."

"And those were?"

For the first time he looked uncomfortable. "I'd rather not say."

Erin lifted a delicate eyebrow. "Any means necessary, huh?"

He almost smiled. "Something like that."

She opened the conference-room door. "I guess it's a good thing I'm a reasonable woman."

"Yes, ma'am, for both our sakes," he mumbled, and followed her back into the room.

"Change of plans. Quinn and Connie, you'll have to handle things without me. Sally, our appointment is still on for three. If there are no other concerns, meeting adjourned."

People began picking up their papers and filing out of the room.

"Now, let's hear the plan," Erin said and went to sit down.

Erin had dreaded this moment for the past six weeks. For the first time since she had taken charge of Cortland Innovations, she had shied away from being the one to make an executive decision.

It was after six, most of the office staff had gone home, and she was meeting with the last candidate for the vice-president's position. She couldn't put it off any longer.

Looking across her desk at Quinn's confident expression, she leaned forward in her chair, placed both hands atop her desk, and said the words she had dreaded for weeks. "Quinn, after a lot of deliberation, I've decided to appoint Sally vice-president.''

Shock registered on his handsome face. ''What?''

''I'm sorry.''

He sprang to his feet. ''You can't mean that?''

''I'm afraid I do. Believe me, it wasn't an easy decision to make. Frankly, I've put it off because I knew how it would affect you.''

''I've worked my butt off for that position. I deserve it,'' he riled.

''You're brilliant when it comes to hammering through a deal or pacifying a client, but your interpersonal relationships with your coworkers are almost null.''

He planted both hands on her desk. ''That's their problem.''

Erin rose. ''Not when you have a multi-million-dollar company to run, and the loyalty and cooperation of every employee is important in getting the job done. We need each other, Quinn. You forget sometimes.''

He straightened. ''How could I forget? I work with them every day.''

''Not always in harmony.'' She came around the desk. ''I left you in charge when Sam and I went to Chicago, and came back to find some of my key people threatening to quit.''

''They didn't want to take orders,'' he defended.

''Sally didn't seem to have that problem while I was busy with the trial and Sam had to go to New York,'' Erin said.

''She doesn't have the pressure of bringing in and keeping the six-figure accounts, either,'' he shot back.

''I realize that. A vice-president's position would only increase the pressure.'' She searched her mind for a way to be objective, and take the hurt from his face. ''You're tops at what you do, Quinn. You thrive in working with people you consider your peers, your equals. A vice-president has to be willing to work with everyone.''

''I know I get impatient sometimes. It's not intentional.''

''If I thought it was, I would have fired you long ago.''

His head jerked up. ''Instead, you're going to make me the

brunt of office jokes. Everyone knows I expected to get that position."

"They'll soon find something else to talk about. You just helped land us a multi-million-dollar deal with Mystique, and you're still the best account executive in the business."

He looked at her with measuring eyes. "Is that all I mean to you? A way to get more revenue for Cortland?"

Erin held his gaze. "I told you a long time ago there could never be anything between us."

His gaze hardened. "There could have been, if it wasn't for Hunter. I don't know what you see in him. He's not from our world. He has no class, no breeding."

"That's enough, Quinn."

"No, it isn't. He's practically worthless as a bodyguard. He's all muscle and no brain. A child could outwit him," cried Quinn.

"You don't know what you're talking about."

"Yes, I do. If he's so hot, why hasn't he found out who's been calling you?"

Erin gasped, then went cold inside. "How do you know about the phone calls?"

Triumph changed to wariness on Quinn's handsome face. "You must have mentioned them."

"No. I didn't. Not even my father knew."

He shrugged. "Someone else must have told me."

"Only the police and Hunter knew," she whispered, betrayal knotting her stomach.

"Erin." He reached for her. She shrank from him. "Please let me explain. He was coming between us. You were caught up with him, just like all the women around this place. You've even started dressing differently. I had to do something."

"So you decided to frighten me?" she asked in disbelief.

"Not intentionally. You've got to believe me," he pleaded, his hand falling to his side. "I'd been trying to call you all day but, each time, he answered the phone."

"I wasn't up to receiving phone calls. I'd been scared out

of my wits the night before. You should have realized that, better than anyone, and understood,'' she said.

''That's why I was trying to call. To apologize.'' His face hardened. ''Hunter sounded annoyed when I didn't say anything and I decided to nettle him a little bit.''

''With no consideration of how it would affect me. You were only thinking of yourself,'' Erin said, in rising anger. How could she have been so wrong about him?

''That's not true. I was trying to protect you from him. I wanted you away from him.'' Misery showed in Quinn's face.

''You miscalculated badly.''

''Please try to understand. I was losing you to him.''

''You never had me to lose.''

He stepped toward her. ''Erin, I can make you—''

''Don't touch her.''

Erin and Quinn swung toward the chillingly threatening voice. Hunter, his muscular body radiating barely suppressed fury, stood in the doorway. Quinn took an uneasy step away from Erin as Hunter closed the door and advanced farther into the room.

''Tell her the rest,'' Hunter ordered the frightened man.

Eyes wide, Quinn backed up another step. ''I . . . I don't know what you're talking about.''

''Yes, you do.'' Hunter matched Quinn's movements, his hard gaze never leaving Quinn's. ''I couldn't figure out how Scanlon found out about the shoot. There was only one explanation. It wasn't him. Someone else had to be following us.''

''No.'' Erin shook her head in denial. ''There must be some mistake.''

''Tell her,'' Hunter ordered again.

''I don't know what you're talking about,'' Quinn said defensively. ''He's just trying to shift the blame for his incompetence onto me.''

''If you want to do this the hard way, so be it. The bartender at one of Scanlon's old watering holes mentioned a well-dressed man asking questions,'' Hunter said, his voice as ruthless as his face. ''I checked with Grimes and came up empty-handed.

I started thinking about the car following us. Quinn usually sticks to you like glue, yet he wasn't there that night.''

Quinn pulled a handkerchief from his pocket and wiped the beads of moisture from his forehead. ''You know I had an appointment. Besides, if some car was following you, it wasn't mine. You have both seen my car.''

''That's why you rented one.''

His mouth fell open. The silken square fell unnoticed to the floor.

Erin shut her eyes against the betrayal she felt. ''Quinn, how could you?''

''It's his word against mine,'' he shouted, his eyes wide.

''The evidence speaks for itself. The credit card you used to rent the car, the addresses of the pay phones within a four-mile radius of your house, the bartender at the Star Club identifying your photo.'' Hunter clicked off point after point.

''I admit to trying to help find Scanlon,'' Quinn quickly said, trying and failing to flash one of his charming smiles. ''I was trying to help.''

''You might have been, then, but your objective quickly changed,'' Hunter told the other man.

Quinn became incensed. ''You don't know anything. You just want Erin dependent upon you. I could take care of her better than you. I showed you up.''

''You only showed yourself up, Quinn,'' Erin said, feeling ill.

Quinn swung frantically toward her. ''I did it for you.''

''You did it for the vice-president's position,'' Hunter said tersely.

''That's a lie. It's Erin I'm concerned about.''

''Bull,'' Hunter shouted, keeping his hands clenched to keep from grabbing the other man and showing him what it was like to be afraid. ''If you wanted her, cared anything for her, you wouldn't have put her through the worry of the phone calls or following us in a car.''

''I did it to show you up. This is your fault,'' Quinn accused hotly, his gaze flickering between Hunter and Erin. ''None of this would have happened if you hadn't tried to keep Erin to yourself."

Erin's arms tightened around her waist. "Hunter didn't make you use deception. You did that on your own. Did you try to frighten me the night of the Kings' party? Was that you behind me on the walkway?"

"No; you've got to believe me. I was waiting for you in the garden room," Quinn said.

Erin nodded. "At least you didn't stoop that low. But I can't work with someone I can't trust. Please clear out your desk."

Stunned, it took Quinn several seconds before he was able to speak. "You can't mean that?"

"I might have overlooked the phone calls, but you crossed the line when you rented a car to follow us." She gazed dispassionately at the man she had once called her friend. "That was premeditated and smacks of stalking."

Angrily, Quinn turned on Hunter and sneered, "Erin, you can't want this nothing."

"You know nothing about him," Erin said, shock becoming fury. "He's more man than you'll ever be. He doesn't use lies or deception to frighten me. Can you say the same?"

Defeated, Quinn stared at the hostile face of Hunter, then moved to Erin's unrelenting one. Shoulders slumped, he moved to the door, then glanced back toward them. "What about a letter of reference? You said yourself I'm good at what I do."

"Don't push it," Hunter warned, not believing the audacity of the man.

"I need a reference. Erin, please," he pleaded, defeat clear in his face.

"A letter will be mailed within the week," Erin told him finally.

His hand on the doorknob, he stopped. "I never meant for this to happen. What will I tell people? Where will I go?"

"Whatever you choose. Despite what you tried to do, I don't want to ruin your career or your life. I just want you out of mine," Erin said with unbending finality. There was no way she wanted him near her again.

His head fell forward for a moment, then lifted. "Erin, I'm sorry."

"I am too, Quinn." She looked straight into his eyes. "Good-bye."

"Mathis?" Quinn froze with the door half open. "Try to contact Erin or come near her in any way and you'll have to answer to me. Pick up your handkerchief and leave while you're still able to under your own power."

Quinn quickly did as he was told. The door closed behind him.

"You okay?" Hunter studied Erin intently.

"I guess. I know what he did was wrong, but I can't help but feel sorry for him," she admitted.

"You've got to be kidding." Hunter said in astonishment.

"You didn't know him before his father declared bankruptcy. Losing everything changed him. I always hoped he could accept what had happened and go on." Erin sighed. "He hasn't. He wants it back. Badly. He got impatient. Maybe now he'll learn that he can't hurt people to get what he wants."

"I doubt it," Hunter rasped. "People will think he left because he didn't get the position. He'll come out of this with only a minor setback in his climb to the top."

A delicate eyebrow arched. "That bothers you?"

"You're darn right," Hunter said with heat. "I wanted to rearrange his face for what he did to you."

"At least we don't have to worry about Scanlon," she told him with visible relief.

Hunter's eyes narrowed with a mixture of anger and regret. "Quinn may have muddied the waters, but there's still the cigarette butts."

"The police couldn't get any fingerprints for a positive identification."

"He's still out there," Hunter persisted.

"Yes, but he doesn't know my phone number or where I live, and he's not following me." Erin smiled. "I'd say that calls for a celebration."

"Erin, I don't—"

"Please. We could go to a nice quiet place for dinner and dancing." She pirouetted, a beguiling smile on her beautiful face. "You have to admit I'm dressed for it."

Hunter did something he had promised himself all day he wouldn't do. He looked at Erin, really looked at the teasing smile on her beautiful face, the way the red dress clung to her lush curves and sleek body. He remembered the satin texture of her skin, the drugging taste of her lips, the way she had come apart in his arms.

"I know just the place. Please, Hunter," she smiled, in an open, playful invitation.

He was captivated by her animated face. He had never seen this side of Erin. He wanted to give her something besides fear, but it was too risky, in more ways than one. "No."

She crossed her arms over her chest. "Either we eat out and have at least one dance, or I'm going to stop being so cooperative."

"Is that a threat?"

"Take it any way you want." Turning from him, she went to put on her coat, then picked up her attaché case. "Home, or dinner and one dance?"

He could probably circumvent any plans Erin had for thwarting him. He didn't want it to come to that. "How about home, dinner, and dancing?"

She seemed to consider. "Depends."

"On what?" Hunter asked suspiciously.

She beamed. "Only if I don't have to help with the dishes."

Hunter took the case from her hand. "You drive a hard bargain. I think I can manage."

"Never doubted it for a moment."

Chapter Fifteen

Erin insisted on the works. Linen, silver, candlelight, fresh flowers. The soulful voice of Teddy Pendergrass.

The fact that dinner was set up on a card table in front of the fireplace didn't matter to her. What mattered was that she and Hunter were alone. Now, if she could just get that frown off his face, and get him to relax.

"I'm glad you suggested this, Hunter."

"I'm not sure I suggested *this.*"

Erin smiled and took a sip of wine. He certainly hadn't. He had fought this intimate setting all the way. She would have liked to have eaten on the floor, but she didn't think he was that ready to let go. In time, he would be.

"More wine?" She refilled his glass before he had a chance to answer.

He watched her through narrowed eyes. "One glass is enough when I'm on duty."

"You never forget and drop your guard, do you?" she asked, enjoying the way the candlelight danced across his strong features. He was a handsome, complicated man.

His expression hardened. "Not anymore."

Erin understood those two cryptic words, and recalled their previous conversation. Something had happened in Hunter's past that had left him scarred. Until he learned to deal with whatever it was, the chances of getting through to him were slim to none.

She set her glass aside and stood. Time for phase two. "Well, dancing shouldn't affect your concentration."

Hunter studied the strikingly beautiful woman smiling down at him and knew, with an unshakeable knowledge, that holding Erin would shoot his concentration and his control to hell. He had watched her all through dinner, and with each second his hunger for her had grown.

"You aren't going to back out, are you?" she asked, a winsome pout on her sensual lips.

"The thought had crossed my mind," he answered honestly.

"You can't tell me you can't dance, because I know better."

"You should have slugged me for acting that way in Chicago," he said, disgust in his voice.

"The thought didn't occur to me until later," she told him, staring down at her fingers plucking at the white tablecloth.

Hunter came to his feet. A shy Erin was a novelty. Strong fingers lifted her chin. "Why not until later?"

Long black lashes swept downward, to hide her eyes, then upward, revealing the uncertainty in their dark depths. "I was so caught up with you that all I wanted to do was get closer."

A splinter of heat rushed through Hunter, centering in his groin. "I felt the same way, but it didn't excuse me for acting like a Class A jerk." His thumb stroked across her lower lip, caressing her on the only place he dared. Her breath fluttered across his thumb. His entire body tightened. "I'm sorry about that night."

"It was as much my fault as yours. I shouldn't have let you kiss me," she whispered.

"I don't think either one of us had any choice."

Her hands came up to rest on his wide chest. "No, I don't think we did, then or now."

Hunter felt the truth of her words deep in his soul. There

was an unmistakable something drawing them together. "I don't want to hurt you."

She rubbed her cheek against his hand, which was holding her chin. "Then don't push me away."

"Erin, don't you understand: it's tearing me apart to push you away, but it would be just as agonizing to make love to you again and know that, when this is over, I won't be staying," he said.

Erin held his hard gaze with difficulty, glad the candlelight hid the hurt she knew she couldn't completely hide in her eyes. "I know, Hunter. That's why our time together is so important. You've made me feel things I never thought possible. After you're gone I'll never experience them again."

"You'll find somebody else," he told her roughly. Even as he said the words he rebelled against the thought of another man knowing her as intimately as he had.

She smiled sadly. "Do you think so little of me, or of yourself?"

"God, woman. Don't do this to either of us. Can't you understand it's too late for us?"

"Only if you want it to be, Hunter. Only if you want it to be." Her arms looped around his neck. Despite the stiffening of his body, she pressed closer. "You promised me a dance, remember?"

"You're Marcus's daughter, all right," Hunter muttered as he settled his hands on her small waist. "Stubborn as a Louisiana mule."

Erin chuckled. "We hate to lose an argument."

He felt the lushness of her breasts, and squirmed in discomfort. There was only so much a man could take. "That I can believe."

"Ummm, I love this song," she murmured, humming the melody, her hands massaging his neck, her lower body brushing enticingly against his.

"Ah, Erin?"

"Shhh," she admonished. "My favorite part is coming up,"

she told him, and went back to driving him slowly out of his mind.

Hunter gritted his teeth and tried to think of anything but the enticing woman clinging seductively around his neck. Her woman's softness, pressed against his male hardness, made coherent thought impossible. By the time Teddy sang the last note and the music stopped, Hunter was more than ready either to explode or take Erin standing up. His hands were trembling.

Releasing him, Erin stepped back. ''Good night, and thanks for a wonderful evening.''

Hunter held his body rigid as she walked away. She couldn't have done that intentionally. Erin wasn't a tease.

At the door, she looked back at him, then went inside her room. She left the door open.

It was up to him.

Unconsciously, he took a step toward her, then stopped. A shaky hand rubbed across his face. As much as Hunter hated to admit it, Quinn had been right about one thing: compared to Erin's accomplishments, he was a nothing. His business was growing, but it wasn't in the league with Cortland Innovations.

He glanced around the candlelit room. His tiny apartment in Chicago was a world apart from this. As fantastic as their loving had been, it couldn't make up for the difference. Besides, he wasn't going to risk Erin's life because he couldn't keep his pants zipped.

After snapping on the light, he began clearing the table. He was going to protect Erin from everything, including himself.

She had lost. Arms wrapped around her body, Erin sat on the edge of the bed and stared at the partially open bedroom door. She wasn't going to kiss him into submission this time. He had to come to her.

What if he doesn't?

Erin refused to believe he wouldn't. He had to feel something for her other than desire. He cared.

What if he doesn't?

She bounded up from the bed, refusing to listen to the nagging voice inside her head. She admitted she didn't have a lot of sexual experience, but she was intuitive enough to know that what she and Hunter shared was special. They had shared more than their bodies. They had forged a bond.

Thunder rumbled. Lightning flashed across the sky. The night seemed to be as turbulent as her feelings. Going to stand by the window, she ran her palms up and down her arms. She wasn't so much chilled as she was restless.

Lightning crackled. The wind kicked up. Tree limbs rustled. Leaves scurried across the patio. The security lights blinked on.

Automatically, she searched the back yard. Nothing. She absently wondered if any motion, no matter the density, could activate the lights.

She glanced toward her door. She wasn't about to go ask Hunter. He'd think she was coming on to him. She looked back out the window. A shadow moved near the pool. Was it a tree limb or—The lights went out, surrounding her in utter darkness.

A scream formed and burst from her throat.

''Erin.'' The sound of Hunter's voice reached through her fears.

He came barreling through the door. A flash of lightning illuminated the room. He crossed to her and drew her into his arms. Shivering, she clutched at him.

''It's okay, honey. The power went off, that's all.''

She burrowed closer. ''I . . . I thought I saw a shadow outside.''

Hunter stiffened. ''When? Where?''

''Just before the lights went out. By the gazebo.''

Gently, he eased her from him. ''I'm going to check it out.''

She clutched at his bare arm, only then realizing he was shirtless. ''You're not going out there.''

''I have to,'' Hunter told her. ''If anyone is out there, he'll be at as much of a disadvantage as I will.''

''Why don't you call Detective Grimes, or the police?''

''I plan to, but I'm not going to wait. When the power went, so did the alarm system.'' With an uncanny sense, he took her to the bed, picked up the phone, and called the police.

The second call was to Marcus. He answered the phone on the second ring. Hunter quickly explained things to him, then handed the phone to Erin. ''Keep talking to him. If you hear anything suspicious, tell him, and he'll use his mobile phone to dial nine-one-one again. Whatever you do, don't hang up, and *stay here.*''

''I don't want you to go.''

''I have to.'' His hand touched her cheek, then he was gone, the door closing behind him.

She whimpered. ''Daddy, I don't want him hurt.''

''Don't worry, baby. I already dialed nine-one-one again.''

''Thank you. I just hope they hurry,'' Erin said, sitting in the dark room.

Silently Hunter let himself out the front door and relocked it. He moved around the side of the house to the back. A flashlight tucked in his pants, the gun in his hand, he opened the side gate to the back yard.

His eyes and ears were strained as he dropped to a crouched position. Nothing. It was pitch dark, and the incessant wind drowned out most sounds. Thunder rumbled overhead. Lightning struck again. Poised, Hunter counted to five and waited for the thunder to follow.

It came, followed by another jagged stalk that lit up the dark sky and pierced his ears. Nothing. There were too many places to hide . . . the gazebo, the trees, the waterfall. If Hunter flashed his light, he'd pinpoint himself. All he could do was hope that, if there was someone out there, he'd get restless and move.

In his years as a police officer, more times than not, he had used that technique to his advantage. Most criminals were the nervous type. Waiting wasn't their strong suit.

The lights came back on. Hunter rolled and came up behind a bush. His mouth thinned. He didn't like hiding. The only thing that kept him in place was the knowledge that he was the only one that stood between Erin and whoever might be out there.

Voices. The police must have arrived. It could be Grimes or another tired, overworked police officer. Hunter placed his gun on the ground and waited. The flashlight streaked across his body, then seconds later he heard a gruff voice order, ''Don't move.''

Almost at the same time another lighter voice said, ''Stand up with your hands in the air.''

Hunter bit back a sarcastic comeback. He couldn't do both. Some police officers had no sense of humor. ''I'm Jake Hunter, Ms. Cortland's bodyguard. My ID is in my back pocket.''

''Stand up and let's see it.''

Rising slowly, Hunter handed the older policeman the ID. After studying it for a few seconds, he gave it back. ''You should have stayed inside.''

''If there's someone out here, I don't want him getting away.'' Hunter picked up his weapon. ''Now that you're here, I can look.''

The policeman eyed the gun. ''Hold on a minute. This is police business.''

Hunter held his temper, with difficulty. ''Ms. Cortland is my responsibility, as well. You can check with Detective Grimes. In the meantime, if one of you would stay with her, I'd appreciate it. The motion lights are functioning, and since none have come on since the lights came back on, if there was someone out there, he left while the lights were out, or he's still hiding.''

''If,'' the policeman repeated. ''I thought someone saw a prowler.''

''She wasn't sure,'' Hunter said, seeing the annoyance creep across the other man's face.

''She wasn't sure,'' the policeman repeated again.

''That's right,'' Hunter said, his own impatience growing. ''When the police let a convicted killer that you'd testified against escape, and then the judge who sentenced him is killed, I guess you have a right to be cautious,'' Hunter told him.

''She's that Cortland?'' asked the senior policeman.

"Yes."

The sergeant turned to the younger police officer. "Simms, go back and stay with Ms. Cortland. Hunter, you take the right, and I'll take the left."

"Sergeant Floyd, isn't that against police procedure?" the younger policeman asked.

"We'll discuss it later, now move."

Hunter watched the younger man hurry back around the house. "Thanks. How long has he been out of the academy?"

"You're welcome, and two weeks," the policeman confided. "The department owes Ms. Cortland one. I should have recognized the name sooner. But this isn't our regular beat."

"No problem. Ready?"

"Ready."

Erin jumped when she heard the doorbell, then started toward the door. Officer Simms stopped her. "Who is it?"

"Sergeant Floyd."

Erin rushed to the door and opened it, her gaze going beyond the policeman to Hunter. His face was grim. "I . . . is everything all right?"

"We didn't find anything," he answered.

Relief and embarrassment swept through her. She faced the policeman beside him. "I'm sorry. I guess I overreacted."

"No problem," Sergeant Floyd said. "Good experience for Officer Simms. If you have any more problems, just call."

Thanking the policemen again, Erin said good night and closed the door. For some reason, she was reluctant to face Hunter.

"You better go call Marcus, and I'll reset the alarm," Hunter told her, then he moved toward the kitchen.

Erin headed for her bedroom. She called her father and, after repeatedly assuring him that she was fine and that he did not need to come over, especially with a storm moving in her direction, she finally hung up the phone.

Agitated, she glanced out the window. Maybe if it finally rained, she wouldn't feel so jumpy or restless.

The knock on her door startled her. "Yes?"

"Can I come in?"

She bit her lip. "I'm rather tired. Can't it wait until tomorrow?"

"No." The word was flat, inflexible.

Dragging her hand through her hair, she folded the other arm around her waist. She didn't want to see him. She wasn't up to seeing the indifference in his eyes again, not when she so desperately wanted him to hold her.

The thought reverberated through her brain. That was the reason she was restless. She wanted Hunter. And he wanted no part of her.

"Erin?"

Her hands went to her sides. Hunter wasn't moving. "Come in."

The door opened. Powerful and dangerous, Hunter filled the opening. The dark shirt he had put on remained unbuttoned, displaying matted black hair over a muscular chest above a flat stomach. Her fingers tingled with the need to touch and explore.

Her hands clenched. "Please, get this over quickly."

The door closed. His gaze hooded, he crossed to her on soundless feet, stopping only inches from her. "Are you sure you want this over quickly?"

Erin blinked. She must be imagining things. She couldn't have heard the sensual undercurrents in his deep voice, nor have seen it in the glittering black depths of his eyes. "W . . . what is it you wanted?"

"For starters . . . this." His lips gently brushed across her forehead. "And this." Over her cheek. "And this." And they finally settled over her lips.

By then Erin's arms were around his neck, straining to get closer. Questions formed, to ask what had changed his mind, but they stumbled on the sensual onslaught of his lips, his hands, his body.

''I'm glad you kept this dress on. I've wanted to take it off you since this morning,'' he said huskily.

Erin shivered. The shivers intensified as she heard the rasp of the back zipper.

Hunter gently eased her away from him, his eyes intent on her body as he slowly peeled the red dress over the smoothness of her shoulders, the tantalizing swell of her breasts in a lacy red demi bra, past her thin waist, over a racy red garter and scant bikini, until the garment fell and pooled around her feet.

Her breath held as Hunter's hot gaze slowly took his fill of her. ''You're the most beautiful thing I've ever seen.''

Erin gloried in his words. ''I feel beautiful when you're looking at me.''

Lifting her up in his arms, he carried her to the bed and stood her beside it. ''Good, because I plan to do a lot of looking.''

''So do I.'' She peeled the shirt from him, then pressed her lips against his chest.

He trembled. ''You make me feel as weak as a baby.''

''Then it's a good thing we're so near the bed.''

His face grew serious. ''You're something else. I don't know how or why we're together, but I can't fight it any longer.''

A trembling hand palmed his cheek. ''I don't want this to make you unhappy.''

He caught her hand in his. ''That's not what I meant. I . . .'' He searched for words. ''I thought I could keep you compartmentalized, but I can't. Tonight when the police left and you refused to look at me, it felt like someone turning a jagged knife in my gut. I thought of all the times I had turned away from you, and I wanted to weep.''

''Don't. Some things are easier for some people than for others. I know that.''

''Erin,'' his voice roughened. ''You deserve so much more.''

She smiled. ''You've given me so much. You've helped me to face my fears, and experience the ultimate in making love. Without you, I couldn't have achieved either. Don't blame yourself because it's all you had to give.''

Hunter closed his eyes. Regret and agony shimmered through him. Warm lips on his chest caused his lids to fly upward. He stared down into Erin's upturned face.

"Are we going to spend the time with regrets, or something far more pleasant?"

"How much sleep do you need?"

She blinked, then laughed. "I've been known to get by on five hours, four if I have to."

"That should just about give us enough time." He took her lips and they tumbled into bed.

Hunter stared down into Erin's sleeping face and could find no regret in his heart or in his mind. How could anyone regret sharing something so undeniably special?

Making love to Erin was like nothing he had ever experienced. He understood that that uniqueness was because of the sleeping woman in his arms. She fascinated him, annoyed him, scared him. Most of all, she humbled him with her ability to love and understand.

His hand swept back the sheet to reveal her dusky nipple. Finger and thumb plucked. Immediately, it blossomed. Asleep, her body still responded to his.

Lowering his head, he replaced his finger with his tongue. The moment he heard Erin murmur his name then felt her begin to slide her arms around his neck, he joined them with one smooth stroke.

Passion replaced the sleepiness in her eyes. "G . . . good morning," she murmured huskily.

He grinned roughishly. "It's gonna get better."

Chapter Sixteen

Erin, grinning from ear to ear, stepped off the Cortland elevator, looking as if she had won the Texas lottery. To her way of thinking, she had won something much better. Hunter's open affection.

He'd never be kissy-face, but the sizzling looks he sent her, the subtle touches, the murmur in his deep voice, were enough. She knew she was desired and wanted. He had proven that last night and this morning, to the satisfaction of both of them.

"Don't you think you should wipe that smile off your face?" Hunter said from beside her.

"Daddy was delighted to see me happy this morning."

Hunter winced. "Don't remind me."

Erin laughed. "It was your idea to drop by to show him I was fine."

"I know. He kept thanking me, and I felt like a heel," he said.

Erin paused at the door to Nancy's office. "You have made me happy. No regrets, remember?"

"No regrets."

Opening the door, she entered the office. "Good morning,

Nancy. I want all of the executives, department heads, and managers in conference room C in thirty minutes. No exceptions, and no excuses for being late.''

Nancy's puzzled gaze went to Hunter before she said, ''Right away.''

Inside her office, Hunter took Erin's coat and hung it up. ''I think Nancy got the wrong idea.''

Erin shrugged her shoulders beneath a tailored black wool suit with a slim mid-calf skirt. ''I didn't notice anything.''

Hunter leaned back against the armoire. ''You were too busy giving orders.''

''Impressed you, huh,'' she said, then crossed her legs and shuffled through the files she removed from her attaché case.

Hunter caught a brief glimpse of her long black stockinged leg from the tantalizing side split of her skirt. ''Other things about you impress me more.''

Erin's head lifted. ''If you don't stop distracting me, I'm going to make a flub of things.''

''You're too sharp for that.'' He said it and meant it.

Happiness washed across her face. ''Thank you.''

''You've accomplished a great deal. Your employees respect and like you. You can't get much better than that.'' He pushed away from the armoire and crossed to the window.

''I thought so once, but I'm not sure anymore.'' Erin laid the files on her desk. ''I get a lot of satisfaction from what I do, but I can't talk over my triumphs or my failures to a layout, or curl up with one, either.''

Hunter glanced over his shoulder. ''That would be a good way to end up in a padded cell, or with a nasty paper cut, but people have survived both.''

''Life is more than surviving. It's living,'' Erin said softly.

''For some, surviving is all there is.''

Erin accepted the words for what they were, a subtle warning. Hunter may have dropped his guard, but he was still wary of a commitment. ''Life is what you choose it to be.''

She picked up the folders and her portfolio. ''We better leave for the meeting. I wouldn't want to be late again.''

His eyes narrowed on her lips. He remembered her applying the lipstick the morning he had let her sleep late. Apparently, she wanted him to remember as well. "You never give up, do you?"

"You don't win by walking away."

"Did you learn that from Marcus, or the Victim Recovery group?"

"It's a lesson I've had to learn and relearn from both my parents, from the recovery group, from life, from history." She crossed her arms over the materials in her hands. "From you."

"From me?"

"You took a job you didn't want, and never once balked at putting your life on the line for mine." She held up her hand when he would have spoken. "If you're going to say it's your job, don't. How much is a person's life worth?"

His face harshened. "You're going to be late for your meeting."

Erin saw the fury mixed with misery in his dark eyes, and she wanted to weep at the suspicion creeping through her like a cold wind. "She died, didn't she?"

Rage like she had never known before stared back at her. "Leave it alone, Erin."

"I wish I could."

"Because we slept together, you think you have a right to know my whole life story?" he snapped.

"I slept with you because I care about you, and that entitles me to ask. It's up to you whether you want to tell me or not."

Broad shoulders sagged beneath the leather jacket. "You get to me quicker and calm me down faster than anything on this earth."

"It's a knack."

Taking a deep breath, he shoved his hands deep into his pockets. "You're right. She died. She trusted me, depended on me. I got her killed."

The buzzer on her desk rang, and she ignored it. "What happened?"

"It's not a pretty story."

''Life seldom is,'' she answered quietly.

His hands came out of his pockets, and one shoved over his head impatiently. ''She was the only witness in a high-profile murder case. She worked as a waitress in one of the upscale clubs in Chicago. One night she saw her boss, Ed Lawrence, kill one of his drug dealers for holding out. She came to the police. Since I had been working trying to get a case against Lawrence, I was assigned to her. Word leaked about the witness and I took her to the DA's house in the country.

''She was very pretty and she made it no secret that she was attracted to me. One night I let myself forget procedure and policy and let things go too far. Professionally and ethically, I crossed a line I had no business crossing.'' His face harshened. ''That it was the first time I had crossed that line didn't make any difference. I'm sorry is a poor excuse for taking advantage of someone who is scared and looking for comfort.''

His voice filled with anguish. ''The next morning she called her mother. The lines to her mother's house were tapped. Sondra said she had just wanted to talk to someone who loved her. An hour later she was dead.''

Erin made herself hold back the tears stinging her eyes. Tears for the dead woman, tears for the man who was still haunted by her death.

The buzzer rang again, impatiently. Erin stalked across to her desk. ''I don't want to be disturbed for anything.''

She turned to Hunter. ''I'm sorry; please continue.''

His broad shoulders hunched forward. ''Maybe we better go.''

''I'd rather stay and hear what you have to say.''

Solomnly, he nodded. ''I tried to get us out of the mountains, but they ambushed us on one of the narrow roads. She tried to protect me, and paid with her life.'' He lifted haunted eyes to her. ''I resigned as soon as the inquest was over.''

''If they'd tapped her mother's phone how did the criminals get to you so soon?''

Admiration glinted in his dark eyes. ''Lawrence had a cop in his pocket. A police dispatcher. He leaked the information about Sondra and our location. Lawrence wanted the cop's hands to be as dirty as his. They both came off the mountain in body bags."

Erin laid her hand gently on Hunter's taut shoulder. She hadn't missed the similarities between Sondra's case and hers, but Erin wasn't about to start doubting herself or Hunter after the night they shared. "You're not responsible for her death."

"I am," he raged. "If I hadn't made her think she cared about me, she wouldn't have jumped in front of me and taken that bullet."

"How old was Sondra?"

"Twenty-nine."

"Were you her first lover?"

His jaw tightened. "She was a good woman."

"I didn't mean to imply she wasn't. You're assuming she confused love with some white-knight syndrome. I think you're wrong. She wouldn't have given her life for you otherwise. She wanted to protect you. I know how she felt." Erin paused. "You see, I love you."

Shock registered on his face, then sorrow.

"No regrets, Hunter. I give you my love freely." Her lips brushed across his cheek. "We better get to that meeting."

His hands curled around her arms when she would have turned away. He stared down into her upturned face. "The more I try to push you away, the closer you get, and the more I want you to stay."

"Is that so bad?"

"I thought it was, but I'm not so sure." His thumb stroked her arm. "I want you safe, and I can't help remembering Sondra's death."

"There's no one leaking information, and you've taken every precaution to protect me," she soothed.

"No one can think of everything," he said grimly.

"You give Scanlon too much credit and yourself too little. He's probably hiding in some dingy hotel room." She glanced at her watch. "Speaking of rooms, I'm ten minutes late."

"Us walking in together late again is going to give rise to a lot of speculation," Hunter said.

Erin tilted her head to one side. "I wonder if the gossip will be as good as the real thing."

A reluctant smile tugged the corners of Hunter's mouth. "You're incorrigible."

"You bring out a side of me I didn't know existed."

He ran a finger down the smooth brown curve of her jaw. "You do the same thing to me. Scary as hell, isn't it?"

"Only sometimes." She nipped his finger. "Other times it's quite intriguing."

"Come on; we better get to your meeting before you're *really* late and they won't have to speculate." Grasping her arm, he led her out of her office.

Erin knew how to handle people.

Hunter was slightly amazed by the way she marched into the conference room, quieted the murmurs with a look, then apologized for her tardiness. The meeting was underway by the time she reached her seat. She was an amazing woman.

He was still slightly stunned by her announcement that she loved him. Her love was a heavy-duty responsibility that he wasn't sure he knew how to handle. The last woman who had said she loved him in a similiar situation had died in his arms.

His face tightened into resolve as he took his usual post by the door. That wouldn't happen to Erin. She wouldn't pay with her life for loving him.

As he expected, there was a round of cheers for Sally's appointment, and stunned amazement when Erin announced Quinn's resignation. By the time everyone had piled out of the room, Erin had traded the work-load of the vice-president's position for that of the account executive.

"Don't you think you have enough to do?" Hunter asked.

"Goes with the territory." Gathering up her things, she met him at the conference room door.

"That may be, but we're getting out of here by six tonight."

Erin merely looked at him. "Wanna bet?"

Hunter opened his mouth to say yes, then closed it. Erin wouldn't leave until she was finished. He wouldn't make her leave, because he respected her and her work.

"How about before dark?"

"That, I think, can be arranged."

They stepped off the elevators between dusk and dark. "You almost didn't make it," Hunter told her.

"In my business, I'm used to cutting it close." She looked at him intently. "Your old profession, too, I bet."

"There never seemed enough time to help all the people who asked for it," he said, opening her door. "For a while, I thought I was making a difference as a policeman."

Erin placed her hand on his arm. "If you helped one person, you made a difference."

"You're quite a woman, Erin Cortland."

"You're quite a man, Jake Hunter."

"Come on, I better get you home." Helping her inside, he got into the car and exited the parking garage.

"I like your car," she mused, half turned in her seat to face him.

"Sure took you a long time to figure that out."

Erin chuckled. "I thought it was too slow, among other things."

Hunter snorted. "It can reach ninety, and with the modifications I plan once I get back to Chicago, it'll easily do one hundred and ten."

The teasing smile left Erin's face. "When do you plan to leave?"

"Not until Scanlon is caught and you're safe."

She clasped her hands tightly in her lap. "You do the repairs yourself?"

He threw her a questioning glance as he exited the freeway. "Most of them. A friend of mine has a garage. He lets me use it when I need to."

"That's nice of him."

There was a long pause, then Hunter said, "Maybe when you're in Chicago again, I could take you for a test drive."

"Maybe." Twisting around in her seat, Erin stared out the window. Casual friendship was all he was offering. She wanted so much more, but she had promised: no regrets. Without Hunter, though, her life would be filled with little else. She had played a dangerous masquerade, and lost.

Hunter's hand flexed on the steering wheel. She had withdrawn from him. What had happened? If she really loved him, she'd want to see him again. He had thought Erin was too grounded to throw out words like "I love you" without meaning them. Had he misjudged her that badly? He glanced at her tense profile again as if seeking an answer. Strangely, he received one.

Erin was too honest for subterfuge and lies. The chill sweeping through him receded. Something else was bothering her. She cared for him, just as he cared for her.

His affection for Erin wasn't going away after they made love, or a week from now, or after Scanlon was caught. The emotion would grow stronger and last a lifetime.

The sudden revelation of the depth of his own devotion stunned him, so much that he almost missed seeing the black sedan behind him. He had caught sight of the BMW when they exited the parking garage, then again on the freeway. The car had pulled ahead of him a couple of times, but here it was behind him again.

Quinn drove a black BMW.

"I think we're being followed again." Hunter stopped at a signal light on a two-lane street. "Black BMW three cars back."

Erin twisted around in her seat. Her lips pursed. "It's probably Quinn. Pull over."

Hunter sped through the light. "Quinn wanted to sneak off, not get into a fight."

"That was last night. He had all day to think of some way of getting back at both of us."

"I don't think so. Hang on." He took a sharp left as the

light turned green. He glanced in the mirror to see the BMW behind him and getting closer.

The luxury sedan was faster. He couldn't outrun or outmaneuver it on the two-lane street. "Get down and call nine-one-one."

"Hunter—"

"Now, Erin." He heard the panic in her voice as she talked to the 911 dispatcher and thrust it to the back of his mind. Scanlon knew how to handle a car, and only a couple of car lengths separated them.

If Hunter could just get out of the resident—

The first shot that hit the back windshield sounded like a loud pop. The next one shattered the rearview mirror on the passenger side. Huddled in the seat, Erin whimpered.

"The glass is bulletproof," Hunter said, but at the moment it only gave him a small amount of comfort. He knew it wasn't accidental that the bullets had struck the passenger's side of the car.

He eased off the gas just enough to keep from going into a spin as he took the next curve. He headed toward the freeway, service stations, lights.

The freeway lights were in sight when he heard the next shot. Almost simultaneously there was a loud pop, as if someone had burst a paper bag full of air. Hunter didn't have time to curse or pray. The Mustang went into a wild spin.

Scanlon had shot out the back tire.

Hunter used all his concentration and skill to keep the car from turning over. The vehicle came to a stop at an angle, two hundred yards from the freeway.

Except for two streetlights spaced fifty feet away on opposite sides of the road, they were in complete darkness.

Shutting off the headlights, he opened the door with one hand and grabbed Erin with the other. "Come on."

He heard her grunt. The gear shift. Turning back, he lifted her out. Hands clasped, they ran down the embankment.

Hunter knew they had a good chance of coming out of this in one piece if they could make it to the covering of the weeds on the underdeveloped acreage. Scanlon had given them an edge by hanging back after he shot out the tire. That miscalculation had given them enough time to escape.

A spear of light raked across them. Hunter grabbed Erin and pushed her in front of him, intending to dive for cover. A gun spat twice. He grunted as he felt something tear into his left side.

Chapter Seventeen

Pain lanced through Hunter. He stumbled, fought to regain his balance, and knew he had failed when the jarring impact of his knees hitting the ground sent a searing pain tearing through his side.

Blinking his eyes to keep them focused, he tried to see Erin. Although he was surrounded by a bright white light, he couldn't see her.

Panic engulfed him. He had to protect her. Keep her safe. She had to leave. She couldn't die like Sondra. He tried to form the words, but his mouth wouldn't cooperate.

"Hunter. Hunter, please. Look at me. Get up. Please get up."

Erin. Her words were hammering into him. Stubborn. She wanted something and he was keeping her from having it. He wanted to smile. He groaned instead.

Pain. A hot poker in his side.

"Hunter. Please." She was making the pain worse. He wanted to tell her to stop pulling at him, but it seemed more important for her to stop crying.

"D . . . don't cry."

"Then come on. Move!"

Hunter blinked again. The pain remained, but the lights weren't so bright. Most importantly, he could see Erin. He didn't like what he saw.

Stark terror and panic marred her beautiful face. He didn't ever want her to be afraid. He had to protect her. This time when he moved his fingers they cooperated. Good. He just had to keep concentrating.

"Goin' someplace?"

Sheer horror lanced through Erin as she looked up into Harry Scanlon's thin, sneering face. She pulled Hunter closer, careful to keep pressure over the wound in his side.

"Touchin', but wasted. He ain't gonna make it. He's bleedin' to death."

"No!" Erin screamed the denial. Her hand pressed the folded tail of his coat harder against his side.

Scanlon's features harshened. "You shouldn't have tried to run from me. Told you I'd be back. The judge first. Then you, bitch."

"You won't get away with this."

He laughed, a thin, hollow sound. "People will drive by his car with only a few curious glances. As for the stupid Austin Police Department, I've been sittin' under their noses for the past ten days just three houses down from the judge's. I broke in and set up housekeepin' while the owners are in Europe. Nice of them to leave me a car and a gun. But the calendar on the 'frigerator says they're comin' home tomorrow, so tonight was my last chance."

Erin felt Hunter's hand move on her arm around his chest. He still had a chance. She just had to make sure she gave the police enough time to get there. "You were at the party, weren't you?"

He sneered. "I saw that silly woman on the TV talkin' 'bout some benefit. I was gettin' ready to change the channel when she said your name. People shouldn't call TV the boob tube. It got me you." His menacing gaze settled on Hunter. "Or it would 'ave if he hadn't come."

Her hands closed more protectively around Hunter. ''He was only doing his duty.''

''His duty,'' Scanlon growled. ''Just like the judge said it was his duty to send me to prison for the rest of my life. I've been hearin' that crap ever since I can 'member. It's my duty to punish you. It's my duty to take your priv'leges. It's my duty to make you a ward of the state.'' His eyes gleamed. ''I got out of the foster home and made it on my own. I was headin' for a place to belong until you got in my way.''

He took a threatening step closer. ''If it hadn't been for you, I wouldn't have gotten caught.''

''Two innocent people died that night.''

''They were nothin',''' he shouted. ''People die every day. At least theirs was quick. I wanted you and the judge's to be slow and agonizin'. In jail I learned all I could about both of you, before I was sentenced. I knew where you worked. I knew he liked to jog.''

Grinning, he rocked back on his heels. ''I planned to kill him after he came back from his jog, but I changed my mind when I heard him and his neighbors talkin'. Gave me an idea. I could off the judge, hide and wait for the police to think I wasn't involved, then come after you.''

Erin shivered. That was exactly what had happened. Only Hunter hadn't been fooled. ''You could have been in Mexico by now.''

He cocked the gun. ''But you'd be livin'. Beautiful, successful, a family. You had everything I never had. But you took what little I had from me.''

Hunter stirred in her arms. She tried to hold him closer.

Scanlon's cold eyes locked on Hunter. ''Maybe I should let you know how it feels.''

''No.'' She renewed her slipping hold. Faintly she heard a police siren.

''Yeah,'' Scanlon said softly as if coming to a decision. ''He's gonna pay, then you're next.''

Letting Hunter go, she scrambled to her feet. She had to protect Hunter. ''It's me you want. Not him.''

"You'd take a bullet for him?"

"Yes." The words were instant and sure.

Scanlon grinned. "Good." He pushed her aside.

Erin's desperate hands grabbed for him and missed. She heard the report of a gun. She screamed. The sound echoed again and again in her heart.

Her palms pressed against her face; she cried out her agony. Agony turned to fury. He had killed Hunter.

With a wild cry, she sprang up, her hands spread like talons. Scanlon was gone. A low moan sent her gaze downward. Hunter was drawn up in a ball.

She dropped to her knees, her arm going around him, repositioning the pressure bandage. She bit her lips and fought tears as she felt the wet stickiness. "Hang on, please."

Overhead she heard the drone of a helicopter, then they were surrounded by light. The police siren pierced the night.

"We're safe. Scanlon must have heard them and run like he did the last time."

Across the field, she saw several spears of light coming quickly toward them. She kissed the top of Hunter's head. "Everything will be all right."

"Lo . . ."

"Don't talk. Scanlon is gone." She pressed her cheek to the side of his face.

"L . . . love you," came the whispered words. "C . . . cold."

She tried to hold him tighter. Tears ran unheeded down her cheek. Somehow she knew he was telling her he loved her because he didn't think he'd survive. "I know. I love you too, sweetheart. Please save your strength. We'll have the rest of our lives to tell each other."

One of the beams of light was almost to her when she heard a man curse. The light fell. She thought the person must have stepped into a hole.

In a matter of seconds, she was surrounded by several policemen. "Please. He needs an ambulance."

"One is on the way, Ms. Cortland. The police chopper

already radioed for one." He reached for Hunter's still form. "We'll take it from here."

"No. I'm not leaving Hunter," she cried frantically.

The uniformed men glanced uneasily from one to the other. "Ma'am. He's in pretty bad shape."

"He can hear you. Don't you dare say that," Erin admonished. "He'll be fine. We just need to get him to the hospital."

"Just go with this officer. Detective Grimes is on his way."

"Don't touch me," she yelled, more afraid than she had ever been in her life. Their pitying faces weren't helping. "Go find the person responsible for this. Go find Scanlon. He's hiding three houses down from where Judge Hughes lived."

"What?"

"You heard me. He ran when he heard you coming."

The police officers exchanged looks again. "Ms. Cortland. Scanlon is dead." He nodded toward the area where the policeman had fallen.

"Dead?" she repeated. "But how? He tried to shoot Hunter again. Scanlon must have miss . . ." Even as she said the words, she knew they couldn't be true. He was standing too close.

She looked down. Tears fell like rain. Hunter's hand clutched his gun. Using the last of his depleted strength, he had protected her. She could do nothing for him.

"Let us have him."

"No." Some part of her realized she was being irrational, but another part of her believed his life was connected to hers. If she stopped holding him, Hunter would die. She had to keep holding him until they reached the hospital.

In the distance she heard another helicopter. Hunter's breathing changed, grew more labored.

"No. God, please, no."

"Ms. Cortland, please."

"No, please—"

She wasn't given a choice. Firm but determined hands moved her away. No matter how she fought, they were unrelenting. She was still screaming for Hunter when the care-flight helicopter lifted off the ground and took him away.

* * *

Erin was crying. The sound disturbed Hunter, as much as it—oddly—comforted him. She was close and alive. The bright lights were gone. The pain throbbing in his side was not.

He needed to remember something. Something important—*Scanlon.*

''Erin, run,'' he cried and tried to jerk upward. He only managed to move his head an inch from the pillow.

''Shhhh. Scanlon won't hurt anyone again. We're both safe. You're in the hospital.''

His gaze finally focused on Erin, noticed the dark smudges beneath her eyes, the moisture on her cheeks. ''You're crying.''

''Because you scared me half to death. Don't you ever do something like that again,'' she told him, smiling despite her tears.

He wanted to tell her not to cry, to tell her he had no intention of getting shot again, then he decided he didn't have the energy. He wanted to touch her, but his hand got no farther than his head. His eyelids were getting heavy.

Her hands squeezed his. ''Go back to sleep, my love. I'll be here when you wake up.''

''Promise.''

''Promise.'' Warm lips brushed across his forehead.

Hunter lost count of the times he drifted in and out of consciousness, but, each time, Erin was always there. He wanted to tell her to go home and get some rest, but he couldn't. He had almost lost her.

The next time when he woke, he saw her sitting by his bedside in a stiff-backed chair, her watchful gaze on him. ''I'm fine,'' he croaked.

Getting up, she gave him a sip of water, then set the glass aside. ''Of course you are.''

His hand lifted and finally succeeded in touching her cheek. ''Then stop worrying.''

Her hand closed around his. Her smile trembled. "Barely awake and you're back to giving orders."

Before he could answer, the door opened, and in came a stocky, bald-headed man in a white lab coat and a nurse with a blue jacket over her white uniform.

"So you're awake again, Mr. Hunter. You probably don't remember me; I'm Dr. Lawson," greeted the man.

"No. I don't."

"Understandable. You were barely alive when they brought you in."

Erin's hand jerked in his.

The doctor looked at her. "I don't suppose it will do any good this time to ask you to wait outside, will it?"

"No."

"She stays."

The gray-haired doctor smiled. "I love being right. Let's see my handiwork." Drawing back the covers, he completed his examination. "I do admire my work when everything comes together."

Hunter sent him a hard look.

"A little joke, young man." Dr. Lawson wrote on the chart, then handed it to the nurse. "You'll be able to see the humor once you see my handiwork."

"How many stitches?"

"Thirty-two." We'll discuss the details when you're stronger. If all continues to go well you'll be out of ICCU in a couple of days, and in your room." The doctor cast an appreciative glance at Erin. "I can certainly see why you'd fight to wake up. Five minutes, then he has to rest. Now that you know he's going to live, you'll have to follow regular visiting hours. You've broken enough of the hospital rules." Smiling, he left the room with the nurse behind him.

Hunter frowned. "What did he mean?"

"I refused to leave you . . . after . . . after you came out of surgery. Daddy is on the hospital board and he pulled in some favors for me." She folded her hand over his. "You were in surgery six hours."

His gaze flickered around the small, pristine cubicle. Tubes from two bottles of clear substances were connected to his arm. A machine beeped each time he moved. "How long have I been in here?"

"Two very long days."

He smiled. "They found out how stubborn you can be, huh?"

"I wanted to be with you."

She had fought and broken rules to be with him. He'd walk through hell for her.

His fingers curled around hers. "I heard you talking to Scanlon. I managed to get my gun while his attention was on you. I wanted you to move, but, instead, you lunged for him."

She shivered. "He wanted to kill you."

"He would have killed you," Hunter said. "You scared me half to death. Don't *you* ever do something like that again."

"You made sure I wouldn't have to."

"Mrs. Hunter, it's time to leave."

Hunter's eyes widened, but he didn't say anything until the smiling nurse closed the door. "Did I miss something while I was unconscious?"

She refused to meet his gaze. "It was the only way they'd let me stay with you or see you. Your parents and brother didn't seem to mind."

"They're here?"

"Since the first night." She bit her lip. There was something she wanted to ask before she left, but he needed to rest. Then, there was the distinct possibility he didn't even remember telling her he loved her. "It's almost three. I'll go home and change and be back by the next visiting hour at four."

His eyebrows bunched. "Aren't you going to your office?"

"Sally can handle things," she said, then frowned. "Unless I'm making a pest of myself."

Something finally clicked in his foggy brain. "It hasn't been just a coincidence that, every time I woke up, you were here, has it? You haven't left the hospital since I've been here."

"I couldn't. Daddy brought me a bag Georgia packed and

the nurses let me use their lounge to shower,'' she admitted quietly.

His chest hurt. His throat felt tight. She had fought him and everyone else to stay and run Cortland Innovations, downplaying the danger, refusing to give in to her fears.

Yet, when he had been hurt, she had chosen to stay with him, then used that same determination and stubbornness to make sure she'd be able to. His hand tightened on hers. ''What did I do to deserve you?''

''You're just lucky, I guess.''

He gazed up at her tremulous smile, read the love she didn't try to hide, and something inside him shifted, loosened. All his doubts slipped away. ''I just realized how lucky. You're an amazing woman, Erin Cortland, and I love you.''

Sheer joy radiated across her face. Her brown eyes sparkled. She bent to throw herself into his arms, paused, and kissed his lips instead. ''What took you so long?''

His hand brushed across her cheek. ''Now that I think about it, I probably loved you from the moment I walked into your father's study for the first time. Scanlon and the difference in our bank balances kept getting in the way.''

She made a face. ''You're going to pay for that last remark when you get well.''

''I'll do any kind of penance just as long as you keep loving me.''

''Oh, Hun—''

''Mrs. Hunter, your husband needs his rest.''

Erin and Hunter both threw disgruntled looks at the nurse who stood in the doorway. Ovbiously, she wasn't leaving this time.

Leaning over, Erin whispered, ''Just wait until I get you in a private room.''

''For all the good I can do about it,'' he grumbled.

Erin grinned. ''I better go before they throw me out.''

His fingers refused to relinquish hers. ''Nurse, can you give me one minute with my wife? Please. It's important.''

The woman nodded. ''Make it snappy—and be glad I'm a sucker for romance.'' The door closed.

''Your car is safe in my garage,'' Erin said, trying to fight the warm rush she had felt when Hunter called her his wife.

''Not even close. This is more important than anything to me. I can't ask properly, but I don't want to wait.'' He paused as if gathering his strength and his courage. ''Will you marry me?''

A wild cadence of joy swept through her. Her heart boomed. Tears sparkled in her eyes. ''Yes. Oh yes.''

''I love you, Erin. I'll make you a good husband. I can open a branch office here so you can run Cortland and me.'' His eyes darkened with promise. ''We'll have our sunshine and laughter together. Almost losing you made me realize material things don't matter if the love is strong enough. Ours is. I love you, Erin, with all my heart, with all that I am or hope to be.''

''Oh, Hunter,'' her voice wobbled.

''Go get some rest and start planning our wedding. Because, as soon as I can stand on my own feet, we're getting married.''

''I'm holding you to that.'' She kissed him on the cheek.

''Please ask the doctor to come back in.''

Her eyes widened in alarm. ''What's the matter?''

He tucked his head. ''Nothing. I just need to ask him a question.''

''Maybe I know the answer. He's kept me informed, since he thinks we're married.''

Hunter's head remained bent. ''I don't think so.''

''I might—''

''It's about the honeymoon,'' he blurted. The monitor went wild.

Erin smiled. ''Right away. Be sure to let me know what he says.''

Hunter grinned. ''You'll be the first to know.''

Epilogue

Laughter floated up through the canopy of oak trees. In one of the trees, a brown squirrel stopped and reared up on its hind legs, its nose twitching. The gleeful sound came again, punctuated with squeals of delight. The small animal took flight, scampering quickly to the next tree, then the next, putting as much distance as possible between the noise and himself.

Beneath the oak trees, dapples of sunshine shone on the happy couple as the man chased the woman around the back yard filled with blooming, rainbow-hued flowers. Droplets of water from the nearby pool glistened on their skin.

His large hand reached out and caught the one remaining string tie that secured her wet bikini top around her neck. She squealed. He roared with triumphant laughter as the tiny piece of cloth came loose in his hand.

Grinning, she looked back over her shoulder, her eyes shining with love and challenge. In two long strides, he caught her, his arms going around her slim waist. Protecting her slender body with his larger, more muscular one, he fell on the soft grass.

He rolled on top of her, his leg slipping between the notch of her thighs. Her nipples brushed against his naked chest and hardened. Through the scanty cloth of her bikini bottoms and his swim trunks, she felt a similar response in his lower body. Delicious shivers raked through them both.

All laughter stopped. They stared into each other's eyes, anticipating, savoring, remembering.

A narrow platinum band glinted on the third finger of her left hand as she gently touched his face. The next instant, his head dipped, his lips settling tenderly over hers. Her other hand entwined with his left one, and she felt the matching wedding band on his hand.

The kiss deepened. His body settled more firmly against hers.

Someone moaned softly. Desire, like a sensuous mist, curled through them both. They had kissed and made love a hundred times, but each time was new and different and precious. A gift they gave to each other. The scar on the man's left side was there to remind them, in case either of them forgot, that life wasn't promised.

Erin and Jake never forgot.

Picking Erin up in his arms, Jake held her close as he started for the house. Kissing had ceased to be enough. Her arms curved around his neck. She nipped the strong line of his jaw.

"We made it, Hunter. We have our sunshine and laughter and—"

"Each other," he finished, pulling her closer. "I love you, honey." Entering the house, he closed the door securely behind them.

"And just to show you how much I love you, I'm going to let you prove it in some mighty interesting ways," Erin teased impishly. "Dr. Lawson was right. You recovered quite nicely."

Jake whooped, his chest shaking. His wife's laughter joined his as he hurried down the hall to the waiting bed.

Dear Readers:

I want to share some wonderful news with you. ONLY HERS went to number one on *Blackboard,* the African-American national bestsellers list, for paperback fiction. All of my *Arabesque* titles have made the list, previously, but ONLY HERS is the first to reach number one. I was thrilled! I couldn't let this opportunity pass without thanking you and booksellers across the country. This accomplishment could not have happened without your continued support.

I hope you enjoyed INCOGNITO and the adventures of Jake and Erin. Coming to bookstores in mid-July, '97 is SILKEN BETRAYAL, the story of a man caught between love and duty. To those who have written to ask about Daniel and Addie's story, I'm working on it now. Take care.

All the best in love & life,

Francis Ray

Francis Ray

ABOUT THE AUTHOR

Francis Ray, the bestselling author of FOREVER YOURS and UNDENIABLE, is a native Texan and lives with her husband and daughter in Dallas. After publishing sixteen short stories, she decided to follow her love and write longer works which would show the healing power of love. She launched the Arabesque line with FOREVER YOURS and was included in the Arabesque December anthology, SPIRIT OF THE SEASON. A school nurse who cares for over 1500 children, she is also a frequent speaker at writing workshops and is a member of Women Writers of Color and Romance Writers of America.